NORTHERN EX

Further Novels by Colin Campbell

DARKWATER TOWERS
THROUGH THE RUINS OF MIDNIGHT
GARGOYLES – SKYLIGHTS AND ROOFSCAPES
BALLAD OF THE ONE-LEGGED MAN
BLUE KNIGHT WHITE CROSS *
NORTHERN EX *

available from Severn House

NORTHERN EX

Colin Campbell

This first world edition published 2010
in Great Britain and in the USA by
SEVERN HOUSE PUBLISHERS LTD of
9–15 High Street, Sutton, Surrey, England, SM1 1DF.
Trade paperback edition published
in Great Britain and the USA 2010 by
SEVERN HOUSE PUBLISHERS LTD

British Library Cataloguing in Publication Data

Campbell, Colin.
  Northern eX.
  1. Ex-police officers – England – Yorkshire – Fiction.
  2. Murder – Investigation – England – Yorkshire – Fiction.
  3. Detective and mystery stories.
  I. Title
  823.9'2-dc22

ISBN-13: 978-0-7278-6871-8   (cased)
ISBN-13: 978-1-84751-229-1   (trade paper)

All Severn House titles are printed on acid-free paper.

Severn House Publishers support The Forest Stewardship Council [FSC],
the leading international forest certification organisation. All our titles that
are printed on Greenpeace-approved FSC-certified paper carry the FSC logo.

Mixed Sources
Product group from well-managed
forests and other controlled sources
www.fsc.org Cert no. SA-COC-1565
© 1996 Forest Stewardship Council
FSC

Typeset by Palimpsest Book Production Ltd.,
Grangemouth, Stirlingshire, Scotland.
Printed and bound in Great Britain by
MPG Books Ltd., Bodmin, Cornwall.

For Edna

Acknowledgements

Although I wrote the story alone I did not write this book. What you see before you is the result of hard work by a lot of people. I owe everyone at Severn House many thanks, especially my editor, James Nightingale, and copy editor, Steve Gove, who made sense of the bad grammar and mistakes. And as always, to my agent, Janet Reid. Thank you.

'There is a house in New Orleans
They call the Rising Sun
And it's been the ruin of many a poor boy
And God I know I'm one'

The House of the Rising Sun

PART ONE
Many a Poor Boy

'I once told you Von Ryan. If only one gets out it's a victory.'

ONE

Once a cop always a cop. Vince McNulty thought about that as the woman massaged scented oil into his shoulders, leaning so close that her naked breasts teased his shoulder blades. Once a cop always a cop. Except this was the UK not the USA, so for cop you'd have to read policeman. Or, more accurately, this was Yorkshire not the UK, so maybe it should be copper instead of policeman. Copper, or any number of other, more colourful things that McNulty had been called during the last eighteen years. But somehow the phrase only worked with cop. Had a certain rhythm to it. Rolled off the tongue. So, whenever it crossed his mind, it was always once a cop always a cop.

Something else rolled off the tongue briefly as he lay face down on the massage table. The woman leaned over him and flicked her tongue up the side of his neck and jiggled it behind his left ear. Her breasts flattened against his back. He felt a familiar pulse way down in the engine room. And then she was up and massaging his shoulders again. Teasing over for now. Strong hands kneaded the muscles across his back and squeezed up either side of his neck. A knot in his spine cracked. He shifted his head on his folded hands, defining the shape of his upper arms as the elbows jutted out from the bed. The woman's hands moved from his neck to his right arm as if drawn by the tightened bicep. It was the arm nearest to her. Her fingers first squeezed then caressed the muscle, the oil preventing the friction from being uncomfortable.

McNulty closed his eyes. Even lying naked except for a white towel draped strategically across his buttocks he retained a certain poise. An animal thing that had alpha male written all over it. Self-confidence oozed out of him like sweat and he was surprised nobody ever realized he was a copper when he went undercover. The grey sweatshirt and faded blue jeans thrown carelessly on the floor in the corner might have something to do with it. That and the gothic house tattoo up the side of his neck. Branches of a long-dead tree climbed like witch's fingers, stopping just short of his left ear.

Natasha – that was the woman's name, according to the badge pinned to the white smock she no longer wore – changed her attention to his left arm. She followed the same routine of squeezing and caressing, leaning across the table so her hands could reach down his arm. Her breasts touched his back just enough to send tiny sparks of electricity through his body. Too much contact would have dissipated the effect. The engine-room pulse grew stronger and he had to shift position to accommodate the bulge. Natasha's eyes caught the movement but she said nothing. That was how he liked it. Too much talk dissipated the effect as well.

With his eyes still closed, he mapped the layout of the building in his mind. Important for future operations and for any report submitted later. Professional. Only way to do the job proper. Remain detached and don't get too involved. Something under the towel was struggling to stay detached. He concentrated on the layout instead, helped by the subtle odour of damp carpet and talcum powder.

Main entrance at the front of the two-storey terraced house. Up a short flight of external stone steps to the heavily studded wooden door. This opened into a small reception area complete with counter, porter's bell and a telephone. A single doorway stood open beside the counter with multicoloured plastic strips dangling from the top to obstruct the view. A narrow corridor led from the doorway to the bottom of the main stairs and just beyond, two stripped pine doors into the ground floor massage rooms. The stairs led up to a first floor lounge decorated in dark red and furnished with three leather settees. A corner bar offered non-alcoholic refreshments. Two more massage rooms to the rear. Fire exit.

The damp-carpet smell came from downstairs. Beyond the two ground floor rooms, carpeted steps descended to the cellar. Again with dark red wallpaper. A large pine cabin took up half the room, the sauna blasting heat into the cellar that could not overcome the damp from the Jacuzzi sunk into the floor. White towels were laid around the bubble bath for customers climbing out, but the carpet was still damp. Still smelled. It was mildly off-putting, but McNulty liked to relax in the Jacuzzi before getting down to business. Not the sauna. Always gave him a headache.

A cold line of scented oil ran down the base of his spine and put paid to his mapping of the layout. Natasha had finished with his shoulders and was recharging the oil in the small of his back. She moved halfway down the table and placed both hands at the base of his spine, thumbs in the middle and fingers fanning out so they looked like a butterfly. She leaned forward and pushed her hands all the way up his spine to the shoulders. Her weight forced the air out of his lungs in a gentle sigh. Coming back down his spine, she worked her thumbs into each vertebra one at a time. Then she repeated the process, crushing his lungs and tightening his skin. He twisted his neck so he could look along the table to where she stood. When she leaned forward this time, he watched her breasts sway above him.

Once a cop always a cop. Had there ever been a better assignment in the police force? Not bloody likely. True, it didn't have the benefit of team spirit he'd enjoyed as a uniformed officer, sitting in the back of a police van swapping jokes or kicking in doors to make an arrest. And there was a definite excitement at murder scenes and serious crimes that the man on the street would never experience. But for sheer hands-on perks of the job this had them all beat.

Silky hands slid from working his spine to massaging his left side. Natasha moved up the table to McNulty's right and leaned forward. Her hands built up a rhythm, one hand sliding forward and then pulling back, drawing the skin tight over his rib cage, sliding forward again as the other hand pulled back. Forward and back. Forward and back. Moving down his body from ribs to hip. The force of her pull back raised his left side off the table slightly with each stroke. The rocking motion teased the pulse throbbing beneath him. Three more circuits and then she turned her hands on their sides, performing gentle karate chops along the area she'd just worked. The pounding brought blood to the surface like an embarrassed blush. She moved round the table and did the same along his right side.

Somewhere in the background he heard the front door close. A few minutes later a female voice escorted another punter upstairs to the lounge. McNulty could picture him being offered tea or coffee or a soft drink; alcohol wasn't encouraged, since it could lead to problems later. The remaining girls would make small talk as the punter took his time drinking whatever he chose to drink. The delay was built into the service. It allowed the customer to choose his masseuse without being so obvious. None of that line-'em-up-like-a-cattle-market stuff while you made your selection at the Sauna Kabin. That was for the more low-rent establishments. Not for the Northern X chain.

A deep voice sounded from the lounge above him.

The downside of having a communal lounge was that you some-times came face to face with the next customer. That didn't bother McNulty, but some punters found it intimidating. The shy type of punter. The cheating-on-their-wives type of customer. Single men on the prowl didn't mind. It was no more embarrassing than taking a leak at the next stall. All part of being a man.

Natasha finished his right side and went to the foot of the table. McNulty forgot about the lounge as she spread his legs, carefully moving his feet to the corners. More oil dribbled along the back of each leg. Cold and sensual. Firm hands worked his right foot, careful not to tickle.

They did each toe and then slid up the back of his calf muscle. She
kneaded and caressed it half a dozen times. Same with the left foot and
calf. She was dragging this out. As her hands reached the back of his
knee, McNulty felt a surge of electricity run up his thighs.

Muffled words from upstairs. Something banged on the bar.

The woman known as Natasha, although her name almost certainly
wasn't Natasha, moved into the closing stages of the massage's first
half. The half that involved lying on your front. She drizzled more oil
along the back of each thigh. The cool liquid sparked extra senses
right up the top of his legs. The towel was gently raised a couple of
inches so the oil didn't stain it. Now the hands worked the right thigh.
Thumbs together and fingers down either side. They pushed up
the muscle all the way to the top and then slid back down. Push to the
top. Slide back down. With each stroke the fingers of her inner hand
touched forbidden fruit, then came away.

McNulty glanced at the crumpled jeans on the floor. Focused on
the back pocket where his wallet protruded slightly. His other wallet
was hidden in the left training shoe.

His badge wallet.

Soon.

The hands switched to his left leg. The same motion. Push to the
top. Slide back down. Push to the top. Slide back down. Her right
hand was on the inside this time and its fingers touched what they
intended to touch. Briefly. Almost a butterfly kiss, it was so gentle.
The butterfly kissing his balls, no matter how briefly, sent the engine-
room pulse into overdrive. It throbbed so hard he could barely lie flat
on it. Now she switched to one hand per leg, thumbs running up
the inside of his thighs while her fingers caressed his buttocks on the
upstroke. Her breasts brushed his calves as she leaned forward to reach.
Once. Twice. Three times a lady.

Then she stopped.

'Turn over please.'

It was the first time she'd spoken since instructing him to lie on his
stomach. No matter how hard she tried, Natasha, or whatever her real
name was, could never be described as posh totty. Polite, yes. Posh,
no. She sounded like she should be working down the pits, if there'd
been any pits left to work down. Rough as a bear's arse, with short,
clipped vowels that definitely didn't roll off the tongue. He took a
deep breath and rose up onto his elbows. Natasha moved to his side
and gripped the towel so it wouldn't slip off. McNulty spun expertly
onto his back and she laid the towel across him again. It wouldn't lie
down but she knew that anyway. She was good at this.

The room felt very warm, and it had nothing to do with the sauna in the basement or the steam from the Jacuzzi. Even the woman was sweating, her flat stomach and swaying breasts glistening under the dim wall light. She drizzled oil onto his chest and the liquid cooled him. Her fingers worked harder now they were into the second half. They kneaded his shoulders and neck. They massaged his chest and stomach. They karate-chopped gently down both sides of his torso and with each change of technique they came closer to the meat of the massage.

But never quite reached the towel.

McNulty thought he would explode. If he wasn't careful, part of him probably would. Into the endgame. At the foot of the bed and oiling his thighs. This time when she raised the towel a couple of inches, what she was staring at wasn't McNulty's buttocks. He glanced over his shoulder at the training shoe on the floor.

Soon. Wait for the offer and price.

Natasha gave his shins a cursory rub and then proceeded to the thighs. Right leg first. Thumbs together, fingers on either side. McNulty could feel the pressure building inside him. The fingers working along his inner thigh slid all the way to the top. They accidentally-on-purpose brushed hot flesh. Electric. Left leg now. The fingers did the same again. Barely a touch, but enough contact to suggest what was to come. At a price.

Offer and price. Nearly there. The point where he would reach down and flick open his badge wallet and hold the warrant card in her face. Make the arrest. There was never any trouble. Working girls were aware of the risks and knew if there was an undercover on scene then backup was covering the exits. No one had ever made a run for it. No half-naked female wearing high heels being chased down the high street. This was where elation and frustration met. The buzz of the arrest followed by deflation at missing the best part of the massage.

But it was different now.

McNulty closed his eyes and waited. Slick hands squeezed twice more along his thigh and then the inner hand slid right under the towel and oiled his shaft. Just once. Soft and gentle, but a firm grip. The shock, even though he'd been expecting it, almost sent him over the edge. He was rock hard and hot to trot. The thing that held him back was the depression that usually set in at this point. The realization that things would never be the same again.

The badge wallet wasn't in the training shoe. His warrant card was no longer valid. The team spirit enjoyed by the brotherhood of blue didn't embrace him any more. He was an outsider. Alone. An ex-cop.

Ex-policeman. Ex-copper. Worse, he was a disgraced ex-copper. He squeezed his eyes tight shut and hoped Natasha would mistake the moisture for excitement. He forced a positive slant on the situation. At least when the offer came this time he could accept. He could fulfil his potential in that regard at least. The woman withdrew her hand as quickly as she'd slipped it along his shaft and stood back. Offer and price would come now.

Shouting from upstairs. A deep voice followed by a stifled female scream. A very young scream. The worst possible timing. He might not have the badge any more, but eighteen years of service didn't just evaporate overnight. Before the offer was even made he was off the table and pulling his jeans on.

McNulty was slightly out of breath when he reached the lounge. Taking two steps at a time while fastening his jeans was more difficult than a straight foot chase. Factor in the energy he'd expended on the table and it wasn't something you trained for. When McNulty entered, slowing down so as not to burst in, the man had his back to him. First rule of a potential violent encounter was, defuse it as much as you can. Fast movement and aggression caused more injuries on duty than anything else. Standing back and taking stock worked every time. Even when he'd been in uniform he used to talk his way out of more trouble than he got into.

'Any chance of a cold drink? Hot as fuck in here.'

No point being too polite. This fella needed to know that McNulty wasn't a cheating-on-his-wife type of customer. The shy type of punter, afraid to get involved in case his wife found out. McNulty asked the question but the girl didn't answer. Fear robbed her of speech. The look in her eyes made that clear. And the grip the man had on her wrist.

A middle-aged woman in a white smock stood near the corner bar. McNulty couldn't read the name badge. Natasha came in behind him. The young girl and the bullying man were standing in front of the hallway to the massage rooms and the fire exit. The fire door was partly open for fresh air and McNulty could just make out the rusting metal of the outside stairs. He'd scouted them out as well. Never go in undercover unless you know your exits. The fire escape zigzagged up the rear of the house with a door on each floor. The basement had its own door, since it was one floor lower than the front of the house. The small paved yard backed onto a cobbled back street giving access to the entire row. It looked like that was where the bully intended to go.

'Orange'll be fine. Still, not fizzy. Fuckin' bubbles get up me nose.'
Again the rough edges to his speech. McNulty was sending a
message. The man glanced over his shoulder to gauge the threat level.
The alpha male thing. The pissing contest kind of thing to see who
was hardest. Seeing McNulty, six foot three of tattooed muscle, gave
him pause but didn't appear to scare him. He was shorter but broader,
and McNulty could sense bodybuilder muscle beneath the threadbare
rugby shirt. His scruffy jeans should have been baggy but seemed tight
over strong legs. The ripped knees went one better than McNulty's
casual look. McNulty smiled at him.

'Pardon my fuckin' French.'

The man smiled back. With his mouth. The smile didn't go anywhere
near his eyes, which remained cold and hard and wary. The girl's eyes
pleaded for help but she said nothing. She was thin and pale and very,
very young. Early teens, McNulty would guess. Although it was hard
to tell these days. She had the breasts and white smock of the other
staff, but if she was legal age McNulty would show his arse on the
town hall steps. Not that anything about the Sauna Kabin was legal,
but in McNulty's eyes some things were more illegal than others. And
he'd detested bullies right back to Crag View. He adopted the hands-
in-pockets pose, partly to appear unthreatening but mainly to hide his
hands balling into fists.

The woman nearest the bar stepped behind it to pour the drink.
Tension hung in the air thicker than the damp towel and talcum powder
smell. The bottle rattled the glass as she poured Robinson's orange
barley water and ran the cold tap. McNulty reckoned all he had to do
was be in the room to prevent the situation escalating. A few more
minutes at most before the bouncer came out of his back room and
ejected Mr Muscles from the premises for manhandling the staff.

McNulty accepted the drink but stayed away from the bar. The
woman brought it over. Her hand was shaking. The shouting must have
been pretty explosive for McNulty to hear it downstairs. Explosive
enough to stun the woman into silence. Even Natasha kept her distance.
McNulty swigged half a glass of orange and felt the cold drink refresh
him to the core. It was warm in here even with the fire escape door
open. Normally he would sit down for his post-massage drink, but he
didn't want to surrender the high ground. To avoid appearing threatening, he faced the open door and closed his eyes. Took a deep breath.

'Boy. Fresh air'd be better with some breeze.'

He was acutely aware of being alone. No police radio. No backup.
Not even a badge he could flash to back the man down. Taking another
swig of orange, he glanced at the wall clock. Ten minutes since he'd

come up here. Where the hell was the heavy mob? The hired muscle that every parlour employed to stop young tearaways getting too excited on the late shift. A few beers before the massage. A big mouth after.

Well, Mr Big Mouth had one of the girls in his grip and the bouncer needed to pull his finger out. Right now. The situation was beginning to bubble again. McNulty could sense it like static before a storm. The man tightened his grip and the girl winced. Her eyes watered but she gritted her teeth. Refusing to cry in front of strangers. McNulty admired her for that. Hated the man even more. A jerk of her wrist and the man propelled the girl towards the fire escape.

'Come on.'

'No. Please.'

Her voice was small. Pleading but without any strength in the plea. Not really believing it would make any difference. McNulty felt heat flush his neck. Anger fuelled the pressure building inside him. Different pressure than before. More destructive pressure. A short temper that had dogged him from Crag View to Mean Wood. And a sense of injustice that had haunted him before that. He despised bullies of any description. Big men who picked on young defenceless girls even more.

The bouncer. Where was he?

Neither of the women said anything. Natasha hung around at the top of the stairs. The other woman retreated behind the bar. The girl knew there would be no help from her colleagues. Didn't look like there was much help from the customer with the tattoo up his neck either. McNulty could sense her resolve vanish. The acceptance of her fate. The look in her eyes as the man guided her away tore McNulty apart. Once a cop always a cop.

Time to act. Keeping his voice low key and friendly, McNulty stepped towards the bar and passed the empty glass over. He nodded for a refill. The woman began to pour. He looked at the girl and then her captor.

'Is she goin' to be free anytime soon?'

Enough orange. Now running the tap.

'I mean. How long you goin' to be?'

The man turned away from the fire escape as if he couldn't believe this idiot was even talking to him. The level of his arrogance edged the odds in McNulty's favour. The glass of orange squash slid across the bar and McNulty picked it up. The drink had become a non-drink. Something so inoffensive it didn't even register as the man glared at McNulty.

'She isn't ever going to be free.'

McNulty took a mouthful of cool orange and flapped his free hand.

'Sorry. Didn't mean free, like gratis.' The flapping hand indicated apology. 'I know there's a price.'

It distracted the man's attention from the glass.

'You do know what gratis means, don't you?'

McNulty gripped the glass tight. His free hand flapped again and the bully's eyes followed the more obvious threat. He was getting annoyed, but his eyes dulled as he tried to think of a witty retort. McNulty didn't think he did know what gratis meant. There was a slight lull in the tension as the man decided what to do next. And then McNulty lunged at his face with the glass.

The man was quick. He let go of the girl's arm and brought both hands up to deflect the glass attack, and it was only then that he realized the glass wasn't in McNulty's hand any more. Ice-cold orange splashed in his eyes but the glass dropped harmlessly to the floor. His eyes stung and he blinked them clear. The man was quick but McNulty was quicker. He grabbed the man's lead hand below the wrist, yanking it towards him and up. He bent the joint down into a gooseneck and the man had no choice but to follow or get a broken wrist. He lost his balance and toppled forward. McNulty slammed the heel of his free hand into the exposed throat.

And that was it. Game over. The man hit the ground like a sack of potatoes, both hands gripping his throat. Unable to breathe. McNulty dropped to his knees beside him and moved the man's hands away.

'Slow down. Shallow breaths. You'll be all right.'

The man did as he was told. Shorter breaths helped but he was still struggling against the fire in his throat. His eyes were watering. All the fight had gone out of him. McNulty used his other get-out-of-trouble technique. He talked to the man.

'You know, if this was a film I'd be asking what movies you'd been in. Like in *Get Shorty*. Remember? After Travolta gut-punched Gandolfini – before he did the *Sopranos* – and asked what movies he did? 'Cos Gandolfini's character had been a stunt man.'

The man was breathing better now. McNulty looked into his eyes.

'You aren't a stunt man are you?'

The man shook his head. McNulty stood up and helped the man onto the nearest settee. Asked for another drink. The aftermath of violence always made him thirsty. His hands shook with adrenaline dump. The anger had gone and for a moment he struggled to remember what had set him off. When he did, he looked around for the girl to see if she was OK.

She had disappeared.

A waft of cool breeze came in through the fire exit door. It was wide open. He tried to remember in which films the hero had rescued the girl from thugs only for her to run away. And couldn't come up with any.

TWO

By the time the adrenaline dump had cleared McNulty was back in his hotel room. Cheap and cheerless and as faded as his jeans. The sun was down and evening drawing in. Being a creature of habit, he preferred late afternoon for his massage parlour visits, mainly because that's when they used to do them when he was still in the job. Less trouble on an afternoon than at night. Fewer drunks to deal with.

Thinking about that depressed him. Happy days doing the job he was no longer a part of. He was thirty-six years old, thirty-seven by the end of the year, and taking into account his eighteen years' service that meant he'd spent half his life in the police force. Add on the year since he'd left under a cloud and he was only just into the debit side.

Damn.

He looked out of the window at the thin wedge of view between the building behind the Victoria Hotel and the pub that was already pumping out mind-numbing music. Park benches around a patch of lawn the size of a snooker table. Metal railings with ten coats of black paint to hide the rust. Half a dozen trees already shedding leaves and turning the branches into spindly black fingers as autumn began to bite. He touched the tattoo up the side of his neck. The house silhouetted against the red sun.

He stripped off his sweatshirt and jeans and went into the tiny boxroom the hotel called en-suite. He drew back the shower curtain and twisted the control. Water belched out of the mixer tap into the bath. McNulty examined the complicated plumbing and pulled the chrome knob on top of the tap. The plumbing burped, stopped, and then water spurted out of the shower attachment. He adjusted the temperature and went back into the bedroom.

His suitcase was on the bed. It was medium sized with zipper compartments and a pullout handle. A pair of wheels. The sort of case that flight crews pulled behind them at the airport. McNulty never used the wheels. Unless you were part of the flight crew you just looked a prat. Anywhere other than airports the cases should be banned, but for McNulty it was the ideal size. He didn't have a massive wardrobe, just two pairs of jeans and an assortment of polo shirts. One faded sweatshirt.

The midsize zipper compartment held his toilet bag. He took it out and the dog-eared map caught in the zip. It fell on the bed. A folded Ordnance Survey map of the North of England. He considered checking his progress now but decided to wait until after the shower. He turned the bedside radio clock on instead and froze as the familiar guitar intro flooded the room.

> *There is a house in New Orleans*
> *They call the Rising Sun*
> *And it's been the ruin of many a poor boy*
> *And God I know I'm one*

Hot water stung his face as he ducked under the showerhead. As with most of the hotels he'd stayed in, the shower above the bath was intended for midgets or extras from *The Lord Of The Rings*. He stepped back and squirted a dollop of Foam Burst shower gel into the palm of his hand. Soaped himself all over while he sang his way into one of the verses.

> *'Oh mother tell your children*
> *Not to do what I have done*
> *Spend your lives in sin and misery*
> *In the House of the Rising Sun.'*

McNulty didn't agree with the sin and misery part going hand in hand. For him the misery came from somewhere else. The sin made him happier than a dog with two dicks. And who was to say what constituted sin anyway? As far as he was concerned sex was the best thing since sliced bread. Provided it occurred between consenting adults, where was the sin in that? In any case, for him, 'House of the Rising Sun' meant something else. Somewhere else. A place he tried to forget but would always remember. Whenever he heard the song.

He turned his back to the shower and rinsed the lather off. He had to duck again to catch his shoulders. Then he faced front and blasted the spray into his eyes. Stood like that for a few minutes. Massage parlours had come into his life through his work in the vice squad but stayed because they satisfied his urges without the hassle of dating, drinking and dining out. You even got a free shower. Most times. He stepped back so the spray hit his love muscle. Swilling that off too as he sang the final verse.

'Well, there is a house in New Orleans
They call the Rising Sun
And it's been the ruin of many a poor boy
And God I know I'm one.'

Only it wasn't brothels or New Orleans he was thinking about. His eyes closed but his mind opened up as it remembered a house on a hill. A darker place. Darker times. Where there had definitely been many a poor boy.

Sitting naked on the bed, McNulty flicked channels with the TV remote. This being a downmarket hotel, that meant five terrestrial channels and Sky News. Two of the terrestrial channels were fuzzy and unwatchable and the rest had gone into the evening soap opera hour, so he settled for the news. He turned the volume low and dropped the remote on the pillow. The map was spread across the bedspread with a red felt-tip pen.

International news washed over him in the background. Famine. Terrorism. An eight-lane motorway bridge that had collapsed into the Mississippi. Big stories with zero impact on the seedy hotel room in the northern mill town. McNulty concentrated on the map. It was part of a two-map set covering England, Scotland and Wales. This part covered the North of England and all of Scotland. Main roads and motorways stood out like veins across a body so you could get from one town to the next, but the minor roads were barely visible. That was OK for McNulty. He had his own routine once he arrived at a new town. This map was simply to get him there. And record where he'd been so he didn't double up. It was amazing how many massage parlours some of these small towns had.

Rescue workers in fluorescent jackets tried to winch survivors to safety on Sky News. The info bar scrolling across the bottom of the screen said seven were confirmed dead but the death toll was expected to rise. To remind viewers how tragic this was they kept replaying footage of the dramatic collapse.

McNulty picked up the felt tip pen. The map was spotted with red dots like one of those join-the-dots magic pictures. He wondered what shape it would reveal if he joined the dots from number one to number whatever-he-was-up-to-now. In the order of his massage parlour visits over the last six months. Each dot represented a town or city he'd visited. Within each town there had been several parlours, some more memorable than others.

The dots ranged from south of Leeds to the east coast and then north along the coastline. He took in the seaside resorts of Bridlington and Scarborough and darted inland occasionally to Pickering and Thirsk. Each time he stayed in back-street hotels and parked his Vauxhall Astra in the hotel car park, if they had one. Apart from the parlours, he took in some of the local highlights and always walked past the main police station just to feel connected. It worked a treat. He felt like the best-travelled tourist in the north and the most exclusive undercover copper in Yorkshire. Ignore the fact that he was working well out of his jurisdiction.

Morecambe, Lancaster and Blackpool led him down the west coast, with a few other calls on the way, and then it was the big cities of Manchester and Liverpool. Those had taken longer because the choice was enormous. From small independent parlours to the more exclusive Northern X chain. He had encountered their premises in most of the larger towns and they were always worth a visit.

He picked up the felt tip pen. Finding Halifax on the map, he marked the spot with another red dot. Almost full circle. Like Michael Palin going round the world for TV, McNulty had gone round the north for sex. He reckoned he'd got the better deal. God's best invention. Sex and the cinema were his favourite pastimes. Sitting on the bed in this seedy hotel room he felt like Michael Caine in *Get Carter*, coming back to his home town for revenge. He could almost hear the familiar beat of the main theme, one of the coolest film themes ever along with *Bullitt* and *The Ipcress File*.

The TV caught his eye and he knew even before looking up that it was local news. Two police officers in fluorescent jackets were wrapping crime scene tape around a lamp post and across a road. Blue lights flashed on their patrol car and in the distance a three-car pile-up revealed it was a fatal accident. Boys in blue. The thin blue line. He watched with the sound turned down and still felt a part of them.

The map again. The rash of red dots. They covered most of northern England, thicker in some places than others, but missed out Leeds and Bradford altogether. His home patch. He'd been travelling non-stop for almost six months, the second half of his year out of the job. It would soon be a full twelve months. Some kind of anniversary there if you like. McNulty didn't. He felt a hollowness in his stomach. And something drawing him back. Not like Jack Carter coming home to avenge his brother's death. Just the power of familiar surroundings pulling him home.

Maybe it was time for a rest. With a stab of the pen he scrawled a circle around Leeds. His next port of call.

THREE

'**Y**ou'd normally have four to choose from but the new girl hasn't turned in.'

McNulty sat in Gemini's lounge and sipped his orange juice. Rest for him meant another massage. Another massage meant trawling the local paper as soon as he got back into town. Not even back into town because the local paper covered all of Yorkshire. It was just the personal ads and cinema listings that changed with the regional editions. As soon as he reckoned he was close enough for the ads to cover the outskirts of Leeds he'd pulled into a petrol station and bought an *Evening Post*, even though it wasn't evening yet. Mid-afternoon.

The orange juice was chilled to perfection. Ice clinked in his glass as he took another sip. A nice touch. The ice. One of the small things that made the Northern X chain the best in the business. That was why he'd chosen it for his first punt on home soil. Turnover of staff in this game was so rapid that he didn't think it would be a problem working the old patch, but he thought it best to avoid the parlours he'd busted himself in his former life. He didn't recognize any of the women in the lounge.

'Then I guess the third time's a charm.'

'I guess it is.'

McNulty leaned back in the leather settee and swirled the ice around his drink as he watched his three choices milling about. Relaxed. Not cattle-market. Another plus for Northern X. If the chain had one of those tick-box surveys with five boxes for every question, number one being very satisfied and number five being very unsatisfied, then most of the answers would be on the number one side. Gemini's even managed to make the rooms above a parade of shops feel like they'd been purpose-built just for this business. Rear entry – not anal fisting – for customers too shy to use the front door, and stairs up to reception. Extensive lounge decorated in dark red with subdued wall lights. Sauna and Jacuzzi. And three massage rooms, one with a mirrored ceiling and en-suite shower.

Traffic rumbled past outside. The only box that scored less than a number one. Maybe a three. Position. A busy high street. He concentrated on the staff, all wearing the traditional white smocks as if they worked the perfume counter at Debenhams. Plastic name badges over their right breasts. No point checking the names until he made his selection, and even then it wouldn't match their birth certificate. *'Names is for tombstones, baby.'* Yaphet Kotto popped into McNulty's head. Playing Mr Big in *Live And Let Die*.

Forget the names and study the form. Like picking a winner down the race track. The form was looking pretty good, two out of three. The woman who'd told him about the staff shortage was an attractive brunette with enormous breasts. Late thirties but with a face that suggested she'd had a hard paper-round. The one who served him the orange juice was a little older but better preserved. She didn't speak but had a cheeky smile that was almost hidden. Slimmer. Less well stacked up front. Blonde hair tied back in a ponytail. The third was the youngest. And biggest. Everywhere. She obviously catered for the Tellytubby brigade and was immediately struck off McNulty's list.

That familiar feeling began to creep over him. The calm before the storm. The sense of anticipation that preceded any operation he'd ever been on, either in uniform or plain clothes. Apart from the sex it was the main reason he was doing this. The sense of connection with his old life. Of still belonging. The police force was the only place he'd ever felt like he belonged. He never belonged at Crag View. Despite what some might have said. Nobody did.

He finished the orange juice and made his selection. Melissa behind the bar. It was the cheeky smile and silence that did it. The other two didn't seem too disappointed. There would always be another punter. As he stood up and put his empty glass on the bar he wondered briefly about the new girl who hadn't turned in. A chill ran down his spine but he put it down to the breeze from the window. The warning flags wouldn't come until later.

Melissa drizzled oil into the depression at the small of McNulty's back, having already worked his shoulders, and leaned into the massage. She was strong and toned and definitely the best choice. Lacked some of the finesse moves that Natasha had possessed but made up for it in sheer quality. Her hands swept up his back and down again, sliding under the towel across his buttocks without pausing. Then back up his spine again, driving the breath out of his lungs.

He shifted his head on his hands and looked down the massage table. Melissa leaned forward as she worked up his spine again and her breasts didn't even move. They weren't exactly small but they were tightly muscled and firm. Her stomach was so solid it almost had a six-pack. This woman was a gym junky for sure. And she enjoyed her work.

He glanced at the white smock with the plastic name badge hanging neatly behind the door. A complete contrast to the pile of clothes discarded on the floor. Faded jeans. Screwed-up sweatshirt. A single training shoe peeping out from under the jeans. The badge wallet hidden from view containing the warrant card he'd managed to keep when they sacked him. Not his current ID card – he'd had to hand that in – but the tatty, split card that he'd washed with his jeans too many times. When they issued the new card he'd been allowed to keep the old one since it was too battered to be of any use. Except for now. He could flash the badge wallet and it would still pass muster if he played it right.

He wasn't planning to flash it today. He enjoyed the build-up towards the arrest but fully understood that he wouldn't be arresting anyone again. That twin pang of sadness and elation as the loss of one thing led to the gaining of another. No arrest but a definite bonus. He was glad there were no noises from the lounge to distract him this time. No bullies beating up young girls.

Melissa moved down the table and began to work his legs. Her fingers were stronger than Natasha's. When they accidentally-on-purpose touched what they intended to touch, it was less of a butterfly kiss and more of a slippery snake rub. His slippery snake tensed and electricity surged through his body. He couldn't resist letting out a satisfied, 'Mmmmm.'

When he turned onto his back he was sure Melissa was licking her lips. In the dim glow of the wall light it was difficult to tell. The cheeky smile was definitely there. And a twinkle in her eye. She certainly enjoyed her work. And why not? You've got it. You sell it. And you've still got it. Must be the best economics in the world. He wondered if there was a male equivalent. Her hand brushed his trouser snake again and he surrendered to the moment. Why over-analyse?

Yeah. No mistake. That's fuckin' him. Traffic was heavy on the high street but the ex-copper was clearly visible across the road between a passing double-decker bus and an *Evening Post* delivery van. Second edition. The man collecting his daily methadone dose from Lloyds Pharmacy watched through the gaps as rush hour commuters made their way home. He saw Detective Constable McNulty come out of the back alley and walk down the street.

Well, you cheeky little bastard, he thought. *You're still at it, aren't you?* He popped a mint to cover the disgusting methadone taste and crossed the road. Followed McNulty from a distance. He didn't need to look down the back alley because he knew where the ex-copper had been. The same sort of place the ex-copper had been when he'd arrested him and ruined his life. Three times.

Keith Tellez ignored the fact that being caught three times displayed not only bad luck but a decided lack of initiative and laid the blame for his decline squarely on the arresting officer. He had lost his job, his wife and his self-respect, and along the way developed a drug habit that he was still trying to kick. Reading in the papers that the very same officer had been sacked a year ago was the only good news he'd heard since becoming part of the local pond life.

Until now.

Catching his tormentor still frequenting massage parlours sent the old grey matter into overdrive. The germ of an idea began to form.

The ex-copper turned down a side street and then stopped. He turned round suddenly and scratched the back of his neck. Looking directly at the man who was following him.

McNulty turned the corner to his car and suddenly felt a prickle up the back of his neck. The old spider sense he hadn't engaged for over a year. Something was wrong. He turned back and watched a crowd of passengers boarding a bus out of town. Traffic was heavy and cars squeezed past the bus, causing a bottleneck in the teatime rush hour. A gaunt-looking man in his forties joined the back of the queue. There was a smattering of pedestrians but nobody stood out.

Even though he'd had a shower and another glass of orange juice, he still smelled of scented oil, and that reminded him where he'd just been. Something wrong. He quickly patted his back pocket but his wallet was still there. The bulge in his other jeans pocket was less pronounced. He took out the badge wallet and flicked it open. Unlike NYPD Blue, the West Yorkshire Police didn't provide detective shields but simply plastic warrant cards like every other police authority. A photo ID card that was about as impressive as a bus pass. McNulty's looked even less impressive since he'd washed it so many times the laminated sheets were splitting apart.

But it was still there. So were his car keys. In his front pocket.

He scratched the back of his neck. The feeling had gone. After a few moments he turned back to his car, parked halfway down the street. He put the bad vibe down to returning to his old stomping ground. Maybe using parlours so close to home was a mistake.

Tellez got stuck in the bus queue. Three more passengers crushed in behind him. He shuffled forward helplessly as the detective flicked open a thin black wallet and then took a set of car keys out of his pocket. Having the ex-copper stare right at him shook him up, but seeing the car keys confirmed his suspicions. He had a car parked nearby.

The vice squad cop turned the corner again just as Tellez was boarding the bus. The driver waited for his fare. Tellez fumbled in his pockets but was craning his neck to see the corner. Overgrown bushes blocked his view. The passengers behind him grew impatient, nudging forward. Tellez felt impatience tugging at him and he barged his way back off the bus.

Red mist descended and he knew the anger was working for him. It was helping shape the plan. *Revenge is a dish best served cold.* An old Klingon proverb. What he needed to see was the detective's car. He closed in on a woman carrying a Morrisons carrier bag and used her as a shield round the corner.

Fuckin' shitty death. The detective had gone. Leaving an empty car space halfway down the street.

FOUR

The old stomping ground. Nine beats covered by uniform patrols from Ecclesfield Police Station. The last place McNulty had worked before being unceremoniously dumped out of the West Yorkshire Police. Not so unceremoniously in fact, since he remembered there being quite a lot of ceremony at the time. Quite a lot of publicity too. The Chief Constable had gone on record that he wasn't going to stand for such behaviour from his officers. Had covered his back by throwing McNulty to the wolves.

A bitter taste flooded McNulty's mouth as he swung the Astra into Queens Road. He couldn't understand why, if it was such a bitter taste, he was heading towards Ecclesfield instead of West Park, where his flat had stood empty for the last six months. But he already knew the answer to that. Because he missed it, that's why. The place. The people. The job.

Early evening traffic was lighter once he was off the main roads. He slipped effortlessly into patrol speed. Cruising speed. Driving around the estate while keeping an eye out for anything unusual speed.

Simply slowing to patrol speed made him feel better. He decided to postpone returning home for a while and go on a nostalgia trip instead. The only thing missing was the police radio bleeping and squawking constantly in the background. Coming back reminded him just how much he missed this.

The wash of nostalgia left a warm glow in McNulty's stomach. The smile was permanently stitched on his face. He felt like Mr Incredible sitting in a car with Frozone listening to the police scanner. How sad was that? How happy? Eighteen years working his beat, whether that be uniform patrol, CID or Vice Squad. It all added up to the same. Serving the public. Protecting the weak. Punishing the bullies.

In a flash the nostalgia rush vanished. He turned a corner and saw Ecclesfield Police Station silhouetted against the blood-red sky. Sun glinted off the windows of the custody suite, but what McNulty saw was a gothic house on a hilltop.

The slap sounded like a gunshot in the quiet office. A gunshot followed by a heartbreaking whimper. A wounded animal kind of whimper. The man in charge of Crag View Orphanage stood back and leaned against his desk, sunlight from the window glinting off his glasses.

It was early evening and the teatime rush had subsided. Everyone in their rooms while the dining room was cleared. One of the rules that was strictly enforced. Only one resident had permission to be in breach of curfew. And only one member of staff was out of the dining room. The headmaster. Mr Cruckshank. Just the two of them alone in his office at the bottom of the stairs. But not quite alone.

The gunshot echoed in young Vincent McNulty's ears and his eyes burned as the implication sank in. Anger filled him like hot oil, changing the normally docile teenager into a raging bull. None of the other staff knew of the rights-of-passage scenario playing out in the dingy office. Nobody else saw Vincent McNulty leaving childhood behind and becoming a man. A man with a very short temper.

The office was lined with bookshelves. A dying rubber plant stood in the bay window. A painting of the Queen hung above the fireplace opposite the desk. And the man who had become the focal point of Vincent's hatred turned to face him as if surprised he had the cheek to even be there.

'Go back to your room.'

Mr Cruckshank pushed off from the desk and his bulk hid the bench seat in the alcove. It didn't matter. It was already too late. Vincent picked the biggest book he could find from the bookshelf and hefted it in both hands like a baseball player preparing to swing. The anger boiled over.

'Go to hell.'

The whisper carried more weight than a thousand shouts.

Mr Cruckshank blinked as if slapped, and the irony of that would have pleased Vincent if he'd understood what irony was. He stepped forward and swung the book with all his might. The headmaster couldn't believe what was happening as the leather-bound Bible crashed into his face and broke his nose. One lens from his glasses popped out of the frame and shattered on the floor.

McNulty absent-mindedly fingered the tattoo on his neck. The gothic house and the long-dead fingers of the tree. His eyes were wet from staring into space without blinking. He blinked now, wiping his eyes dry with the back of one hand. The sun had set behind Ecclesfield Police Station but the bruised sky looked as sore as a smacked arse.

Protect and serve. He'd been doing that ever since Crag View Orphanage. Even before the slap and the broken nose that got him kicked out. He slipped the Astra into gear but kept the clutch down. The custody suite windows, with their bars and thick glass, were in shadow but now that he understood irony it seemed ironic that it was another slap that got him kicked out of the police force. He let the clutch out and pulled away from the kerb. Time to go home. Or what passed for home these days.

FIVE

Weetwood Court was a sixties complex built like Lego and designed like a Rubik's cube. McNulty could relate to the little red bricks that reminded him of the Lego set at the orphanage but he'd always found Rubik's cubes confusing. Finding an address at Weetwood Court for the first time was just as confusing. Finding your way home after six months was nearly as bad. McNulty turned the same corner twice and went down the wrong corridor three times before reaching the sanctuary of Flat 7 on the second floor. Rear.

Each flat was a self-contained box with a bedroom, living room and kitchen to the right of the entrance hall and a bathroom and storage cupboards to the left. The architect had decided on a rather liberal approach to design, simply piling the boxes haphazardly and then joining them with covered walkways and communal entrance halls. This made the complex look like someone had spilled their building blocks in the garden and then added parking spaces for the residents. Curved lawns and flower borders calmed the stress levels and trees gave a colourful backdrop to the boundaries, but neither did anything to make sense of the place.

The entire thing stood in the shadow of Weetwood House, a gothic monstrosity with steepled rooftops and blackened chimneys that reminded McNulty of somewhere else entirely. Was probably the reason he'd chosen the flat in the first place. A little bit of self-punishment. Or a dig in the ribs never to forget.

It was dark when he turned the key in his door. Knee-high patio lamps illuminated the pathways outside. The brooding monster of Weetwood House wasn't illuminated at all, apart from several windows of the flats that the house had been split into. The communal landing had two wall lights on the rough brick walls and a window box filled with various succulents overlooking the car park.

The door wouldn't open.

For a moment McNulty thought he'd not turned the key enough, but when he used it again he found that he had. A cold shiver ran down his spine. The first thing he did was check the door frame. There were no splinter marks or indentations. Over the years he'd attended numerous burglaries and if the doors had been forced there were always tell-tale signs around the frame. The frame was intact. No damage. The door still wouldn't open.

The cold shiver changed into a hot flush. Sweat beaded on his forehead.

There were no windows into the flats from the landing and the door was the only way in. He bent down and looked through the letterbox. Darkness inside. No hint of a breeze or movement. If the flat had been burgled from the rear it would have to be through the windows and burglars rarely shut them on their way out. Especially if they had bolted the front door in case the occupier came home early. It had been six months. Not exactly early.

But there was no breeze inside. No flicker of the curtains.

He glanced over his shoulder. Had there been some movement along the path outside? A shifting of the shadows near the trees? He stared into the darkness between the patio lamps. Nobody there.

Turning back to the door he depressed the handle and pushed. This time there wasn't so much resistance. The door gave a little then stopped. Something heavy behind it. This time the sweat did more than bead on his forehead. It trickled down his face and stung his eyes. The last time he'd come across something heavy behind a door it had been at a concern-for-a-neighbour call when he'd worked uniform patrol. The something heavy had been a pensioner who'd collapsed picking up the mail. But there were no pensioners in McNulty's flat.

Who then?

He wiped the sweat from his eyes and pushed again. More give. A one-inch gap as the door opened slightly. Enough room to see a dead pensioner behind the door. Or a dead anyone else. There was no dead arm laid across the gap. No body parts at all. Another look through the letterbox but he couldn't see downwards enough to see the floor. He pushed one more time and . . .

There was a rustling noise behind the door. The shock sent electricity shooting up the back of his neck and the short hairs bristled. The door finally opened despite the weight holding it shut and a mountain of mail spilled out of the gap. Six months' worth of letters and packages that had become wedged beneath the door as he'd tried to open it.

The sharp exhalation of breath was almost a laugh as the tension vanished. McNulty kicked the mail to one side, flicked on the light switch beside the door, and stepped into his hallway.

'I once told you Von Ryan. If only one gets out it's a victory.'

The back of the train disappears into the tunnel as Frank Sinatra lies dead on the tracks, one arm reaching out for the train he can't quite reach. Jerry Goldsmith's poignant theme tune, swelling into the closing march before the end credits roll.

That scene played in McNulty's head as he read the advert in the *Evening Post*. The bag of shopping was unpacked in the kitchen. The mail was sorted on the dining table. And McNulty whistled the Von Ryan march as he stirred his cup of tea. The end-title march, not the first rendition that played during the burn-the-uniforms scene. That had been jauntier and a little tongue in cheek. The end title began more sombrely, building to an uplifting crescendo. That's how McNulty felt having returned to Flat 7, Weetwood Court. Sombre, but building to something better.

He was sitting at the dining table in the living room with a cup of tea at his elbow and a pack of custard creams open on the table. The *Evening Post* was folded back to the personal ads, which coincidentally were on the same page as the cinema listings. *Von Ryan's Express* was showing at a late-night performance at the Hyde Park Picture House tonight. Part of the Classic War Film season the old cinema was running to try and keep the place open.

McNulty dunked a custard cream in his tea and plopped it into his mouth before it dissolved and broke off. He had purposely bought the Rolls-Royce of custard creams instead of the budget variety because he'd fished enough of the cheap shitty things out of his tea in the past.

Tonight he wanted the real deal. *Von Ryan's Express* was the real deal. And later in the week it was going to be *The Dirty Dozen*. He felt like he'd died and gone to war movie heaven.

His eye caught the Northern X advert at the bottom of the page. The massage chain had five parlours in and around Leeds and so far he'd only visited one of them. There were also half a dozen independent parlours that hadn't been bought out by Northern X yet. The way the chain was growing, that was only a matter of time. If only because Northern X parlours were far superior. McNulty thought he'd probably take in a couple of the independents as well, but would mainly stick with Northern X. Not for a few days though. Now he was back there was some catching up to do.

He dunked another biscuit and popped it in his mouth. A whisper of breeze shifted the full-length curtains. He'd opened the balcony windows to air the flat and he went over to them now. Weetwood House loomed above him, a hulking shadow in the darkness. The familiar guitar intro played in his head and he found himself murmuring the words.

> 'There is a house in New Orleans
> They call the Rising Sun
> And it's been the ruin of many a poor boy
> And God I know I'm one.'

He wondered if the old place was still standing. His own personal House of the Rising Sun. Many a poor boy had definitely been ruined there. Some catching up to do. Yes. He considered driving past on his way to the cinema but dismissed the thought. He knew Crag View had been closed years ago following a scandal that rocked the local authority. Stuff he'd been railing against all the time he'd lived there but hadn't come to light until later. Too late for him certainly. No. Crag View was a place to visit during the day, when the ghosts of his past couldn't harm him.

He tried to change the tune in his head but found he couldn't remember the Von Ryan march. His whistle was tuneless and harsh and even looking at the Hyde Park Picture House advert didn't help. He turned the TV on instead and went back to the Northern X section. Tomorrow maybe. One down, four to go. He checked the locations and picked one on the other side of town. Sunshine Supertan. He doubted there was much tanning going on there, unless it was tanning your backside with a table tennis bat. Not his cup of tea, but one of the extras on offer.

Five to ten. The film started at eleven. Now that he'd made his decision he felt more relaxed. Thinking of the sunny side of life helped dispel the dark side that occasionally crept up on him. He sometimes wondered if buying a flat next door to a facsimile of Crag View Orphanage had been a wise move. Whatever. There was just enough time for a shower and a change of clothes before Von Ryan helped six hundred Allied prisoners of war to escape on a stolen express train.

'I once told you Von Ryan. If only one gets out it's a victory.'

He supposed that was true. He had escaped from Crag View, but what about the ones left behind? Maybe that's why Frank Sinatra had taken all six hundred with him. McNulty felt guilty that he hadn't been able to do the same. Protect and serve? At a time when he should have been protecting he'd ended up looking after number one. That was a scar that ran deep and he doubted he would ever outrun it.

A final swig of his tea and then it was strip off and shower. The water hissed against his closed eyes as it washed the past away. For the moment. In the living room the TV played to itself. The ten o'clock news came on but McNulty couldn't hear it. Breaking news. A girl's naked body had been found upended in an oil drum behind Kwik Save downtown. It was early days but speculation was that she had been working as a masseuse at Gemini's parlour.

Part of the Northern X chain.

SIX

'**N**o. You're going to have to seal off the whole thing.'

Detective Constable Jimmy Tynan shouted across the waste ground behind Kwik Save, but the patrol officer couldn't hear for the mobile generator powering the arc lamps that lit the crime scene.

'There's going to be a fingertip search in the morning.'

He couldn't hear that either, so Tynan skirted the car park of the late-night shop and told him up close. The constable's shoulders sagged. This had been a long shift and he should be off in an hour, but now there was a murder scene to protect, so going home wasn't looking good any time soon. Tynan glanced towards the white scene tent that was being erected over the oil drum.

'You the first unit to arrive?'

'Yeah. Me and Pat over there.'

The constable indicated another uniform wrapping blue and white crime scene tape around a lamp post on the side road. Tynan nodded at the traffic cones that had been placed in a rough line from the car park to the oil drum behind the shop.

'Good work staking out a common approach. That the only path anyone took?'

'Yeah. Bloke who found her'd gone round back for a piss and thought the legs were a shop dummy. Wasn't until he saw her furry third eye winking at him he took a closer look.'

'Not surprising. Round here any chance of a bit of pussy and they'll take it.'

'Yeah.' The constable only had one sentence opener. 'Anyway. That's the path he took as best he can remember. Was panicking like mad when he phoned it in. Caught his foreskin in his zip as well. That didn't help.'

'Ouch.'

Tynan sympathized but was already turning his attention to the waste ground behind the parade of shops. It was a misshapen triangle of land about the size of half a football pitch that had been cleared for building over a year ago. The ground had been bulldozed level so that the topsoil formed an embankment along the two sides that bordered City Road and Hillside Terrace. The third side sloped gently up to the brick and plaster gable ends of the terraced houses up the hill. An eight-foot retaining wall blocked off the bottom of the streets, giving the impression of a prison enclosure, with broken glass cemented across the top. The gable ends had no windows.

Dull orange street lamps poked out above the walls but the light only breached the waste ground by ten feet or so. Building work had never begun, another inner city project stalled due to lack of funds. The mounds of earth were now overgrown with grass and weeds, and the cleared space covered with gravel, dog shit and broken bottles. A stray dog scampered across, pausing to sniff the dried turds before laying a fresh one.

The parade of shops stood at the junction of the main road and Hillside Terrace. A fairly modern development with four shops and a cash machine. Two of the shops stood empty, unlet following a spate of vandalism from customers of the third, Kwik Save. The fourth was a nail and hair salon but that too would be closing soon. Nobody around here had enough unchewed nails to need manicuring and most people's hair came in bottle blonde or shocking black. Access to the ten-space car park was from City Road with a narrow exit onto Hillside

Terrace. The rusting oil drum stood six feet from the back wall of the shops.

Tynan watched two Scenes of Crime Officers struggling with the tent that would protect any evidence at the immediate scene not already lost to the elements. At least it was a dry night. Not too windy. He glanced up at the overcast sky. Thin cloud. Not likely to rain. Then he looked at the expanse of waste ground stretching into shadow and at the car park the patrol car was blocking. Blue lights flashing but ineffectual against the arc lamp behind the SOCO van. Kwik Save was still open. There were three other cars in the car park. He turned to the constable, whose name he still hadn't asked.

'Scene tape along the road on all sides, including the car park. The three cars are going to have to stay. You shouldn't really be parked in here but at least you're blocking the entrance. Not easy when you're first on scene. As good as you could make it.'

He nodded towards Kwik Save.

'Any customers come and gone since you arrived?'

'No. The cashier pretty much threw a dickey fit and shut up shop.'

'Good. I'll give him the bad news later. Staying shut until everything's checked. CCTV. Last customers he can remember.'

'He's a she.'

'Whatever. Go tell her to switch the main lights off. Don't want to encourage anyone else to pop in. Last post office robbery I had, customers kept trying to cash their Giros despite the shotgun blast in the counter. Fuckin' idiots.'

The constable rolled the blue and white tape up and set off towards the shop door. Tynan stopped him with another question.

'SIO turned up yet?'

Even the mention of the Senior Investigating Officer made the constable shiver. Some long service chief superintendent who would chew the scenery and any lowly copper not doing his job right.

'Not yet. ACR called him though.'

Tynan nodded. The Area Control Room Operator was on the ball.

'Better get a clipboard and start a scene log then. He'll go ballistic if you're not standing cap in hand ready to salute and sign him in.'

'Yeah. Thanks.'

'Get times of arrival for you and SOCO from the control room.'

He glanced at his watch and backtracked.

'Me. At ten twenty-five. DC Tynan. MCU.'

Tynan turned towards the oil drum. Time to take a closer look. He left the constable struggling with what to do first, get the cashier to turn the lights off or start a scene log. In the back of his mind he wondered why a detective constable from Major Crime Unit was here instead of the divisional night detective.

Tynan approached the tent, careful to follow the path indicated by the cones and not stray into virgin territory. At every major incident there was always an initial route taken by either the first person to discover it or the first officer on scene. Unavoidable. If you turn up to a robbery your first thought is to see if the robber is still there and arrest the son-of-a-bitch. If it's a body then first thing is to find out if it's a dead body or someone needing urgent medical treatment. Three main rules of policing. Protect life and property. Prevent crime. And arrest offenders. It said so on the back of his warrant card. Arresting criminals came last. If you could prevent crime then the world would be a better and safer place and you wouldn't need number three. Number one came into play tonight. First unit at the scene needed to establish if the girl was alive or dead. Hence the initial hasty route into the scene. After that, anyone else entering should use the common path in order not to ruin any more evidence than they had already.

Looking at the legs sticking out of the top of the oil drum he didn't think it had taken long to establish she wasn't alive. Unless she enjoyed dunking for apples in a rusty oil drum half full of water. They would still have to go through the formal procedures of having the police surgeon pronounce life extinct when he arrived but there was no need to stand on ceremony before getting the scene investigation started. First part of that being having a look at the deceased.

The deceased had nice legs. That was Tynan's initial reaction. And a trim quim. Strictly speaking, it wasn't the furry third eye the constable had described because there was a decided lack of fur. He wasn't sure if it was classed as a Brazilian or a full wax, but the hairs were short and fine and probably as soft as the inside of a dormouse's ear. The legs were smooth and tanned. No tights or stockings. A pair of pink knickers around the knees.

She wasn't naked, as they'd said on TV. Tynan had caught the beginning of the news as he was setting off and was always annoyed at how quick the newshounds got a story out to the public. There were often times when you could do with a little leeway at the beginning of an investigation and having important information blasted all over the TV and papers was downright unproductive. Especially when some of that information was wrong. Although that could work in their favour later if they got a suspect who tried to cover his knowledge by saying he'd seen it on TV. Well, the knowledge he'd be covering tonight was the fact that the dead girl wasn't naked. She was wearing a white T-shirt that was just visible above the water line. He could understand how they'd got it wrong this time though. A white smock like that of a nurse or dentist's assistant hung over the side of the oil drum. He could see how they'd come up with the link to the massage parlour too. Whoever had tipped the press – probably the bloke who found the body or the girl at Kwik Save – had seen the plastic tag pinned to the smock. According to that, the girl was called Samantha. And she worked at Gemini's Sauna and Massage.

Reading the scene of a crime was interesting in a sort of stamp-collector's, train-spotter's, computer-geek way but it wasn't Tynan's forte. He was more of a hands-on, fly-by-the-seat-of-your-pants kind of detective. His gut feelings and common sense solved more crimes on his workload than forensic evidence and the CSI effect pissed him right off. As far as he was concerned, unless the crook left his bus pass with his name and photo at the scene then forensics didn't help you find the bastard. Fingerprints and DNA excepted of course, provided he'd been caught before and recorded. By the time you moved up to serious crime that was usually the case. The age-old plea of, 'It was my first time, officer,' was bollocks. That just meant it was the first time they'd been caught. No. The value of forensic evidence was linking the suspect to the scene. That was all. After that, good detective work and interview technique made sure he didn't come up with a credible excuse for being there.

He remembered a burglary once where the blood donor centre had been screwed. The offices ransacked. The centre was on a back street beneath the bus station and you had to go down three steps to the reception door. All the examination rooms were just below ground level but the windows, high in each room, were just above the pavement outside. One window had been forced open and yanked upwards, breaking the frame. The intruder had climbed through the window and come out of the front door leaving it open, the curtains billowing out with the wind. SOCO had found point-of-entry prints inside the window where it had been pulled outwards but the surfaces in the office were too rough and well used. Prints had overlapped so much they were just a black mess.

Still, the point-of-entry marks were identified and the burglar arrested. Tynan hadn't been quick enough into interview because disclosure had already been given to the solicitor. It is a requirement that you disclose what evidence you have before interview, but it's up to you how much you feel necessary to reveal. You might have to state that there was forensic evidence but not exactly what forensic evidence.

When you booked him into custody you'd already have explained your grounds for suspecting him, so at that point they would know you had evidence linking him to the scene.

What Tynan didn't want to reveal was the exact evidence and where it was. The fingerprints on the window and their direction. On the inside, pulling the window open. The burglar might be able to explain marks on the outside if he was quick enough – 'Just happened to be passing and fastened my shoe, officer. Leaned on the window.' But he was too late. A young detective had already given the details and the solicitor came up with a cock-and-bull story that the jury swallowed. The suspect had indeed been passing by when he noticed the curtains billowing out of an open window. In a public-spirited gesture he had simply pushed the curtains back into the opening but, gasps of amazement, had to pull the window open wider to do so. Hence his fingerprints on the inside. Acquitted. Free to go.

Tynan didn't want the scummy bastard who'd done this getting off on a technicality. The press's release of information about where the girl worked was annoying. He needed to keep a lid on anything else until his instinct told him when to tell them. Watching the SOCO begin examining the rim of the drum for fibres, blood or semen before removing the body, he glanced at the floor around him.

'No sign of a bus pass or anything, is there?'

The SOCO gave him an old-fashioned look.

'Very fucking funny.'

Tynan put his hands in his pockets.

'*I* thought so.'

He heard movement outside the tent and went through the flap. A plain CID car had parked on the road and the night detective was talking to the constable with the clipboard. Tynan took his hands out of his pockets and flexed his shoulders. Overstepping your authority could cause friction if not handled carefully. He prepared to eat humble pie for the cause and waited for the DC on the common approach next to the first cone. Detective Constable Stuart Exley, an old-timer with plenty of service who Tynan had known for years, gave a rueful smile as he turned his collar up against the chill air.

'JT. A bit late for you MCU boys isn't it?'

Tynan nodded but didn't shake hands. Never touch a new arrival after you've been at the scene. Cross-contamination issues.

'Stu. You too. Thought you'd have put in for days by now.'

'Naw. Where's the fun in that? Have to see the wife more'n twice a week then, wouldn't I? Can't afford another divorce.'

'That good, eh?'

'She's already said, only reason we're together's 'cos we're never together.'

Tynan shrugged his shoulders and turned his hands palm upwards in a that's-life-but-what-can-you-do-about-it gesture. It was an old story on the job. A combination of unsocial hours and too many opportunities to stray, especially in plain clothes when shagging on duty was almost second nature. It was more difficult to hide a marked patrol car while on the nest, not to mention the constant badgering of the radio controller.

'I hear Black and Decker are back together again. You should be more like Steve. Married to his partner.'

'And that's gonna help me how?'

Good point. Tynan nodded towards the tent.

'Haven't done anything but watch. Hope I'm not stepping on your toes.'

Exley followed Tynan's nod but made no move towards the crime scene.

'No skin off my nose. SIO could be a problem.'

'Who is it?'

'Bulldog.'

Chief Superintendent Drummond. A long-standing murder investigator who'd worked on everything from the Yorkshire Ripper to the schoolboy shot in the head playing street football. His nickname had nothing to do with Bulldog Drummond and everything to do with the fact that when he got hold of anything he hung on like a dog with a bone. Crushed it until the marrow flowed. That included any piece of evidence he thought was important, and any DC overstepping his mark. Tynan might be considered to be overstepping his mark.

'I'd better get going then.'

Tynan moved to sidestep the night detective but Exley went with him. He talked on the way to Tynan's car.

'You're on the scene log. Easier for me to cover that if you tell me why.'

They walked around the edge of the car park, avoiding Kwik Save's front entrance, which was going to be fingerprinted in case the suspect had been a customer before he became the killer. Chances were the girl had been in the shop too. CCTV would determine that in the morning. Tynan shrugged his shoulders.

'Just nosy, I guess.'

'Nosy and couldn't sleep?'

'It's only quarter to eleven, Stu.'

'So, not sleep.'

'Not sleep.'

They were dancing around the question but Exley had something of the bulldog about him too. He shook the bone with a few choice words.

'This anything to do with those missing girls?'

Tynan stopped in his tracks and faced the night DC.

'Missing girls?'

Exley tilted his head to one side and raised his eyebrows.

'Don't get fat mixed up with stupid.'

'Hear that in a film, did you?'

'I did actually. Can't remember which one though.'

'Well, don't worry. You're not fat anyway.'

'Not stupid either. I read briefings.'

'Hasn't been on briefings.'

'I read between the lines on briefings.' Exley tapped the side of his nose with one finger. 'This tells me the rest. Massage parlour girls. Just like this one.'

Tynan sunk his hands deep in his trouser pockets.

'Just like this one. Yes.'

'How many is it now?'

'Dead? One. Missing? Seven that we know of. But who's counting? That line of work. Not everyone gets reported missing. Like winos. How many can disappear before you start noticing?'

'Sad but true.'

They stood in silence for a moment, each reflecting on the unfairness of life. The SOCO went into the tent with a small plastic bucket and lid. Time to get a sample of the water before draining the oil drum. Exley was aware that he should be paying attention to the crime scene and not chatting to the intruder, but things needed to be said.

'Don't hold back on me with this. You have anything that'll help?'

'Nope. Was hoping there'd be something here to break it loose a bit.'

Exley indicated the taped-in area around them with his arms.

'This all going to get folded into your investigation, you think?'

'Doubt it. Murder's murder. We're not that far gone with ours yet. Still only missing girls.'

Exley did his little head tilt, don't-get-fat-mixed-up-with-stupid gesture. Major Crime Unit didn't get involved in simple missing persons cases.

'Come on. Throw me a bone here. SIO's gonna be after my balls about you.'

'Tell him my boss'll be in touch tomorrow. For now, only link we've really got is they're all massage girls.'

'That's it?'

Tynan took his car keys out of his pocket.

'Different parlours. But all part of the Northern X chain.'

SEVEN

F rank Sinatra still didn't make it to the train. Sun baked the aggre-gate beneath the sleepers as he chased the final carriage along the viaduct. The bleached stones crunched beneath his feet and his breath came in ragged gasps. He reached a hand out but it was too far to reach the guardrail along the back of the carriage. Trevor Howard, a young actor named John Leyton, and the padre leaned over the rail to grab the outstretched hand.

Machine-gun fire crackled behind him but Frankie kept on running. The train entered the tunnel and was swallowed by the darkness one carriage at a time. The sound of the wheels echoed in the hollowness. The only other sounds were the shouts of encour-agement from the guardrail and the crackle of gunfire. Then the train outdistanced the pursuing German soldiers. They stopped, panting, in their tracks and the commanding officer gestured for a Schmeisser. One of his troops handed him a machine gun and the officer aimed carefully, then fired. Von Ryan almost caught the train. His fingers almost brushed the outstretched hands trying to help him.

Bullets ripped into his back and he stumbled.

The world went quiet. No more shouting. No more firing. Just the hollow echo of the wheels as the last carriage disappeared into the tunnel. Von Ryan lay in the dust, one arm still stretching for the train he couldn't reach. Jerry Goldsmith's poignant theme played in the background as Trevor Howard's voiceover said, '*I once told you Von Ryan. If only one gets out it's a victory.*' Then the music swelled into the closing march as the end credits rolled.

The final scene played out in front of McNulty and light from the silver screen washed over his face as he sat ten rows from the front. No matter how many times he watched *Von Ryan's Express*, from the first time on a rare seaside outing to now, he always hoped that Frank Sinatra would finally catch the train. It reminded him of that old joke.

An Irishman keeps betting that John Wayne won't get killed at the end of a western even though he's seen it a dozen times. His mate asks him why and he says he didn't think John Wayne would make the same mistake again.

Heavy velvet curtains closed across the screen and the house lights came up on the last good old-fashioned cinema in the north. The Hyde Park Picture House. Once the laughing stock of the Leeds circuit, it had been lovingly restored to its former glory by an independent and now looked as good as it had ever done. Velvet curtains. Deep red wallpaper. Glittering chandeliers and alcove wall lights. And best of all, traditional yet comfortable seats, neatly arranged in the stalls downstairs and the balcony up above. Even the sound system had been upgraded to Dolby Surround, although most of the older films barely came with stereo. The exterior façade, with fluted arches and false front above the doors, reeked of a bygone era. Framed posters of classic films adorned the foyer walls.

McNulty stood and stretched his legs as the sparse late-night crowd made its way to the ground floor exits. He took a deep breath and savoured the atmosphere. Dating way back to his life as an orphan at Crag View, he had always been able to lose himself in a good film. Probably *because* of his life as an orphan. God knows there wasn't much else to write home about. He hadn't discovered the joys of sex until later, so the cinema was the next best thing. Still was, but sex beat it hands down, even if it didn't last as long.

He looked up at the chandelier hanging way above him. He used to avoid sitting directly under it in case it fell, but nowadays he liked to tempt fate and sit in the kill zone. Daring God to take him out. He gritted his teeth and dared him again now. He was so engrossed in his private war that he didn't notice the figure watching him from the shadows at the back of the stalls. Didn't see the gleam in the eyes or the white knuckles as the man clenched his fists.

Blood squeezed from his knuckles as he clenched his fists, turning them white as bone, and tears formed in his eyes with the intensity of his stare. The man from his past, who had played such an important role in the path his life had taken, stood less than twenty feet away glaring up at the chandelier as if daring it to fall.

Calm down. Calm down. Take a Valium. His fists unclenched and he dried his eyes on a patched sleeve as he told himself not to let things get the better of him. It was an embarrassing fact that he became weepy at the slightest thing these days. Angry too. It was like his psyche was a seesaw and he was either at one end or the other. Up or down. Angry or weepy and never the twain shall meet. Much of that could be laid at the door of PC Vincent McNulty.

He considered approaching him now, in the middle of the auditorium, but decided against it. Instead, he slipped through the nearest door into the corridor that ran along the back of the stalls. He watched as McNulty walked towards the other door. That meant he'd be entering the corridor at the far end. In between the two doors, and on the opposite side, a set of double doors opened into the foyer, where the crowd was thinning. The man went through there and waited beside the popcorn kiosk. The security grille was down but the display of Sunkist popcorn and Kia-Ora orange squash smiled at him. He smiled back.

A few minutes later the policeman came out. Passed within inches of him and then stood looking at a framed poster of *Casablanca* on the wall. Fists clenched again and the man had to force them to relax. He walked quickly up behind the copper and grabbed him by the shoulder.

'What the fuck?'

McNulty spun round. Lightning quick. Grabbed the fingers of the hand on his shoulder and twisted them as he spun. The man's arm bent against the joint and he had to go with it or risk serious injury. He was kneeling on the floor with his arm twisted sideways before McNulty had fully turned. And then McNulty laughed.

'Donkey Flowers. What you playin' at?'

'Doctors and nurses if you don't let go my arm, Officer McNulty.'

McNulty released the fingers and Don 'Donkey' Flowers stood up. He was five years younger than McNulty and a few inches shorter, but thin as a rail. Barely weighed ten stone soaking wet. He rubbed his fingers and wrist.

'Fine way to treat an old familiar.'

'You should know better than to sneak up on a copper. Arrested you often enough.'

'Yeah. And my mum used to thank you every day.'

Back in McNulty's formative years on the beat, when he was still a teenager himself, he had apprehended the fourteen-year-old Donald Flowers for every kind of antisocial behaviour before it was even known as antisocial behaviour. Drunk and disorderly. Breach of the peace. Minor criminal damage. You name it, Don had done it. And each time McNulty had taken him home to his mother with a few choice words and a smack round the head. He'd been nicknamed Donkey because he was a bit of an ass and didn't learn his lesson until it was too late. He preferred to tell his mates it was because he was hung like a donkey.

Eventually taking him home wasn't enough and McNulty had to arrest him. He didn't go to prison, but spending time in the police station cells was just the short sharp shock he needed. In order to keep out of trouble and away from the mates his mother reckoned were a bad influence he joined the Royal Navy and left home. McNulty used to call round for a cuppa at Don's mum's. Keep an eye on her since she lived alone.

'How's she keeping?'

Don went quiet for a moment before answering.

'Oh, she died a few years back.'

That put a dampener on things.

'Sorry to hear that.'

'I still live at the old place. Lots of memories of her there.'

'Yeah, well. You have to know her to have memories of her.'

That put a bigger dampener on things. McNulty felt guilty at having forced his own emotions at not having known his parents onto the grief of his familiar. He checked his watch. It was half past one in the morning.

'Fancy a pint, Donk? Catch up a bit.'

Don cheered up.

'Sounds good to me. You buying?'

They walked out of the cinema looking for all the world like Humphrey Bogart and Claude Rains. All it needed was for one of them to say, 'This could be the beginning of a beautiful friendship,' and they might have stepped right out of *Casablanca*.

Catching up was more of a two-way street than McNulty had expected. He'd been a private person ever since Crag View, so having someone know so much about him was unsettling. It started OK though. In the snug of the King's Arms round the corner.

'How come you're back at your mum's? After the navy?'

McNulty set the pint of Carlsberg in front of Donk and sat down with his Pepsi. Despite the time of night the King's Arms was busy, a testament to the relaxation of the licensing laws a couple of years ago. Half the late show customers from the cinema had come in, together with a handful of scraggy locals. This wasn't exactly the most salubrious part of town.

'That was years ago. Lot's happened since.'

Cut a long story short, what had happened since was shit piled on more shit. Five years in the navy then back out to Civvy Street. Married an American and moved over there for a while. Had a baby. Wife became a drug addict and got a divorce. A bit of wife beating en route. Back to England but a custody battle over the daughter. Wife came to England. A reconciliation and two more kids. Still a drug addict. Back to America to try and work it out. More wife beating. Arrested and deported. Lost wife and kids to her parents in the States. Now living alone with the ghost of his mother's 'I told you so.'

'And now you're back at Mean Wood.'

'Ashes to ashes. Dust to dust.'

McNulty held his glass out for a toast.

'And Mean Wood to Mean Wood.'

Donk clinked his pint glass against McNulty's half-pint. Telling the tale did nothing to dampen his enthusiasm for meeting his old mate, because that's what he thought of Officer McNulty. They'd met more times over the years than some people who *were* friends. Both in the early days and, more importantly, for a period during the middle years. The up and down years. McNulty had known most of Donk's unhappy story but let him tell it again. It had been a while since they'd caught up with each other. A while since Donk used to keep his ear to the ground for him in a professional capacity.

'You still got your finger on the pulse then, Donk?'

'Enough to know you've had your own shit to deal with.'

McNulty wasn't surprised. Donk always had a knack for finding out just what you wanted no one to find out. He wondered how much he did know.

'What shit's that?'

Donk smiled and took a drink of his lager. McNulty probed further.

'Maybe we should have one of those competitions. You know, like the Annual Soap Opera Awards. Vote for the best turd of the year. Because whichever wins they're all shit.'

'Come on, Officer McNulty. You know what shit.'

'Vince. How many times I got to tell you. Call me Vince.'

'Officer Vince.'

'For fuck's sake, Donk. You were my ears. Supposed to be undercover. What the fuck you keep calling me Officer for?'

'What they changed my name to?'

'What?'

'You know. Instead of informant?'

'Covert Human Intelligence Source. CHIS.'

'Intelligence. I like that. Well, my intelligence tells me you ain't an Officer no more.'

'Shit. That's no secret.'

Donk put his glass on the table and waved the interruption aside.

'But it is Soap Award winning shit. And don't tell me you're happy about it.'

'No. I won't tell you that. 'Cos I'm not. But I'm not bitter about it either.'

That was a lie and they both knew it. Losing the job he loved in the way that he had was enough to make anyone bitter. What made McNulty really bitter though was the reason he was wired that way in the first place. Wired with a short fuse. A short temper. The place he'd grown up and learned the hard lessons of life. McNulty kept that little secret buried deep. Donk could only guess what it must be like to have never known your parents, but it was a pretty good guess. It was shit.

'Yeah, I know. Shit happens. Kiddy fiddler wasn't it? On a little girl?'

McNulty shrugged, kept quiet and drank some Pepsi.

'Got what he deserved then. In my book.'

'My book too. But not the Chief Constable's book.'

The post-cinema crowd were thinning out, leaving just three regulars, a pickled egg salesman and a prostitute. Donk looked McNulty in the eye and McNulty met his stare. He shrugged again then replied.

'Can't blame him for that. I knew what I was doing.'

'Just couldn't control it?'

'Control is only an illusion. When the fire gets out none of us can control it.'

'Good job you're still using the release valve then.'

'Release valve?'

Donk held a fist in front of his crotch and mimicked a wank.

'Still pervin' the parlours.'

McNulty laughed. Was there anything Donk didn't know? He held a fist in front of his mouth and when he copied Donk's action he pushed his tongue into his left cheek with each incoming stroke, indicating something more enjoyable than a wank.

'There's nothing perverted about it. Good clean fun between consenting adults of the opposite sex. If I messed with dogs or little boys, *that*'d be perving.'

'And you do get a free shower after. Right?'

'Like I said. Good clean fun.'

Donk finished his lager and stood to get another. McNulty covered his glass with one hand and shook his head. When Donk sat down with a fresh pint he continued as if he hadn't been away.

'Not good clean fun in the Chief Constable's book, I bet.'

'I'm not on the Chief Constable's books any more.'

'But you sometimes still feel like you are. Don't you?'

Again, that feeling that Donk knew more than he should. It was amazing. And the main reason he had been such a valuable resource back when he was in the job. He not only knew things, but he was very intuitive about things he didn't know. The best educated guesser he'd ever met.

'Not sometimes. All the time. Watch stuff on the news. See a patrol car in the street. My mindset's that I'm still one of 'em.'

He stared into his drink as if dragging a memory from the soothing black Pepsi.

'Some bloke was causing trouble the other day.'

Now that the memory was formed he looked across the table at Donk.

'Ragging on one of the girls. Young lass. At a parlour out of town. It was none of my business. They have bouncers for that sort of stuff. And I didn't even think twice.'

He shook his head in disbelief at his own foolishness.

'Just waded in. Floored the guy. By the time I made sure he was all right the girl had gone.'

'Whadya expect? Engraved thank you card?'

McNulty laughed. He did a lot of laughing but it had nothing to do with humour.

'Not engraved. No.'

'You can't protect everyone.'

This time McNulty didn't laugh. He smiled a mischievous smile instead.

'I once told you. If only one gets out it's a victory.'

Donk threw a beer mat across the table.

'Go fuck yourself.'

'Now that would be perverted. But a lot cheaper.'

EIGHT

McNulty should have recognized the warning signals when the shouting started at the Golden Touch, but he simply thought he was getting a touch of déjà vu. The strawberry blonde had already done his back and was working cool scented oil into McNulty's chest and shoulders. The woman, Kim according to the name badge on the smock hanging behind the door, stood beside the massage table

and leaned forward as her hands slid up his chest and began kneading
the muscles either side of his neck. Her breasts swung gently with
each squeeze of his shoulders.

Commotion from the lounge upstairs. A similar layout to the Sauna
Kabin, since the Northern X chain was trying to present a uniform
image like McDonald's and Pizza Hut. Even the décor was the same.
And the solid wooden massage tables. Waist high and easy to move
around. McNulty concentrated on the crinkly aureole around each
nipple, hands behind his head for a better view. The sensuous dark
teats puckered with goose pimples even though it was warm in the
room.

The shouting grew louder. Kim glanced at the door but carried on.
'Sorry about the noise.'

Her mouth formed the words but McNulty couldn't take his eyes
off her breasts. It reminded him of the question why men never look
women in the eye when talking to them. Because they don't have eyes
in their tits. The tits spoke again.

'Probably complaining about the shortage of staff. Having to wait.'

That should have been the second warning signal. The second bout
of déjà vu. While drinking his orange juice in the lounge he'd been
told one of the girls hadn't turned in today so there were fewer to
choose from. Didn't bother him because Kim was an obvious choice.
Nor did it seem to bother him that he was upping his visits since
returning home. He normally paced himself with a couple of massages
a week, but this was his third in three days.

Expert fingers moved down his torso and McNulty was adamant he
wasn't going to interfere this time. More oil. Kim moved further up
the side of the bed and massaged away from his head down his body.
Drawing back up to his chest and then sliding down his stomach. This
was a variation that gave him a different perspective. Her breasts lowered
onto his stomach as she reached forward. Cheeky fingers slid beneath
the towel.

There was a lull in the shouting from the lounge.

Good. Should have been good anyway. The outbreak of peace
upstairs should have allowed him to concentrate on the job in hand,
or almost in hand during that last slide down his stomach, but his mind
kept wandering back to his other visit of the day. Earlier that afternoon. A gothic building on a hillside surrounded by trees.

Damn. Why did that place keep coming back to haunt him?

McNulty had been right to leave this nostalgia trip until daylight. He
felt a chill creep over him even before he turned off the Ring Road

and up the forested hillside towards the building at the top. Crag View
Orphanage was visible to all motorists on the sweeping dual
carriageway, but he doubted if any of the other Ring Road users saw
it quite the same way he did. The house disappeared from sight as he
swung the Astra onto the back road that would eventually cut through
the woods towards the Mean Wood estate, but the song was already
playing in his head.

> There is a house in New Orleans
> They call the Rising Sun
> And it's been the ruin of many a poor boy
> And God I know I'm one

The guitar refrain was as clear as if The Animals were playing in
the car, the deep dark voice of the vocals as black as the house itself.
McNulty stroked the tattoo on the side of his neck. Glimpses of Crag
View flashed between the trees until he was almost at the top of the
hill and suddenly there it was, for all the world to see. Grey stone
pillars stood either side of the rotting gate and the driveway swept
towards the turning circle in front of the main door. One of the heavy
wooden gates had sagged across the drive, hanging by a single hinge.
The first leaves of autumn dusted the ground, still brightly coloured
before they, like everything else here, turned dead and brown.

He stopped the car in front of the gate and walked the rest of the
way. Getting out of the car actually made it worse. At least while he'd
been driving he felt protected from the atmosphere of the place but
now, in the silence of the woods, his feet crunching on dead leaves,
fingers of the past reached out for him.

The first thing he noticed was that none of the boards had been
pulled off the ground floor windows. That surprised him, because
during his eighteen years as a policeman he'd found that whenever a
building closed down the vandals moved in. Windows were smashed.
Doors kicked in. Walls covered in graffiti. But not Crag View. It was as if
even the vandals didn't want to touch this stain on the state childcare
system.

The second thing was the smell. Walking up the driveway there had
only been the pleasant woodland smells of grass and leaves. The occasional nutty scent of acorns and pine cones. As he approached the front
door the smell of putrefying flesh took over. Like the aftermath of a
Rentokil visit before the dead rats had been removed.

The front door was locked but as rotten as the main gate. The
wood was so soft he could push his fingers into the spongy surface.

He shouldered it just above the handle and the door swung inwards. McNulty didn't go in. He simply looked into the gloom of the entrance hall. Over to his right was the dining room, but his eyes stared straight ahead. At the sweeping staircase. And the corridor. And the office door at the far end.

Young Vincent McNulty stood in the corridor for a moment, undecided about what to do. He could hear muffled voices, a girl and an older man. What sounded like sobs from the girl. In the background, plates and cutlery clinked as the dining room was cleared. Apart from that the house was silent. The only movement the bustling dining-room staff and the two people in the headmaster's office. Vincent took two paces forward and listened at the door.

He was right.

They were definitely sobs, and there was a rustling of clothes. So, he had been right about the other thing too. He tried the door handle. It turned easily and he peered through the gap.

The slap sounded like a gunshot in the quiet office. A gunshot followed by a heartbreaking whimper. A wounded animal kind of whimper. The man in charge of Crag View Orphanage stood back and leaned against his desk, sunlight from the window glinting off his glasses.

It was early evening and the teatime rush had subsided. Everyone in their rooms while the dining room was cleared. One of the rules that was strictly enforced. Only one resident had permission to be in breach of curfew. The girl sitting crumpled on the bench seat. And only one member of staff was out of the dining room. The headmaster. Mr Cruckshank. Just the two of them alone in his office at the bottom of the stairs. But not quite alone now.

The gunshot echoed in Vincent's ears and his eyes burned as the truth sank in. Anger filled him like hot oil, changing the normally docile teenager into a raging bull. None of the other staff knew of the rights-of-passage scenario being played out in the dingy office. Nobody else saw Vincent McNulty leaving childhood behind and becoming a man. A man with a very short temper.

The office was lined with bookshelves. A dying rubber plant stood in the bay window. A painting of the Queen hung above the fireplace opposite the desk. And the man who had become the focal point of Vincent's hatred turned to face him as if surprised he had the cheek to even be there.

'Go back to your room.'

Mr Cruckshank pushed off from the desk and his bulk hid the bench seat in the alcove. It didn't matter. It was too late. Vincent had already seen the girl who was too young to defend herself holding the torn dress across her chest. He had seen the bright red handprint on her tear-streaked cheek. He picked the biggest book he could find from the bookshelf and hefted it in both hands like a baseball player preparing to swing. The anger boiled over.

'Go to hell.'

The whisper carried more weight than a thousand shouts. Mr Cruckshank blinked as if slapped and the irony of that would have pleased Vincent if he'd understood what irony was. He stepped forward and swung the book with all his might, protecting the first of many long before he would realize he couldn't protect them all. The head-master couldn't believe what was happening as the leather-bound Bible crashed into his face and broke his nose. One lens from his glasses popped out of the frame and shattered on the floor. When Vincent put the Bible on the desk he turned towards the girl but she had gone. Scampered off as if ashamed of what she had done. Vincent wouldn't understand that for a long time either.

The shouting started up in the lounge again. McNulty snapped back to the present as cool sensual oil was poured along his pulsing manhood. Cool sensual fingers massaged it in and the pulse almost exploded. He watched the strawberry blonde but his mind was listening to the raised voices outside. Kim obviously sensed his lack of concentration.

'It's all right. There's a minder. All the time.'

Not all the time, McNulty thought. *Otherwise I wouldn't have needed to get involved the last time.* He tried to relax and let the masseuse complete their contract. Her hands were slick with oil. Her breasts too, as she leant forward and rubbed them across his stomach.

'Honestly. Northern X provides one.'

She began to work faster and McNulty closed his eyes. He listened to the beat of his heart and felt the pulse of the muscle a man can't live without. Maybe Northern X ought to employ minders who were a bit quicker off the mark. This lazy bastard must be waiting for World War Three before getting his arse into gear.

Something broke in the lounge. A glass or a cup. A squeal from the other girl on duty. Drunken rambling from the male voice. Getting louder. Approaching the point when alcohol tipped the balance from noisy bluster to physical action. McNulty had seen it before. Like flashover in a house fire when the temperature gets so hot it ignites everything. From the sound of things the lounge was about to flashover.

The next squeal was sharper.

McNulty was off the table and pulling his jeans on before Kim knew what was happening. One minute she had his love muscle in her hand and the next she was grasping air. McNulty stepped into unlaced shoes and opened the door.

He didn't bother with the drink-of-orange diversion this time. As soon as he stepped into the lounge he knew it would be a waste of time. Massage room three was on the first floor near the fire exit, so there was none of that running upstairs fastening your trousers shit. He was straight out of the frying pan and into the fire. The fire was overweight and overdrunk. One thing McNulty knew from experience was there is no reasoning with a drunken man. He didn't even try to lull him into a false sense of security, because the man was already up for a fight. McNulty simply gave him a man to fight instead of the terrified receptionist.

Despite going on the offensive with a stiffy in his pants that forced him to limp, McNulty was too fast and too fit for the overweight bully. A flash of Michael Caine popped into his head. *'You're a big man but you're out of shape. With me it's a full time job.'* But this wasn't *Get Carter*; this was Get It Over Quickly. The man had his back turned but heard McNulty coming. Just to make sure McNulty gave him a turn-around-and-face-me-like-a-man call.

'Hey. Fucknut.'

The man saw McNulty and swung a haymaker punch that was all arm and no direction. The clenched fist went high and wide and McNulty stepped under the blow, planted his right leg behind the man's left, and double palm-heeled him in the chest. He went over backwards and hit the floor hard, spilling blackcurrant juice on the carpet. McNulty stamped on his balls once and it was all over. Whatever fight the man had in him evaporated like the breath that exploded from his mouth. A kick in the balls is the single most effective defence against a man with his dander up. Against any man at all.

With his stiffy easing, McNulty knelt beside the drunk and twisted one ear between thumb and forefinger. Twisted hard. The man gasped in pain. McNulty leaned in close and spoke into the ear.

'Pick on someone your own size next time.'

He was still bent over when the back door burst open and the bouncer came in, out of breath after dashing up the fire escape. Brutal eyes assessed the situation in a flash, and got the wrong end of the stick. McNulty let go of the ear and stood up slowly. This was a completely different scenario. Not a drunk. Hired muscle who saw McNulty as the threat. Time to defuse the situation.

'Whoah. That was quick. All them steps. You used to be a fireman?'

The bouncer ignored the quip, planting his feet and hunching his shoulders.

'A bit out of breath though, aren't you? So maybe not.'

Too many words. The minder's eyebrows furrowed with concentration as he tried to decide if he was being made fun of or not. McNulty didn't stop.

'Maybe if Northern X put its bouncers a bit nearer the action you wouldn't have to run so far to sort it out.'

The minder found his tongue.

'Just nipped out for a fag.'

'Didn't take you for the *Brokeback Mountain* type.'

The bouncer understood that and bristled.

'A smoke.'

The drunken bully on the floor was sobering up fast. He saw his chance to slide out from under the trouble he'd caused. With his best innocent voice and sad-eyed look he appealed to the bouncer.

'He hit me for no reason. Only came to get me carrot stroked.'

McNulty caught a glimpse of Kim standing in the massage room doorway.

'Me too. And it was going just fine. You gobby turd.'

As soon as he said it he knew it was the wrong thing to say. Instead of defusing the tension he'd simply added to it. Basic training. Never engage in an argument. It only gets everybody's backs up. The minder had no investment in whose fault it was. Northern X basic training made it easy for him. Any trouble, kick 'em all out. Biggest threat first. That was an easy choice too. The one on the floor was low priority. He took a step towards the one standing half naked in front of the corner bar and clenched his fists.

McNulty took one look at those fists and braced himself. The muscles stood out on his shoulders and across his oil-slicked chest. His body prepared for combat while his mind resorted to appeasement. He knew he could take the bouncer but it would be an uphill battle against a prepared enemy position. Except he wasn't really the enemy. The flashpoint for McNulty was always the bully picking on someone smaller. Tonight, the bully was already out of the picture. The overweight man on the floor. If anything, the bouncer was the cavalry coming over the hill just too late. So he didn't want to fight him. Situation like this it was better to withdraw. He held his hands out palms up and took a step backwards.

'My mistake. But he started it.'

The receptionist, a petite bottle blonde, nodded.

'That's right. He did.'

The danger level dropped. Now the bouncer had time to think and that had never been his strength. They were both still going to have to go. He simply changed the order.

'Oy. Fatso. You first. Out.'

The drunk, who wasn't nearly so drunk any more, struggled to his feet.

'But . . .'

The bouncer raised his voice.

'Now.'

With a hangdog look he went towards the fire escape, but the bouncer blocked his way.

'Front stairs.'

The lounge was quiet for a moment after the front door slammed. Four of them stood frozen like gunfighters waiting to draw. Kim in the doorway of room three. The receptionist in front of the corner bar. The bouncer in the middle of the room. And McNulty standing over the place the bully had been felled. His job done. There was no more fight in him. Never had been, even back at Crag View. Not without the spark that always lit his touch paper. The bouncer recognized it but had a job to do.

'Your turn.'

McNulty didn't argue. He went down the main stairs and out the front door without a word. He was in the street and halfway to his car before he realized he was bare-chested and covered in oil. He thought about going back for his sweatshirt but got his car keys out instead. As he turned down the side street a figure stepped out of the shadows across the road, light from a mobile phone licking one side of his face.

NINE

'Anonymous caller reported it?'

Tynan asked the question while making a morning coffee in the CID office at Ecclesfield Police Station. His unit had been given a corner to run its investigation. The early turn detective giving his report from a message sheet nodded.

'About eight p.m.'

'Where from?'

Bill Baildon had been up since five o'clock and he checked the message sheet again before he realized the answer wasn't there.

'We don't know. It was anonymous.'

Tynan stirred two sugars into his first coffee of the day and opened the fridge door for milk. A carton of doughnuts stared back at him from the top shelf. He ignored them and took the bottle of milk out.

'Anonymous is the caller. Not the call. We get a number?'

'Withheld.'

'Landline or mobile?'

'Mobile.'

'Shit.'

If it had been a landline, they could have done a reverse check on the incoming call even if the number had been withheld. BT was very accommodating that way. Mobile phone companies were notoriously difficult to pin down and Tynan would need mountains of paperwork to force them to give it up. He put the milk back in the fridge.

'What's with the doughnuts?'

Baildon smiled. Doughnuts were his favourite subject.

'Inspector Speedhoff's birthday. He dropped them in first thing.'

'Speedo? Team two uniform inspector?'

The detective nodded.

'What the fuck's he giving CID some for?'

Baildon glanced over his shoulder in case Speedo was in the corridor.

''Cos he's an ass-lickin' cretin who wants everyone to like him. Steve Decker threatened to deck him last week. Probably given the Chief Super a big one all of his own.'

Tynan fingered the little round sugared dough balls.

'What flavours?'

'Apple. Jam. And chocolate.'

'How d'you tell?'

'I'm a detective. It's what I'm paid for.'

'And I'm senior detective. Short of biting every fuckin' one. How do I tell?'

Baildon wasn't fazed by the rebuke. Everyone knew that Tynan didn't come round before his second coffee. Baildon explained as if to a child.

'The butt hole where they squirted the filling in.'

Tynan turned each doughnut until he could see the puckered hole and a hint of filling. He pushed the chocolate one aside and selected jam.

'Better send this brown one back to Speedo. Should taste better than where he normally sticks his tongue.'

He shut the fridge door and took a bite out of the doughnut. Talking with his mouth full he continued getting himself up to date.

'The caller say how he knew the girl was missing?'

'No. Just that she hadn't turned in for her shift yesterday.'

Tynan licked his fingers clean and swilled the last mouthful down with coffee.

'Now that's the thing right there. Who the fuck reports a working girl missing after one shift?'

It was a rhetorical question. Of all the girls on the investigation only two had been reported missing within three days, and that was by concerned parents. Why the concerned parents didn't get worried until their daughters had been missing for three days was a problem for the Good Parenting League. The others had come in dribs and drabs, sometimes a couple of weeks after they were last seen. Prostitutes didn't get reported straight away. Some didn't get reported at all. Their choice of career dropped them off the normal radar and it was one of the main problems for Tynan's team. He still didn't know if the list was complete. There could be plenty more missing but not reported.

Tynan stood in front of the corkboard with its collection of Polaroids and family photos of the missing girls. There was also a name card for each massage parlour and a brief description of opening times and telephone numbers. Lengths of pink string linked the photos to the parlours the girls worked at. Why pink he didn't know, and assumed it was somebody's idea of a joke.

'We got a name?'

'Candy.'

'That's it?'

'Parlour was closed by the time a unit went round. Form one-fifty through the door.'

A Form 150 was uniform patrol's get-out-of-jail card. Volume of calls kept them rushing from pillar to post all night long and they had to prioritize just to keep their heads above water. Immediates were obvious. Robberies. Burglaries. Assaults. Anything that was happening there and then needed urgent attention. Planned Ones were reports of incidents that had happened earlier and needed an officer within the hour to meet divisional targets. A miss meant a black mark against the shift. To beat that the sergeant would often give a quick phone call to meet the deadline and arrange a revisit the following morning. Failing that, or if there was a withheld number, a Form 150 was left through the letterbox for them to call back.

Tynan checked his watch. Nine o'clock. Golden Touch wouldn't open until ten at the earliest. He looked at the board again. The parlour had one previous report three weeks ago. Today he would be adding a fresh photo. He moved to the key cabinet next to the corkboard and picked a set of car keys before the other detectives turned in. He didn't want to get stuck with the shitty Rover again. He turned to Baildon, who was eating his second doughnut of the day.

'Have the CCTV checks come in yet?'

Through a mouthful of apple doughnut. 'Don't think so.'

'I'm going to Golden Touch when they open. Chase up the CCTV while I'm gone, will you?'

Baildon nodded to save wasting doughnut. Tynan sat at the communal desk his squad had been allocated and took out his notebook. Everything that was on the corkboard was abbreviated into his notebook. The girls' names. Where they worked. When they disappeared. And their ages. So far that last was the unifying feature. The parlours were spread far and wide but the ages were all within a five-year range. Between young and very young. He thought about the oil drum murder. How many on his list were going to be found like that? Or never found at all?

'Shit. I need another coffee.'

He went to the kettle and made a fresh cup. Just for safe measure he selected the chocolate doughnut as well.

By the time Tynan pulled up outside the Golden Touch massage parlour the second coffee had kicked in, but the doughnuts sat heavy in his stomach. He parked the CID car on double yellow lines in front of the studded wooden door and put the Police Vehicle sign from the glove box on the dashboard. The sign was unofficial, printed on an office computer in big letters and laminated on the help desk's machine. It simply warned any roving traffic wardens or PCSOs not to ticket the Astra because it was on police business. It also helped if you were nipping in to get your sandwiches or a late-night curry. Police Community Support Officers had been known to ticket CID anyway, but that's because they were more concerned with target figures than using their brains. Hobby bobbies made Tynan cringe.

He stood outside the front door for five minutes. It was part of his routine. Never go barging in anywhere before you get your mind right. If it was a raid type situation that meant preparing for action. Anything else, it meant making sure your thoughts were straight. What questions you were going to ask. What information you wanted them to give.

For now, the five minutes was about checking the CCTV camera high on the front wall, pointing down at the door and steps. He smiled up at it and waved. Grinned an idiot grin. If they were recording this he would seize the tape and show it on uniform briefings; the CID equivalent of baring your arse on the town hall steps. He knew they wouldn't be. This was part of a security system that was all about knowing who was at the door, not recording evidence of a crime for future prosecution. After all, everyone coming in here was committing a crime. Imagine what the customers would think if they knew they were being recorded.

That was frustrating for Tynan. Nine working girls had gone missing from parlours like this one and you could bet your boots that whoever took them had visited each parlour at least once. Collating CCTV video footage would have been invaluable. Instead, they were having to trawl the city's traffic cameras and any office building security tapes near the target premises.

He turned away from the door and looked down the road. A hundred yards away the traffic lights changed to red and the tail end of the rush hour came to a halt. It was a major junction, main road into town with the Ring Road that went around town. The street lamps were tall and wide and very bright at night. Just below each lamp housing a hooded camera pointed along the road. Four cameras. One pointing towards town. One up the Ring Road. One down the Ring Road. And one pointing directly at Detective Constable Jimmy Tynan. He grinned and waved at that one as well. It was too far away to embarrass him.

He made a mental note to add that camera to the list and then tried the door. It wasn't locked. Golden Touch was open for business. He knocked and went in.

'Nobody here reported it, Detective.'

The woman was wearing black trousers under a white smock similar to those the other girls wore. It was the trousers that marked her out as the receptionist. Too many clothes to take off for this business. Too many wrinkles as well. And a paunch that wouldn't look too good if she were leaning over oiling your tool. Tynan reckoned she might have been on the game twenty years ago. But now she answered the phone and took the door fees.

'You working last night?'

'No.'

'So how d'you know nobody reported it from here?'

That stumped her, but he wasn't really looking to trip her up. He didn't think anyone from Golden Touch had reported the girl missing. Not to the police anyway. At best they might have complained to the owner. They were sitting in a cubicle the size of a downstairs toilet, which was what it used to be, behind the reception desk. There was only one chair so Tynan had brought the spare from reception. Strings of linked chain hung from the door frame instead of a door, like the strip curtains used on caravans to keep the flies out in summer. A ten-inch split screen TV monitor stood on a shelf showing four camera views. Outside the front door. Outside the back door. And inside reception. The fourth was blank. Even a business chain as big as Northern X wasn't going to waste money on more cameras than it needed.

'Never mind. You got Candy's details?'

'In the office upstairs.'

That was it. She didn't offer to take him up or get someone to bring them down. Her lips pursed and wrinkled as if she were sucking a lemon. He tried not to think about what else they had sucked over the years. For a brief moment he saw the puckered butt of the chocolate doughnut and shivered. Putting his best good cop face on, he lowered his voice.

'Look, Mary darlin'. I'm not looking to jam you up here. This isn't a vice inquiry. But a girl is missing and I want to find her before she gets in trouble. Christ. Even Vice Squad aren't bothered about massage parlours any more. They're not part of government targets. So how about a little cooperation here? OK?'

The lemon sucking stopped. The lips unpursed and almost smiled.

'OK. I'll just get someone to cover the desk.'

Ten minutes later they were in an office twice the size of the cubicle downstairs. Still too small for more than one chair. There was a grey metal filing cabinet, a waist-high shelf that stood in for a desk and a large tinted window on one wall. The window looked into the first floor lounge and was an ornate mirror behind the bar on the other side. The cushioning on the swivel chair was squashed in the shape of a pair of buttocks. The bouncer's chair. Some no-neck fat lump of lard that Northern X paid peanuts in case there was trouble. A duplicate split screen TV monitor showed the same three views. Front door. Back door. Reception.

Tynan looked at the sheet of A4 paper with the photograph stapled to it.

'Candice Bergen? You kidding me?'

'That's what she gave.'

He read the date of birth that would make her ten years older than the head and shoulders photo looked. She was very young. Sixteen if you were being generous. He wondered how she'd come to know there was an actress called Candice Bergen. He doubted if she'd seen *The Wind and the Lion* or *Bite the Bullet*. The only details on this inquiry that he could swear to were the ones given by distraught parents. That wouldn't come for a few days and even then only if her parents gave a damn.

'Anybody tried ringing this mobile?'

'I don't know.'

Tynan wrote the number down in his notebook. He'd try ringing back at the office, not here. He would need more evidence that she hadn't simply quit her job before the mobile phone companies would set up a trace. If only BT ran all the UK phones. What really baffled him though was who had phoned the police last night. And why? There was some kind of hidden agenda here.

'Where's the bouncer?'

The woman sucked lemons again.

'Security consultant.'

'Where's the security consultant?'

'He's out getting our sandwiches.'

For sandwiches Tynan saw doughnuts.

'Is it his birthday?'

That stumped the woman too. Tynan waved the question aside and tore the photo off the page. He looked out through the tinted window at the lounge. One of the girls was on her hands and knees scrubbing a stain out of the carpet. It seemed that everyone had a secondary job.

'Not exactly Securicor then, is he? What if there's trouble now?'

The woman smirked a humourless smirk.

'We don't get trouble in the mornings, Detective.'

The 'Detective' was a sarcastic full stop. Tynan nodded towards the girl scrubbing in the lounge.

'Get some early morning spillages though, don't you?'

This time the woman put on her most superior expression, the one that said *you really are a silly little man, aren't you?*

'No we don't. That was from a little trouble last night.'

Tynan's ears pricked up.

'Really? What trouble was that?'

The woman looked proud to have her finger on the pulse. Tynan got the impression he could ask her about anything at all and she would come up with an answer, even if she had no idea what he was talking about. She was that type. Knew everything about everything. The look of disdain told him as much as her words. The trouble last night wasn't any kind of trouble they couldn't cope with.

'A dispute between customers. The troublemaker was ejected.'

Ejected before he ejaculated, Tynan thought. Unless that was the stain on the carpet. He wasn't really interested in a punter punch-up but he didn't believe in coincidences. Timing was the key. Now to find out just how much the woman did have her finger on the pulse.

'What happened?'

'As I understand it, the man came straight out of his massage and attacked a customer at the bar for no reason. He knocked him to the floor and assaulted him before our security consultant ejected them.'

'Both of them?'

'Yes.'

'This the same security consultant who's out getting sandwiches now?'

The woman slitted her eyes as if rebuking Tynan for the jibe. She clearly thought the detective wasn't taking Golden Touch's security staff seriously.

'The same security consultant who is *back* with the sandwiches now.'

Tynan heard movement behind him and smelled bacon and egg. The office door was blocked by a squat figure whose head sat right on his shoulders, bypassing the need for a neck. Tynan sniffed the air.

'Did you put brown sauce on mine?'

The bouncer's brow furrowed with concentration and then he realized it was a joke. For a minute there he thought he'd forgotten a sandwich.

'Very funny.'

'*I* thought so.'

No Neck passed a grease-stained paper bag to the woman, making a show of ignoring the copper.

'What's the comedian want?'

A rhetorical question aimed at belittling the detective. The woman accepted the sandwich with a nod of thanks but displayed the first sign that she wasn't as all-knowing as she pretended. Should she explain about the missing girl or go straight to the disturbance they were talking about now? Not realizing the question was rhetorical, she went for the latter.

'The trouble last night.'

No Neck flexed his shoulders and smirked.

'That weren't no trouble. Pair of pussies.'

Tynan was getting tired of this.

'Right place for them then. Since pussy's what's on offer.'

He wanted answers and he wanted them now. Whatever happened last night might have nothing to do with the missing girl but, for certain, whoever was taking them was visiting the parlours first. Maybe even afterwards to see if there was any fallout. That said, any customer was a suspect, and any trouble between suspects on the night an anonymous call came in was worth looking into.

'Let's stop fucking about. What time did you throw the fellas out last night?'

The bouncer bristled and flexed his shoulders again.

'Mind yer own fuckin' business.'

'It is my fuckin' business. And if you don't fuckin' tell me you'll be telling me under fuckin' caution at the fuckin' nick.'

'Under caution for what?'

Tynan ticked off on his fingers.

'Assault. Breach of the peace. Theft.'

He threw that last one in for added effect.

'What fuckin' theft?'

'One of them had his wallet stolen.'

That took a while to sink in, but then the furrowed brow cleared as a light bulb went on inside the bouncer's head. He smiled a knowing smile.

'Nobody reported no assault. You don't got no complainant.'

'That's two double negatives. Makes two positives. Somebody did report an assault. And we do have a complainant. How else would I know about the wallet?'

The bouncer re-evaluated his position. Too many words baffled him and he was way beyond his normal quota. Easier to just answer the questions.

'What was the question again?'

Tynan could see the war was over.

'What time did you throw them out?'

The brow furrowed again and Tynan almost expected him to start counting on his fingers. Instead he checked his watch as if that had the answer.

'About seven. Half seven.'

The hairs on the back of Tynan's neck rode a wave of goose bumps. Half an hour before the mystery phone call. They had to be connected.

'They give any names?'

It might sound like a silly question but punters sometimes liked to encourage a girlfriend-type experience. Starting with the use of first names.

'No.'

'Descriptions.'

Now the furrow deepened and Tynan knew he wasn't going to ID anyone off this guy's description. He prepared to note it in his book anyway.

'Er. One knocked to the floor was about six feet. Flabby. Dark hair. One who knocked him down was taller. Muscles. Younger.'

'Younger than what?'

'Than the fat one.'

'How old was he?'

'Don't know.'

This was going nowhere. Vague physicals and no ages whatsoever. He was about to call it a day when a thought struck him.

'How d'you know he was muscly?'

The bouncer smiled a smug little smile. He had a surprise up his sleeve and he knew it was a beauty.

''Cos he was stripped to the waist. Still oiled up.'

'Stripped to the waist before you threw him out?'

'Stripped to the waist *when* I threw him out.'

'How come?'

''Cos he came straight out of his massage. Surprised he had his trousers on.'

'What happened to his top?'

Tynan held his breath. The back of his neck turned cold. The bouncer nodded towards a black bin liner ready to go out with the rubbish. He opened the neck of the bag. Lying there among the cum-soaked tissues was a crumpled grey sweatshirt.

TEN

The knock on the door was loud and insistent. It slammed McNulty out of a deep sleep and he fumbled for his watch on the bedside cabinet. It was ten in the morning. He rubbed his eyes. Scratched his head and forced himself awake. It was a little worrying how much he was sleeping just lately. A lot more since he'd come home than when he was on his travels. He felt lethargic too. As if everything was too much trouble.

Across town DC Tynan was parking outside Golden Touch.

Again the knock. Angry pounding that threatened to come right through the door of Flat 7. A copper's knock. That thought woke him up fast. He recognized the urgency in the hammering because he'd been on the other side of that door knock many times. It was the heavy pounding of the concern-for-an-elderly-neighbour-who-hasn't-been-seen-for-a-week kind of knock. Or the open-up-you're-under-arrest kind of knock. Three more knocks and they'd be kicking the door in.

McNulty swung his legs out of bed and picked a pair of tracksuit bottoms off the floor. He pulled them up on his way to the door, ignoring the T-shirt and trainers scattered across the bedroom. His mind raced. If he'd still been in the job this might be a last-minute court warning, but he wasn't. His last case had gone to court three months after he'd left and he'd received a witness summons for that. He hadn't done anything recently that might provoke the urgency suggested by the knocking. Vice Squad weren't interested in massage parlours any more and even when they were it was the staff, not the customers.

A cloud crossed his mind as he reached the door. The fat man with the blackcurrant juice and the bouncer. That was all it could be, but he didn't think the fat man would make a complaint and the bouncer certainly wouldn't. He'd done his job and nobody got hurt. Why call the police? Working on the theory that he'd not done anything else, he began composing his answers.

This time the knocking rattled the letterbox.

'All right. I'm coming. Keep your hair on.'

The keys were in the lock. McNulty turned them and opened the door. The face that greeted him was that of Donkey Flowers.

'Have you seen the news?'

Donk's voice was breathless and urgent. It was as if he couldn't breathe until he'd got his message across. Weak autumn sunshine flooded the communal hallway, glinting off the rubber plant in the window. He imagined the neighbours twitching behind closed doors at the disturbance. McNulty waved him in and shut the door. His mind was still foggy.

'News?'

'The news.'

McNulty went into the living room and opened the curtains. Sunshine hurt his eyes as it suddenly filled the room. He turned the TV on to see what all the fuss was about. An effeminate male presenter was explaining what colour dress an overweight female should be wearing this autumn. On the other channel Jeremy Kyle presided over a dispute between members of an inbred family. The tattooed daughter, with nose rings, lip rings, and a stud in her tongue, shouted at her tattooed mother for sleeping with her tattooed boyfriend. The mother and the boyfriend were shouting too. Kyle shouted them all down and McNulty changed channels. A pair of train spotters wearing matching red fleece tops walked around a car boot sale with a posh antiques expert. Channel 4 had a rerun of *Friends*, that neverending story of thirty-something morons acting like children. McNulty couldn't get Channel 5.

There were no news programmes scheduled until midday.

Donk was going bog-eyed and red in the face. Unable to believe McNulty was being so blind, he waved the newspaper in his face.

'No. The bleedin' news.'

He dropped the *Yorkshire Post* on the dining table. A colour photo

on the front page showed a patch of wasteland with blue and white
police tape and a white crime scene tent. A patrol car stood in the fore-
ground and Kwik Save to one side. The headline was stark and black.

MISSING GIRLS LINKED TO MASSAGE PARLOURS

Not just massage parlours. Northern X massage parlours. Not just
in Leeds. All across the north of England. McNulty unfolded the paper
and saw that the lead story took up most of the front page. The photo
went all the way to the bottom, lending it more gravity than the content
deserved. The photographer would have no doubt loved a shot of the
body or a patch of blood, but had to make do with a policeman's fluorescent jacket to add colour. Otherwise they might as well have used
black and white. McNulty was coming round now. He scanned the
story and his first thought was . . .

'So?'

Donk's eyes nearly popped out of his head.

'So? Look at the last two.'

McNulty scanned the story again. He had no patience with the jour-
nalistic licence used in newspapers and on TV that made every news
item sound like a Hollywood thriller. If somebody got killed they
always drummed up enough friends and neighbours to say what a nice
chap he was, or how he wouldn't hurt a fly, or what a loving
husband/father/son he was. There were no bastards in the cemetery.
They could probably find enough people to say Hitler loved his dog.
So the facts as stated in the *Yorkshire Post* didn't grab him as much
as they did some people.

Bottom line was this. A girl had been found dead in an oil drum
off City Road. She had worked as a masseuse at Gemini's. Several
other girls were believed missing from various other massage parlours,
most of them part of the Northern X chain. Vague numbers. Vague
locations. Typical scaremongering journalism. Police were unavailable
to comment. Even more typical. The only hard facts were the last two
parlours. Gemini's and Golden Touch.

Donk could see that McNulty had reached the end.

'Well?'

'Well what?'

'What you gonna do?'

'I'm not going to do fuck all. It's nothing to do with me.'

'Oh yeah? Bet that's what Warren Beatty said in *The Parallax Error*.'

'View.'

'*Parallax View.*'

McNulty sighed and folded the paper.

'Warren Beatty was duped into being prime suspect in an assassination because he was in the right place at the wrong time. Not because he used a couple of massage parlours where girls have gone missing.'

'That's 'cos it's about political assassination. Same principle though.'

'Well, if they ever do The Phallic View I'll start worrying.'

A trace memory drifted into his mind. Something that had happened twice in the last few days. But it wouldn't solidify. What did solidify was why did Donk bring this to him when they hadn't met for years before *Von Ryan's Express*?

'Hang on a minute. What makes you think I used the same parlours?'

Donk looked shamefaced but hid it well. His face went only slightly red.

'Because you're still perving the massage scene.'

'I told you before. It's not perving. I don't go in for any that Greek or Golden Showers. No Hard Sports or anything like that.'

Even the thought of anal sex made him cringe. Being pissed or shit on made him cringe even more. As far as he was concerned there was nothing wrong with a bit of good old-fashioned heterosexual hanky-panky, so long as it didn't hurt anyone. It wasn't like he was going behind some poor husband's back or corrupting a minor. But Donk's answer wasn't good enough.

'Same question again. What makes you think I used the same parlours?'

This time Donk actually looked proud behind the shame.

'Told you I know things. Still got my nose to the ground.'

'Still got your nose in other people's business, you mean.'

'You didn't complain when that nose was working for you.'

'Well, it don't work for me any more.'

'Could be. If you went private. I still know things.'

'Philip Marlowe, *The Big Sleep* private?'

'Yeah. Why not? I could be your ears on the streets.'

'PIs are right up there with PCSOs and Special Constables. Hobby bobbies who weren't good enough to be real coppers. I'd rather have my arse sewn up by Boy George.'

Donk looked deflated. McNulty wondered if this visit was more about rekindling old friendships than bringing a warning that wasn't really necessary. There was an outside chance the police might come calling if they found out he visited some of the parlours, but he'd been a policeman for eighteen years. He knew they'd need more than a tenuous link to start believing he had anything to do with the disappearances. And he didn't have anything to do with them, so he was safe.

That trace memory drifted in again but this time he anchored it. The girl who hadn't turned up for her shift at Gemini's. *'You'd normally have four to choose from but the new girl hasn't turned in.'* Then a second time, the shouting at Golden Touch. *'Probably complaining about the shortage of staff. Having to wait.'* That was twice he could remember when girls hadn't turned up for work. Twice at parlours he had visited, at roughly the time when he visited them. Maybe there was something to look into here. He decided to soften his stance with Donk.

'Anyway. Thanks for thinking of me. I know you only wanted to help.'

'I just thought. You know. Forewarned is forearmed.'

'Yeah. I know. Thanks. But I'm not worried.'

'Glad to hear it.'

Another thought crossed his mind but he kept it to himself. If Donkey Flowers had his finger on the pulse and knew that Vince McNulty had been visiting massage parlours, how many other people might know the same thing? He thought about the battered warrant card in his wallet. It would probably stand up to inspection.

'McNulty and Flowers. Quite a team.'

Donk smiled.

'You could hang it above your office door.'

'Could do. After all these massages I am a private dick.'

Donk squirmed and waved the thought aside.

'Whoah. Too much information.'

They both laughed but the newspaper headline stared up from the table.

MISSING GIRLS LINKED TO
MASSAGE PARLOURS

Yes. Maybe there was something to look into there.

ELEVEN

McNulty parked the Astra three doors up the road from Gemini's, where the double yellow lines became broken single yellow. Parking allowed between times shown on the sign. Off peak. The rush hour had finished and traffic flowed smoothly. Half the parking spaces were empty. It was mid-morning creeping towards noon. Eleven thirty. He turned the engine off and listened to the hot metal tick as it cooled. He didn't have a laminated Police Vehicle sign to put on the dashboard so he couldn't park right outside the door.

Having sent Donk on his way McNulty had decided to strike while the iron was hot, before he changed his mind. That had always been the way for him on the job. Very much an impulse copper. Work the gut feeling as much as the evidence. His gut feeling told him not to start his enquiries at Golden Touch and common sense told him to make them during the day shift. He knew from experience that the receptionists changed around teatime, so if he flashed his badge before then he wouldn't be flashing it at someone who'd served him during the evening.

Golden Touch was the obvious starting point, where the evidence would be freshest and recollections strongest, but that very fact meant he might be remembered. The receptionist would be different but anyone looking at the CCTV upstairs might not be. Northern X employed their bouncers on minimum wage, so they worked long hours with even less brainpower, but that didn't mean they were blind. The muscle who'd thrown him out wasn't going to forget him.

He got out of the car and checked his badge wallet. Split and faded though it was after several washing accidents in his jeans pocket, the warrant card didn't look too bad behind the plastic window when he flipped it open. In truth, it had looked just as bad when he was still on the job before the police replaced it with a fresh one. The one he'd handed in when he left. McNulty looked ten years younger and a damn sight heavier, but then again nobody looked like their ID photo. It had been a running joke in uniform that if you looked like your warrant card you'd better see the force surgeon.

McNulty slipped the wallet in his back pocket and walked towards Gemini's Sauna and Massage. It was part of a parade of shops on the main road. A newsagent and video rental library. A hairdresser. And a greengrocer whose display of fruit and veg spread across half the pavement. Judging by the smell, most of it wasn't today's. He walked past a box of rancid cauliflowers and up the steps of Gemini's. Threw a quick glance at the camera above the door and went straight in. Another part of his technique that kept him moving forward at all times. He didn't stand on ceremony and he didn't pause to collect his thoughts, he simply went with the flow.

A woman he hadn't seen before came out of the alcove office behind the counter, all Stepford Wives smiles. His instincts were right. Different staff. Best time to do this.

'Good morning, sir. And what can we do for you?'

The question dripped sexual innuendo. What she was offering to do for him, not personally, was a lot more enticing than what the green-grocer was selling next door. McNulty took the badge wallet out of his pocket and flipped it open in one quick movement. It was opened and shut and back in his pocket before the woman could see more than a face and the big Police Officer sign above the force crest.

'Morning, love. Just a few follow-up questions.'

The woman's expression changed from alluring sexuality to bored housewife in a split second. He obviously wasn't the first detective to come around asking questions. There had probably been reporters too, and he'd bet his pension she was no happier to see them. Only the most hardened brass would want her face seen in the paper working in a brothel. McNulty gave her a sad little smile and shrugged his shoulders.

'I know. Pain in the arse, isn't it? But it pays the rent.'

She unwound a little.

'Something's got to.'

'Ain't that the truth?'

He leaned on the counter as if having a friendly chat and defused the situation even more. Made it less of a police officer getting in your face and more of an old friend popping in for a coffee.

'This might be easier over a coffee, d'ya think?'

'I think you're a cheeky little monkey.'

The ice was broken. She went into the little back room and put the kettle on, while McNulty prepared to get all the information he wanted. He felt a shiver of excitement run down his spine. This was like being back in the job.

By four o'clock McNulty had visited five parlours and built up enough of a picture to know he was in deep trouble. The five he chose were the nearest ones to Leeds, either from his outward journey at the beginning of his sexual quest or the return leg coming home. That worked out as two from six months ago and three over the last couple of weeks. The rest were too far away for any serious enquiries today, but from what he'd learned he didn't think that would be necessary.

He was in deep trouble.

All five had at least one girl missing and one had two. All six girls were of the very young variety. And all six disappearances were being investigated by the police. That put Vincent McNulty at the scene of the crime five times, too much of a coincidence for even the laziest detective to ignore. If they found out he was a customer of all five parlours.

He put the Astra in gear and pulled away from the Sauna Kabin, his last massage before returning to Leeds. The receptionist had been as helpful as all the rest once she'd seen his warrant card. The adjoining shops' owners too. Three of the shops on the parade used the upstairs as storage but four rented the first floor as bedsit flats. As with the other locations he'd visited, half of the tenants were out at work. Those who were in when he knocked had heard nothing, knew nothing, and wanted nothing to do with the police.

There was no CCTV video at any of the parlours and the girls hadn't been taken from there anyway. They simply hadn't turned up for work one day. The only trouble at the Sauna Kabin during the last couple of months had been somebody getting rough with one of the masseuses and being restrained by a customer.

'But we told the last detective all this before.'

'I know. Just checking we didn't miss anything. Routine.'

Pulling into the petrol station where he'd bought the *Evening Post*, he thought about that. The customer had been him. Goose-necking the bodybuilder's wrist before hitting him in the throat. He filled the tank with unleaded and paid at the kiosk. Didn't bother with an *Evening Post* this time. The electric clock on the wall said 4.15 p.m. McNulty thought about the change of shifts coming up at six. He still had time if he set off now.

The Astra swung off the forecourt and turned left on the main road towards Leeds. He had avoided the Golden Touch because of the trouble there last night but now had second thoughts. It was a dangerous move but he thought he could get away with it. The receptionist would be the daygirl and he didn't intend going upstairs.

As he drove north-east he felt like the burglar he'd arrested after the paint depot job. Way back. It was a local DIY store and the lad lived half a mile away. He'd dropped a tin of white Dulux One-Coat Gloss and panicked. Left his spoils and ran all the way home, after stepping in the spreading pool of white paint. A trail of white gloss footprints led Constable McNulty almost all the way to the thief's house. The reason they didn't lead all the way was because McNulty found him in the street with a bottle of Polyclens and a cloth, scrubbing the footprints out.

He felt like he was leaving a trail of footprints himself. That the police had been told about the trouble at the Sauna Kabin wasn't a problem in itself, but if they'd also been told about the trouble at Golden Touch they only had to match descriptions and they were on his trail.

He was in deep, deep trouble. And it was about to get deeper.

*　　*　　*

'I know. Just checking we didn't miss anything. Routine.'

McNulty thought the woman who looked like she was sucking lemons didn't seem convinced. She'd already given this information twice today and obviously wished the press and the police would simply leave her alone. McNulty tapped the peak of the baseball cap he'd put on.

'Sorry.'

He wrote the missing girl's details in his notebook with a sinking feeling. The description she'd given of the man causing trouble was vague because she hadn't seen him, but he'd bet the bouncer had given a better one. He might even be upstairs now, looking at the CCTV covering the reception area. That didn't worry him. Grainy black and white images of a man in a baseball cap shouldn't flag up trouble, and he kept his head down so the peak hid his face.

'Thanks for your time. Sorry to bother you again.'

He pushed through the dangling chain curtain and round the counter. He was halfway to the front door when the woman came out of the cubicle too.

'Did they get any CSI stuff off the sweatshirt?'

That stopped him in his tracks and he turned to face her. He knew exactly what she meant and his heart sank even further. He'd forgotten about the torn grey sweatshirt that had been left on the massage room floor.

'It takes longer than a fifty-minute episode to get the results back. We'll have to wait and see. But thanks again.'

Then he was out of the door and heading for his car. He needed time to think. And he needed to speak to Donk.

This time the man across the street was ready when the detective came out of Golden Touch. After the news in this morning's paper he knew that McNulty would be snooping around sooner or later. The baseball cap wasn't fooling anyone. It was earlier than last time, so the traffic wasn't a problem as the man crossed the road and followed.

Round the corner and down the side street. McNulty got his car keys out and unlocked a blue Vauxhall Astra. It was parked tight between an ex-Post Office van with the lettering painted out and a new Mini. The detective had to manoeuvre two or three times before driving away. Plenty of time for the man to make a note of the registration number.

Once the car disappeared around the corner the man flicked open his mobile phone and began dialling.

TWELVE

Tynan had just popped another Polo mint in his mouth when he was called away from the post mortem to take the phone call. It wasn't the most disappointing moment of his life. The mints were fighting a losing battle.

It was early evening and the sky was already dark with brooding clouds. The stone-built mortuary looked like it should have gargoyles crouched along the rooftop. The building was a single-storey square block of carved stone and concrete that looked more like the gate lodge of a country house than a hi-tech facility of modern forensic science. It was in a narrow cul-de-sac opposite a Chinese takeaway.

The front aspect had a heavy black door with stained glass leaded windows on either side. Not stained glass like that in a church, with pictures of Our Lord or suchlike, just glass that had become stained with decades of city grime that had never been cleaned off. Delivery entrance was through a double garage door on the right. The coroner's office was to the left of the entrance hall inside the main door. The only other door was to the examination room. A polite way of saying the cutting room.

The cutting room was split in two. The first half was attached to the delivery entrance and had tiled floor and walls with a drainage trough down the middle. Wheeled metal trolleys stood against the left wall in front of the big steel refrigerated cadaver drawers. There were bodies covered by green sheets on two of the trolleys. Taking up one corner was an intermediate office with windows on all sides. From in there you could see the delivery area or watch the post mortems being carried out in the cutting room proper. That room was much smaller, tiled like the other, with two permanent examination tables. Stainless steel with drainage and hot and cold running water. The right-hand table was the centre of attention this evening.

Tynan stood against the back wall with the SOCO photographer. He could have watched from the little office but then he wouldn't have been able to interject if he had any questions. The photographer looked bored. He'd photographed hundreds of post mortems and was only interested in getting everything in focus and, if it was a close-up, including a measuring scale. Once you were taking pictures inside someone's chest cavity or brain pan there wasn't much to give you a sense of size, so interconnecting plastic measures marked in inches and centimetres were used. The electronic flash hung from the tripod, humming gently as it charged up for the next shot.

The naked body of the girl from the oil drum lay on her back on the table. If there was one thing Tynan was certain of, it was that Hollywood film-makers had never seen a dead body being cut open. All the films he'd ever seen had gorgeous dead women with firm breasts and great hair. The girl on the table had probably been gorgeous in life, but now she was a pallid, sunken corpse with no shape and no breasts and, at the moment, no top to her head. What they missed in Hollywood though was the smell. Not antiseptic hospital smells. Nothing clean about it at all. It was the smell of discharged bowels and urine. The worst possible combination of rotting food and diarrhoea, one that clung to your clothes for days. Tynan unwrapped his post-mortem Polos and popped one in his mouth to combat the smell, which was so thick it clogged his throat. Minty freshness flared in his mouth.

A harsh bell rang over the loudspeaker, making everyone jump. The pathologist looked up over his half-moon glasses and his assistant nodded and shuffled out of the room. He reappeared in the glass-walled office looking like Igor from *Frankenstein*. He answered the phone while taking a swig of tea from a chipped mug. He had offered Tynan and the photographer one but Tynan remembered where they kept the milk. Chilled in the refrigerated drawers between a pair of frozen dead feet.

He listened and then waved Tynan over, holding the receiver up. Tynan went through the outer room and into the office. Igor gave him the phone and left. When the door closed the majority of the smell stayed outside. Tynan took a shallow breath and smelled mint. He spoke into the handset.

'DC Tynan.'

'Jimmy. It's Bill Baildon. You on your second pack of Polos yet?'

'I've never needed two packs.'

'I do. Every time they open the stomach.'

Tynan wasn't interested in Baildon's post-mortem blues.

'What's up?'

There was a pause and a noise of shuffling paper.

'CCTV tapes arrived.'

'That why you dragged me out here?'

'No. We've had another anonymous call. Car number.'

Tynan was back at the CID office half an hour later. He'd missed the second half of the post mortem but wasn't going to lose any sleep over that. Strictly speaking it was the investigating detective who should attend the PM, and even then it was more courtesy than necessity. There were no exhibits to bag and label for this one. No murder weapon or foreign objects inserted where they shouldn't have been. He'd made sure of that before he left.

The girl had been strangled and dumped in a drum of water. From behind according to the bruises on her neck. By hand. There were bruises from the fingers around the front of her throat. She'd also had violent anal sex before she died. By definition that had been from behind too. Probably at the time of death, so there was an element of auto-erotic asphyxiation arousal going on. He'd seen it with some hangings. One in particular had happened while the lad's mother was downstairs cooking dinner. While she was basting the meat he was hanging by a belt ligature from his wardrobe door, basting his own meat. He'd slipped beyond arousal and hung himself with a stonk on and a cum-stained porn magazine.

The office was empty apart from Baildon. Late turn CID were dealing with a hostage robbery at a cash and carry warehouse on the industrial estate. Along with one of his staff, the owner had been tied up and gagged with gaffer tape that took half of his beard off when the detective ripped it from his face. Most of the uniform shift were guarding the scene, so God help anyone who got mugged in the next couple of hours.

Tynan dodged between the desks of the darkened office until he reached the pool of light in the corner they'd been allocated. The over-head fluorescent was the only light on. Two computer screens painted blue light across the desktop and Baildon pushed a mug of steaming coffee across the blotter.

'Two sugars?'

Tynan sat down and took the mug.

'Thanks.'

'No more doughnuts. Sorry.'

'Have you been in all day?'

'Yes.'

'Wouldn't expect any then.'

'Cheeky bastard.'

Tynan sipped the coffee. It was too hot for a deep swig. He glanced across the desk at the pile of A4 paper spilling out of a folder in front of Baildon's chair.

'So the CCTV footage. How many hits?'

Baildon shuffled the papers into order and slid one finger down the list.

'Three. And a possible fourth but it was partially obscured.'

Tynan was talking mainly to himself. Putting things in place in his mind.

'Same car parked near four of the parlours then. CCTV doesn't cover all of them so it could be outside some of the others too.'

Baildon waited a few moments while Tynan drummed his fingers on the blotter. Tynan's way of focusing his mind on a problem. When the fingers stopped, Baildon moved on to the next question before it was asked.

'Same reg number the anon call gave us.'

Tynan nodded. He checked his watch, even though he knew what he wanted doing couldn't be done until tomorrow morning.

'Let's run it through Big Fish tomorrow. Three days either side of each disappearance for each parlour. See if we can pick it up in the area.'

'Big Fish operators aren't going to like that. Tons of work.'

Tynan imagined the camera operators in the bunker having to input the car into the Big Fish vehicle recognition computer and trawl through all the hits that the city cameras picked up. Not the standard CCTV cameras but the specialist cameras that recorded car number plates coming into and out of town. Any cars recorded as stolen, wanted for crime or without insurance were flagged up and uniform patrols could be directed to intercept. If they weren't too busy, which they invariably were. This was more of a retrospective enquiry. It would show the vehicle's movement in the areas requested during the period involved.

'Who does it PNC to?'

'I'm waiting for the help desk to get back to me.'

Neither Baildon nor Tynan was trained for Police National Computer enquiries and Tynan thanked his lucky stars every day. PNC operators were constantly being asked to do a quick enquiry by everyone from uniform patrol to CID. It was like being ID Suite trained. You'd spend half your working life doing ID parades for other cases and not getting anything done on your own workload.

Tynan sipped coffee and wrote the relevant sightings in his notebook while they waited for the phone call. Vehicle make and registration number. No colour because the images were black and white. Dates, times and parlours. Ten minutes later the phone made him jump for the second time that night. Baildon answered it, listened and scribbled a few notes on the blotter. Said thanks and hung up.

'It's a blue Vauxhall Astra.'

'Not one of ours?'

The registration number hadn't rung any bells, but blue Vauxhall Astras were standard for CID and other plain-clothes units.

'No. Don't panic. Registered to a Vincent McNulty. Address is a flat over at Weetwood Court.'

Tynan's shoulders sagged. He let out a sigh that emptied his lungs.

'Shit.'

'You know him?'

'In passing. He's ex-Vice Squad.'

'Ex, like back in uniform ex?'

'No. Ex, like out of the job ex.'

'Sorry.'

Tynan picked up the mug of coffee but didn't drink any.

'You should be. Eating all the fucking doughnuts.'

Baildon kept quiet. He knew this was blowing off steam. Tynan took a deep swig of coffee and burned his throat. Didn't pause but took another drink and burped. His throat stung, forcing tears in his eyes. He went back to his notebook. The last recorded sighting of McNulty's car was near the Sauna Kabin a week ago. There was no usable CCTV of Golden Touch.

'Sauna Kabin. There was trouble at that one, wasn't there?'

Baildon flicked through the A4 sheets.

'Yes. Last week. Customer attacked another one in the lounge. Must have been a bit handy according to this. Fancy moves with the arm twist and strike to the throat. Helped him come round after he'd floored him.'

'We get descriptions for them?'

'For what they're worth. Witnesses aren't top drawer.'

'Let me have a look.'

Baildon passed the papers across the desk and Tynan found the descriptions. There was always a possibility that McNulty was no longer the registered keeper of the Astra. Cars were sold on all the time without DVLA being updated. He'd lost track of how many keeper enquiries he'd done for a parking ticket or a speed camera when he was in uniform, only to find it wasn't them. He kept his fingers crossed that the description wouldn't match.

He found them halfway down page two. Baildon was right, they weren't great. But the six foot three, dark-haired, well-muscled man was ballpark near enough to be Vince McNulty. He read the other description just because it was there.

'Shit.'

Baildon leaned forward with no great relish.

'Is it him?'

Tynan didn't answer. He looked at the description. It was Vince McNulty. But that wasn't all. He recognized the other description too. And that made it much worse.

THIRTEEN

McNulty found Donk in the back row of the Hyde Park Picture House. He'd forgotten about the classic war film season and gone round to Donkey Flowers' house first. After driving around for a while to get his head straight. Bad news always took time to absorb and he'd parked outside the place where bad news had been part of everyday life. In the leaf-strewn driveway of Crag View Orphanage. The gate still hung by one hinge. Evening shadows turned the main building into a black smudge in the darkness. It suited his mood.

He forced his mind to ignore the trace memory of the corridor, the office, and the slap that sounded like a gunshot. Forced himself not to think about the immediate consequences of that, or the shocking news that came too late. Instead he worked the facts of his current troubles.

Main thing was, he knew he hadn't done anything wrong. Apart from paying for sex, but people didn't hold that against you these days. He hadn't abducted or killed any of the missing girls and there could be no physical evidence to prove that he had. So he was in the clear.

After eighteen years in the police force he knew it wasn't as simple as that, though. There had been numerous cases where circumstantial evidence had been enough to convince a jury. The twelve good men and true were often twelve gullible morons who believed what they saw on American cop shows. For them, CSI was God and forensic evidence the ultimate tool. Trouble was, they also believed what witnesses told them. Sitting in Crown Court is a sobering experience. Listening to the advocates and experts and witnesses pouring their hearts out, it was easy to believe they were stating the facts. A good solicitor could twist even the most innocent phrase into a noose to hang the unwary copper. Weight of indirect evidence could add up to enough for the jury to believe it must be true.

There was a lot of indirect evidence against Vincent McNulty.

For a start, nobody was going to believe it was a coincidence that McNulty had massages at all the parlours where the girls were missing.

They weren't going to believe that attacking two customers over three days wasn't somehow connected to the girls who had been taken from there. And when details of his violent past were introduced, which they could do now as Bad Character Evidence even before conviction, they were going to believe whatever the prosecution told them.

But he hadn't done it.

Was innocent as the day is long.

So that meant someone else had. Someone else had visited all those parlours. Someone else had scouted the locations and selected the girls for plucking. McNulty had conducted enquiries into all sorts of crimes. When it came to arresting the suspects they all had one thing in common. There was a link between them and the crime scene every single time. Nobody burgled a house they'd never seen before. They never robbed a post office they hadn't scouted before.

And they never abducted a girl they hadn't been watching before the abduction. Whoever had taken these girls had seen them at work, and that meant the massage parlours they worked at. Of course, with missing persons cases there really weren't any crimes until you found the person, because until then they were simply missing. Weight of indirect evidence kicked in here again. It was no coincidence that so many had gone missing from so many similar locations. All from massage parlours. All within a narrow age range. All within a specific time frame. So there was enough to convince the police to start an inquiry. The fact that one of the girls had been found murdered just cranked up the tension. Now it was a murder investigation, with dozens of other possible murders waiting to be discovered.

McNulty sat in the Astra in front of the unhinged gate. He didn't get out. He didn't take another trip down memory lane. The present was more important than the past tonight. Someone had visited all those parlours. And someone knew that McNulty had visited all those parlours. Donkey Flowers.

The house where McNulty had taken Donk home every time he'd arrested him was dark when he pulled up outside. There were no lights on. McNulty remembered Donk's mother being glad he'd been arrested. She'd hoped it would straighten him out. Set him on the right track to a better life. It had appeared to work because the teenager had joined the Royal Navy and travelled the world. It felt sad knowing she was no longer around. She'd been a strong woman. Made fabulous home-baked cakes. But she wasn't here to keep Donk on the straight and narrow any more.

Donk wasn't here either. Then McNulty remembered what day it was. He checked his watch. He'd missed the beginning of *The Dirty*

Dozen but that was good. It meant that Donk would be preoccupied when he arrived.

Jim Brown pulled the pin on the grenade and paused beside the first uncovered air vent. The cobblestones were shiny and wet. Light from the chateau behind him glinted off them in the darkness. Lee Marvin put the can of petrol down and emptied a bag of hand grenades with the pins still in them into the last vent. He climbed aboard the stolen German halftrack and nodded at Brown.

The former American football star turned actor threw the grenade into the vent and set off at a sprint. He threw a grenade into each vent as he passed it. One. Two. Three. Four. When he reached the last vent he stopped. The pin was stuck. Finally he yanked the pin out, slammed the grenade into the hole, and raced across the cobblestones towards the waiting halftrack.

Machine-gun fire cut him down before he got halfway there. He stumbled as he ran full tilt and crashed to the ground. Lee Marvin stared in stunned silence for a split second and then emptied his Schmeisser at the chateau window. A body fell through the broken glass just as the first grenade exploded. It set off a chain reaction and the world exploded in a huge ball of flame.

Light from the explosion lit the cinema. McNulty saw Donk watching with rapt attention in the middle of the back row. He stood beside the door as the mayhem on screen brought *The Dirty Dozen* to a rousing climax. Machine-gun fire. More explosions. Death and destruction. Just what every red-blooded male wanted to see. Forget all that *When Harry Met Sally* shit. Or those stupid teen comedies with nubile females and idiot sons.

McNulty had seen *The Dirty Dozen* more times than he'd seen *Von Ryan's Express*, but not as many times as he'd seen his all-time favourite, *Zulu*; not strictly a war film but with plenty of battle action among the human stories. He wasn't watching tonight though. He kept his eyes on Donkey Flowers and waited for the hospital scene at the end to finish before sidling along the back row and taking the seat next to him. The house lights came up as Frank De Vol's drum roll played over the dozen's frozen image at the dinner table in happier times. Most of them were dead now. Just like Von Ryan. And the girl from Gemini's massage parlour.

McNulty watched Donk for any signs of an adverse reaction.

'Thought I'd find you here.'

'Where were you? Up in the balcony seats?'

There was nothing untoward in the enquiring look Donk gave him.

Just innocent curiosity. They'd talked about *The Dirty Dozen* after seeing *Von Ryan's Express*. It was the closing film of the season. McNulty had been looking forward to watching it on the big screen again after years of being butchered on television. Adverts every fifteen minutes and a half-hour news break in the middle. He wondered if he was wrong about Donk.

'Up to my neck in shit.'

'Oh fuck. What's happened?'

Donk looked genuinely concerned. Like this morning when he'd brought the newspaper round to McNulty's flat. A worm of doubt crawled into his stomach. There was too much going on to be coincidence, but as far as he knew Donk was the only person with knowledge of his massage trips.

McNulty looked Donk in the eye without speaking. It was an old interview technique designed to unsettle the suspect into filling the silence. One thing he'd learned after eighteen years on the job was that guilty people didn't like heavy silences. It suggested the interviewer knew something he was holding back. Suspects often blurted out the first thing that came into their head simply to keep the conversation going. Innocent things, they hoped, but more often than not they dug a bigger hole for themselves. Donk didn't flinch. He just stared back waiting.

'What?'

McNulty was convinced. There was no guile in the face that stared back at him. Never had been all the times he'd arrested him. He was such an open book he made the worst criminal on the planet. That was why his mother had been happy that McNulty finally put him in the system. The short sharp shock had straightened him out. McNulty kicked himself for thinking like a copper. The same thought process that CID were no doubt applying to *him*. There is no such thing as coincidence. Therefore the man who'd visited all the parlours was the man who'd taken the missing girls. Or in McNulty's case, the man who knew that McNulty had visited all those parlours was the man who *knew* about the missing girls. It was a false assumption. He needed to go back to square one.

'I'm in deep trouble.'

'I told you that this morning.'

The crowd had thinned to a few stragglers and two usherettes clearing rubbish from between the seats. The music finished and the velvet curtains closed across the screen. McNulty stood up.

'Want to talk about it over a drink?'

Donk stood up too and they shuffled along the row towards the aisle. McNulty had a lot of questions he was convinced only Donk had the answers to. The *Casablanca* poster was still in the foyer but as they walked out together it felt less like the beginning of a beautiful friendship. McNulty didn't know that his next decision was almost the end of any kind of relationship.

The cold night air cut McNulty to the bone. He'd had too many dark thoughts since returning to Leeds and they were catching up with him. Standing outside the Hyde Park Picture House he suddenly didn't feel like a cold drink in the local pub. He wanted something hot and he wanted it somewhere private. What he needed to talk about shouldn't be overheard by prying ears. He made a snap decision.

'Let's get a coffee instead. At the flat. I'll drop you home after.'

'OK.'

Donk followed him round the corner to the parked Astra. The street lamp was out and the car sat in a pool of darkness opposite a late-night grocer's. McNulty fumbled with his keys and unlocked the door. Like most ex-CID cars it didn't have central locking. That made it too easy to jump out of the back doors, which had child locks. McNulty climbed in and reached over to unlock the passenger door. Donk opened it and paused.

'D'you want anything from the shop?'

'No. I've got stuff in.'

Donk climbed in and shut the door. The internal light went out and they sat in the dark for a moment while McNulty found the ignition. The key missed the hole. He tried again.

Someone came out of the cinema towards the car. A big shape in a long coat. The key slid into the ignition. The man came closer and McNulty paused, his fingers ready to turn the key. A big man. His coat held closed with one hand. McNulty tensed. His hand dropped from the key and bunched into a fist.

The man drew level with the car.

And walked right past towards the shop.

McNulty started the car and slipped it into gear. He was getting paranoid. He turned the headlights on and pulled away from the kerb. Turned right at the cinema and headed towards Weetwood Court.

They didn't talk during the drive to McNulty's flat. Both sat in silence with their own thoughts. McNulty felt pressure building in the back of his head as if something was coming to the boil. He sometimes had a sixth sense for things like that but it wasn't always clear exactly what it was – just an uncomfortable feeling that something was going to happen. How that translated to his current situation he didn't know.

The night had drawn in and turned cold. A touch of ground mist began to form on the fields and grass verges alongside the road as the Astra came out of the urban sprawl into stretches of countryside. The outskirts of town, but not quite all the way out. McNulty followed the main road as it cut through Headingley's student area, passing the shops and pubs that fed the brains of tomorrow. Terraced houses and Victorian giants converted into flats gave way to sports fields and woodland interspersed with groups of houses, parades of shops and a petrol station. Fifty yards past the mini-roundabout he turned right into Weetwood Court.

The headlights swept across the car park. He found a space in the corner facing the communal entrance to his block. The mist had thickened into an amorphous shifting blanket, highlighted every few yards by patio lights along the path. It swirled around their legs as they walked towards the door. He glanced up at the gothic monstrosity behind the flats and shivered. Tonight wasn't the night to be thinking about Crag View. He had enough problems without that.

The grounds were deserted. It was late and cold and misty and nobody wanted to be outside in weather like this. Lights were on in several of the flats but the curtains were drawn. Flickering blue light of TV screens the only sign of life. McNulty took the keys out of his pocket as they approached the main door. Donk was a few steps behind. The main door wasn't latched shut. McNulty made a mental note to ask the maintenance man to tighten the spring that was supposed to close the door and click the lock into place. Visitors needed to push the bell for whichever flat they were visiting, but anyone could get in if the lock didn't work.

He ignored the main key and selected his flat key before heading for the stairs. The door creaked behind him and there was a scuffling noise outside. Donk tumbled into the door as it was closing. Sparks of electricity flared up McNulty's neck. He spun round. Donk got to his feet and waved an 'I'm all right' apology. His shoelace was undone and he'd stood on it in the mist.

'Sorry.'

He knelt down in the hallway to fasten it.

'Be right with you.'

McNulty went up the stairs and turned left into the vestibule of Flats 6, 7, 8 and 9. The rubber plant looked forlorn and limp in the window. The damp compost smelled like gas in the enclosed space. The groundskeeper was supposed to look after the houseplants scattered throughout the hallways but the old woman in Flat 9 watered this one twice a week. It left a musty smell every Sunday and Wednesday and McNulty was sure she was killing it softly with her love.

He had his key ready. Approached the door to Flat 7. Never even wondered why the old woman would water the rubber plant on a Thursday. Footsteps sounded on the stairs behind him.

Donk had obviously tied his laces.

The first thing McNulty noticed was that the gassy smell was stronger. His key slid into the lock but he didn't turn it. The second thing he noticed was the jemmy marks on the door frame. The door was closed but the wood was chewed up next to the handle. He twisted it and the door swung open. The gassy smell wasn't the rubber plant, it was gas. And it was coming from the darkness inside his flat.

He pushed the door all the way open and stepped inside. Didn't turn the lights on. That was the first thing they taught you about gas leaks. He'd been to dozens of burglaries where the gas cooker had been stolen and one thing he knew was that burglars never turned off the gas before stealing your appliances. The smell was thick and heavy. It filled the inner hallway. All the doors were open. Bathroom. Kitchen. Bedroom. Living room.

Holding his breath he walked into the living room. The curtains were open and light from the garden lamps skittered across the ceiling. He paused to allow his night vision to kick in before crossing to open the windows.

He never got the chance.

His mind recorded the gas as a room killer, the fire brigade's name for a room filled from floor to ceiling. If ignited the entire room would go up in flames. Unlike a smoke-filled room there was no hugging the ground for air. Gas was heavier than air. It was down at floor level and everywhere. He was about to open the window when he saw something on the settee. And heard footsteps entering the flat behind him.

A female body lay on the leather sofa. A shadowy figure that was either dead or unconscious. McNulty could make out the white smock and blonde hair but nothing else. Couldn't detect any movement. No rising and falling of her chest. No breathing.

'What you doing in the dark, Vince?'

Donk stood in the doorway and McNulty didn't have time to register it was the first time Donk hadn't called him officer. He saw Donk's hand fumble for the light switch beside the door.

'No. Don't turn the—'

Donk flicked the switch. The light sparked on. And the world exploded in a huge ball of flame.

PART TWO
New Orleans

'Mos Eisley spaceport. You will never find a more wretched hive of scum and villainy. We must be cautious.'

FOURTEEN

Tynan thought World War Three had broken out when he parked on the road outside Weetwood Court. He couldn't pull into the car park because it was full of fire engines and ambulances and smoke. An orange glow emanated from one of the Legoland blocks of flats and steam hissed as a fire tender poured water onto the flames. A section of first floor communal hallway stood open to the night air, its full-length window destroyed and the frame so much splintered wood. A charred rubber plant stood forlornly in the corner, battered by water and scorched by flames.

Tynan slammed the door and leaned against the CID car.

'Jesus H. Christ.'

He could have used stronger language because the gaggle of pensioners being treated near the ambulances couldn't hear over the noise of the pump and the squawk of the radios. It was a hellish noise that drilled into Tynan's head, making it difficult to think. He tried anyway, starting with placing the scene in some kind of order.

Two uniformed constables and a patrol car guarded the outer perimeter. Extra uniforms were being drafted in from Ecclesfield Division but hadn't arrived yet. The single blue lamp flashed ineffectually in competition with the brighter flashes of the fire engines and ambulances. The policemen had taped off the entrance but there was nobody around to keep out. That was more for the morning, if the scene still needed preserving.

Beyond the tape was Weetwood Court's car park. Staggered squares like a chessboard with several cars parked neatly alongside the flower borders and lawns. None of them were damaged. Broken glass from the first floor window only extended as far as the path to the front door. Two fire tenders took up most of the right-hand parking spaces and heavy-duty canvas hose snaked into the entrance and up the stairs. There was none of that long-throw hosing that you saw in films or London Blitz newsreels. This was firefighting up close and personal. One crew doused from the landing. The second was round the back.

Three ambulances were parked away from the excitement in the farthest parking spaces. Their back doors were open and paramedics administered breathing masks for smoke inhalation to a group of elderly residents. None of them appeared to be injured and there were no charred corpses.

That was good. Tynan didn't want to be first detective at another major scene. Murder by oil drum was enough for one week. This was only supposed to be an owner/keeper enquiry about the Astra caught on camera. And testing the water with an ex-copper about a very delicate matter.

Tynan crossed the verge to the patrol car and flashed his warrant card to the nearest policeman. He didn't recognize him. That was hardly surprising. Like most policemen, Vince McNulty had lived off division when he'd been in the job and hadn't moved since. The last thing you want when you're shopping in Morrisons is to bump into someone you were fighting with last week. The badge worked.

'DC Tynan. Just on an enquiry. What happened?'

That might sound like a stupid question but there were all sorts of possibilities, from a terrorist bombing to an exploding fart. He could have asked the fire chief, but that would mean getting closer to the tenders. He doubted if he'd be able to make himself heard over the generator.

'Gas explosion.'

Tynan could feel the heat from here.

'Any injuries?'

'Smoke stuff for the neighbours. Don't know about the flat yet.'

Tynan watched the fire crew playing water around the communal landing. Dousing the door frame of the damaged flat. The interior was darker now, the orange glow barely visible amid the smoke and steam. Next step would be searching the flat for survivors. After that for bodies. And finally clearing the room of debris and furniture, so there was nothing for the fire to take hold of should the heat restart it. That would entail throwing everything into the garden, a bone of contention with neighbours of every fire Tynan had ever attended. The fire brigade could cause more damage than the fires they fought and were constantly axing doors and smashing windows that residents didn't think needed axing or smashing. And if your car was parked in the way, forget about it.

A weight settled in Tynan's stomach that had nothing to do with the doughnuts he'd eaten earlier. It was the certainty that he knew the answer to his next question even before he asked it.

'Which flat was it?'

'Number seven.'

He didn't say, 'Shit,' but he thought it. He thought a lot worse as he watched the first fireman go through the flat door.

'What the neighbours say?'

'Not much yet. They're still in shock. Most of 'em were asleep.'

'About flat seven, I mean.'

'Not much about that either.'

'Shit.'

This time he did say it, piquing the constable's interest.

'What was your enquiry?'

'Vehicle. Owner enquiry.'

'By CID?'

The tone was mocking. Owner enquiries were as low down the totem pole as enquiries came and were usually dished out to uniform patrol when they weren't busy dealing with all the other crap that got shovelled their way. Detectives tended to sit in their ivory towers and direct all the shit down hill. And uniform shifts lived in a valley. Bottom of the pile. Tynan could understand the constable's amusement but it had been a long day. He snapped at him.

'What the fuck's that supposed to mean?'

The constable held his hands up in mock surrender.

'Whoah. Just saying, is all.'

Tynan stepped forward and pinched the button of his jacket between finger and thumb. He pointed the button towards the constable as if he were wearing a wire.

'Well, just speak into the fuckin' microphone.'

The officer laughed and the tension was broken. Tynan smiled. Dismissed the comment with a wave of the hand and stepped under the scene tape. He looked for the senior firefighter but couldn't tell one uniform from the next. A heavy-set crew member stood talking on the radio beside the nearest tender. Seemed to be in charge. Tynan waited until he racked the handset.

'DC Tynan. Anybody in there?'

They both looked towards the flat. The hosing was finished and firemen were going inside. The senior man wiped his smoke-stained face.

'Should know in a couple of minutes. Hang on and I'll let you know.'

Tynan stepped away from the tender and surveyed the car park. This could be tentatively called a keeper enquiry but it really all came down to the car. A blue Vauxhall Astra, ex-police registration. It had been recorded near four of the massage parlours and would no doubt be linked to the rest. That was too much of a coincidence, and Tynan didn't believe in coincidences. No policeman did. Vince McNulty wouldn't if the roles were reversed.

Then there was the disturbance at the Sauna Kabin last week. Disregard the trouble at Golden Touch. That was incidental. The Sauna Kabin was the important one because of the descriptions. Vince McNulty and the other fella. And now this. A gas explosion that had likely taken McNulty down. There was no doubt in Tynan's mind that the whole thing was connected. He just couldn't figure out how.

Blue lights flashed. Smoke drifted around the car park and steam hissed from the breached flat's door. Behind the cubist blocks of Weetwood Court the greater bulk of Weetwood House stood out against the night sky. A gothic horror right out of *Dracula* or *Frankenstein*. Tynan half expected bats to come swooping out of the mist that had mostly withdrawn because of the heat. It was a nightmarish scene. The blue lights glinted off the windscreens of the parked cars.

Parked cars.

Tynan looked at the elderly residents being treated by the paramedics. Most of the cars were obvious pensioners' cars. Safe and economical. Nothing flash. Nothing that looked like an ex-CID car. He began to search for the Astra.

The radio squawked in the tender. The fire chief snatched the hand mike and spoke into it. A few words. A nod. A few more. Then he racked the mike. He looked around and waved Tynan over.

'Flat's empty. Nobody home. Lucky for us.'

Lucky for somebody else too, Tynan thought. He didn't need to search the rest of the car park. The Astra wasn't here. That was a good thing and a bad thing. It was decision time and he really didn't want to do what he knew he had to do next.

FIFTEEN

The dirt track behind Donk's house was pitted and overgrown but at least it was secluded. Tyre tracks that had become deep ruts during the wet season were hardened mud now and McNulty almost bottomed the Astra twice before parking under an overhanging apple tree. He turned the engine off and rested his head on the steering wheel.

Darkness swallowed them when the headlamps went out, the only illumination a feathering of orange sodium from the main road and an occasional security light behind some of the houses. Most of the windows were dark. It was late and even on Mean Wood council estate people had to sleep. The engine ticked as it cooled. The interior smelled of singed hair and smoke. Donk coughed. McNulty looked at him and then over his shoulder at the figure on the back seat. Steam drifted off her in stringy tendrils. His ears were still ringing.

The girl didn't move. McNulty opened his door and went round the other side to open hers. He stood for a moment and tried to get his mouth working.

'Come on, Donk. Give us a hand.'

Donk struggled out of the front passenger seat and closed the door. He had to lean a hand on the roof so he wouldn't fall over. He swayed like a drunk. McNulty swayed too. It was difficult to focus. His sight kept going in and out. If they had smelled of drink instead of smoke they'd display the classic signs of D and I. *He was unsteady on his feet, your worships. His eyes were blurred, his speech was slurred, and he smelled strongly of intoxicants.* Drunk and Incapable.

They couldn't both reach in at the same time so McNulty grabbed the girl's shoulders and pulled her out. Once he'd got enough purchase he swung her up into his arms and Donk shut the door.

'I've got her.'

The mist that had settled around Weetwood Court also slithered around the back gardens. Donk waded through it towards the kitchen door and McNulty followed in his footsteps. The ground was uneven but not too bad. He only stumbled once and that was more to do with his balance. Five minutes later they were inside the house. Donk flicked the switch beside the kitchen door, taking McNulty back to . . .

'What you doing in the dark, Vince?'

Donk stood in the doorway and McNulty didn't have time to register it was the first time he hadn't called him officer. He saw Donk's hand fumble for the light switch beside the door.

'No. Don't turn the—'

Donk flicked the switch. The light sparked on.

Then everything happened at once.

The living room of Flat 7, Weetwood Court, exploded from the ceiling down. Blue flame spread from the light bulb outwards, becoming the driving force for everything in the room. It happened in a split second and lasted a lifetime. McNulty didn't finish the sentence. Even if he had it would have been drowned by the roar of the explosion. He moved fast, diving over the leather settee, grabbing the backrest as he went. With all his strength he heaved it over in one movement. It flipped. Turned turtle. And the shell came down on top of him and the girl. Heat blasted all around him.

Donk stood in the doorway, slack-jawed and gormless. The full force of the explosion forced air into his face as it went the only place it could go. Out of the door. Flames followed. Lightning fast and vicious. He faced it without realizing what was happening. Then everything was on fire. The curtains. The wallpaper. The dining table in the corner. Even the back of the door itself as it slammed shut in Donk's face.

The gush of air. That was what saved him. The blast slammed the door shut. All in an instant. The force of the expanding gas and flames blew it off its hinges and flattened Donk to the floor. The explosion blew out the windows of the communal hallway and torched the rubber plant. The only good thing the blast did was blow the fire out. Most of it. The curtains were still alight and it wouldn't be long before the flames caught again. Gas explosions blow hard and then disappear, but what they set afire stays on fire.

McNulty felt the crushing weight of the settee on top of him. He couldn't breathe. The girl beneath him was even worse. He braced his shoulders and pushed upwards. The settee shifted. He heaved again and it toppled off them.

'Donk?'

The room was a hellish scene. All scorched paintwork and licking flames. Smoke took over where the gas had left. Donk was nowhere to be seen. Then McNulty saw his shoes poking out from under the felled door. He struggled to his feet, ears ringing from the explosion, and yanked the burning door off Donk. A coughing and spluttering Donk, so he was still alive. McNulty rolled him over and pushed him towards the front door. Thought about telling him to get out but reckoned even Donk could figure that.

The girl wasn't coughing. She wasn't doing much of anything. That was when McNulty made the snap decision. There was no time to think, but he thought loud and clear and very, very quickly. The girl was wearing a massage parlour smock. If the police found her here when they arrived, that would be all the connection they'd need. No more coincidences. All wrapped up neat as a bow on an Easter bunny. Missing girls. Repeat customer. Dead girl in repeat customer's flat. Repeat customer dead in the explosion too.

Except nobody was dead. Just badly singed. Apart from the girl. If she wasn't dead she certainly wasn't fully conscious. Drugged, probably, to keep her docile until the explosion.

Shit or bust time. McNulty scooped her up in his arms and followed Donk onto the landing. He needed time to think and here wasn't the place. He hoped his car keys hadn't melted in his pocket. This time he did shout at Donk.

'Down to the car.'

Donk did as he was told, coughing all the way. Smoke streamed off his clothes. McNulty's too, as he carried the girl downstairs.

He laid her gently on the sofa without turning the living room light on, paused long enough to make sure she was breathing, and then joined Donk in the kitchen. The last time he'd stood in this room was ten years ago. Donk had straightened out by then and was away in the navy. Mrs Flowers gave McNulty a cup of tea and three freshly baked butterfly buns. Keeping up with his contacts was only part of the reason for his visit. Donk's mother was a nice woman. The kitchen felt different without her.

McNulty leaned his back against the sink. Donk locked the door and closed the curtains. No point letting the nosy neighbours see more than they had already seen. He nudged McNulty out of the way and filled the kettle.

'Since we didn't get a coffee at your . . .'

He was trying to lighten the atmosphere but couldn't finish. Donk's voice betrayed the shock they both felt. It quivered, bordering on tears. He pulled out a chair at the kitchen table and sat down. His hands were shaking. He didn't put the kettle on.

'Jeepers creepers. What the fuck just happened?'

McNulty didn't feel like joking either. There were times when a throwaway quip could dispel the tension but this wasn't one of them. His flat had been destroyed and the pair of them almost killed, not to mention the girl who had been planted there to convict him of murder or kidnapping or whatever the fuck was going on.

'Put the kettle on, mate. I need to think about this.'

Donk took solace in being called mate and pulled himself together.

'Tea or coffee?'

The question seemed inconsequential under the circumstances.

'Whichever.'

McNulty noticed the décor for the first time. It was exactly as Mrs Flowers had left it. Brightly coloured walls and flowered curtains; yellow and white chequered vinyl table cover; neat little porcelain pots with tea, coffee and sugar printed on the sides. Not a thing out of place. No clutter. No mess. Everything as clean and tidy as if the old woman were still here. Except there were no butterfly buns.

'Your mum would be pleased.'

No witty reply this time. Donk simply nodded. He plugged the electric kettle in and turned it on. Took two tea bags from the caddy and dropped them in the teapot. He busied himself with the routine of brewing a pot of tea. Milk. Sugar. Plate of biscuits. Put them all on a tray and brought them to the table. McNulty spooned two sugars into his cup and stirred the milk in until it was medium brown. Not too strong. He ignored the biscuits.

'How's the head?'

Donk's face was smudged black. There was a lump growing on the left of his forehead. Dried blood clogged one nostril and his nose was swollen but not broken. Everything looked sore.

'Hurts.'

'I'm sorry.'

McNulty didn't mean about the lumps and bruises. He was sorry for thinking Donk had something to do with the disappearances. It had seemed logical, his previous train of thought, but unlike in *Star Trek* logic played little part in police work. All that Sherlock Holmes, Hercule Poirot stuff where they could work out who committed the crime through a process of deduction was nonsense. You couldn't deduce anything from the tangled mind of the average criminal because they didn't follow logical patterns themselves. They just went on instinct.

That instinct had placed an unconscious girl in a gas-filled flat and waited for McNulty to come home and blow them both up. It was a stupid plan because if he'd been alone he wouldn't have turned the light on anyway. The smell of gas was overwhelming. You'd have to be a complete moron not to notice. An even bigger one to flick the switch. If Donk hadn't been with him he'd have simply carried the girl onto the landing and opened the windows. Donk looked downcast.

'No. I'm the one should be sorry.'

McNulty knew what Donk was talking about and on that point they were both agreed. He picked up a biscuit and tapped it gently against his cup. Shook his head in disbelief.

'You stupid arse. Couldn't you smell the gas?'

'Wasn't thinking, was I?'

'You got that right.'

McNulty dunked the biscuit in his tea and held it over the cup to drain. He was about to lift it to his mouth when the soggy end dropped into the cup with a plop. Tea splashed into his eye. Despite everything that had happened he couldn't help but laugh. Sometimes that's all there is to do. Donk snorted a laugh too. Neither of them heard the living room door open.

'What's so funny?'

They snapped shut and looked at the girl standing in the doorway.

In the light from the kitchen she looked even younger than when he'd first seen her. Long blonde hair fell across her face and she brushed it aside. Dark sooty smudges covered her nose and mouth, but seeing her now confirmed what he'd suspected in the flat. She was the girl he'd rescued at the Sauna Kabin last week.

'You know the best way to disable a crocodile?'
  'I beg your pardon?'
They were sitting around the kitchen table, all cleaned up and fresh as they were going to get. The simple act of washing had made each of them feel better but it was the girl who had undergone the biggest transformation. She was beautiful. And definitely under the legal age. Thirteen or fourteen at best. With a woman's body. She didn't understand McNulty's question but Donk did. He'd seen *Live and Let Die* too.
  'You stick your hand in its mouth. And pull its teeth out.'
The girl didn't understand that either.
  'Huh?'
McNulty became less cryptic.
  'Mr Muscles at the Sauna Kabin.'
  'What about him?'
  'Best way to disable a crocodile. Even as muscly as him. Any man. Is a swift kick in the knapsack.'
Donk winced. The girl nodded. McNulty cupped his balls and feigned injury.
  'Works every time. If you're facing him. Knee jerk'll do it. Behind you. Like at the Sauna Kabin. Kick up with your heel. It'll fell a giant redwood.'
The name badge on her smock said Michelle. No surname. She'd given that as Jamison. Michelle Jamison took a swig of coffee, her choice over the tea that McNulty and Donk were on their second pot of, and shrugged her shoulders.
  'That sort of thing happens all the time. Goes with the territory.'
McNulty played with a biscuit but didn't dunk it. He looked at Michelle but saw another girl instead. A younger girl. Cringing on the bench seat of the headmaster's office. She had tears in her eyes but a determined expression on her face. Set jaw. Clenched teeth. She might have said the same thing.
  'This sort of thing happens all the time. Goes with the territory.'
McNulty hadn't believed it then and didn't believe it now. Nothing like that should go with the territory. The muscles in his jaw bulged. A look came into his eye that had got him into trouble before. In the

headmaster's office at Crag View Orphanage and the custody suite corridor at Ecclesfield Police Station.

'Well. If there's nobody to look after you, you should learn to look after yourself.'

Michelle snorted in disbelief. She lowered her head and raised her eyebrows.

'Look after myself? I'm not the one whose flat just blew up.'

'*You* were in it.'

'Only so they'd get to you. Worry about yourself, why don't you? You're in deeper shit than me.'

McNulty overlooked the bad language. He reckoned in her line of work she'd heard plenty worse. What she was getting at he'd already considered though. She wasn't bait to get him into trouble. She was the sacrificial lamb to take him down altogether and close the case before the police got too close. Clumsy as their efforts were, that was obviously the plan.

'Deeper shit than getting blown up? Because if that shit had worked we'd both be just turds in the cesspool.'

She looked down at her feet, her show of bravado spent. They all knew how serious the situation was. McNulty felt guilty for raising his voice at her. He was supposed to protect people like this, not shout at them. He glanced at the curtains and noticed the first lightening of the sky outside. Dawn was just around the corner. He checked his watch. Five thirty.

'You'd better stay here for now.'

Michelle looked up in a flash. Panic in her eyes.

'You gotta be kidding me. Anywhere around you isn't safe.'

McNulty made a calm-down motion with his hands.

'Nobody knows about Donk. I haven't been here in ten years.'

The panic didn't leave her eyes, but it became less vivid. She took another swig of coffee to cover her agitation. McNulty dunked the biscuit and caught it before it fell into his tea. He looked around the kitchen. Clean and tidy. Bright and breezy. As safe a place as there was ever likely to be. Whoever had been watching him had linked him to the massage parlours and even knew where he lived. But unless they were psychic they couldn't know about Donkey Flowers, because meeting him had been an accident. Knowing where Donk lived wasn't an option. Therefore it was safe here. He glanced across at Donk and then nodded towards Michelle.

'You got a spare room?'

Donk got the message.

'There's only me lives here. After that all the rooms are spare.'

He stood up and staggered against the table, spilling tea from his cup.

'Aw shit. I'm knackered. Sorry.'

The apology was to Michelle. For his language, not spilling the tea. Whatever her chosen lifestyle, in Donk's book it still wasn't right swearing in front of a young girl. He fetched a dishcloth and mopped the spillage.

'You look tired as well.'

Again to Michelle. His voice tender.

'Come on. The small bedroom's made up. You can get some sleep.'

Having someone be nice to her seemed to throw Michelle and she didn't know how to react. The first look to cross her face was indignation at being told what to do, quickly followed by a half smile at being treated like a human. It made McNulty feel guilty all over again at raising his voice to her. He followed the tender route.

'We could all do with some sleep. You've been through it more than us though. Go on up. Donk'll see you right. He's a good man.'

She saw Donk fill with pride at being called a good man and seemed to make a decision about the man who'd called him that. McNulty must be highly regarded for this slow-headed fool to be proud of his status with him. Maybe it was OK to trust him too. She pushed back from the table.

'I am tired.'

Donk opened the hallway door and led the way to the stairs. Michelle paused in the doorway, on unfamiliar ground, having to be nice in return.

'Thank you.'

It was said to the room, didn't feel too soppy that way, but encompassed both men. Donk stopped at the bottom of the banister rail. McNulty looked at the girl, who was avoiding eye contact. She simply nodded once . . .

'Thanks.'

. . . and followed Donk upstairs.

Twenty minutes later the kettle was on again. Donk cleaned out the teapot and recharged it with two bags of leaves. McNulty switched on the portable TV that stood on the corner of the worktop and turned the volume down low. It was almost six. Morning news would be on soon.

'What do you make of her?'

Donk kept busy with the mashings.

'Seems like a nice girl.'

McNulty stood shoulder to shoulder with Donk.

'Nice, but rough around the edges. Hard life.'

His shoulders sagged and he spoke more to himself than to Donk.

'And too young for this shit. What the fuck drives a girl that young into the massage game?'

Donk spoke to the teapot, not looking at McNulty.

'You mean the massage game you keep perving with?'

McNulty stood upright and faced his accuser.

'Told you. It's not perving. No little boys or donkeys or shit like that. Just good clean sex between consenting adults.'

He wasn't sure he believed that any more and Donk proved himself more astute than McNulty had given him credit for.

'She'll be a consenting adult one day. Depending how long she stays in the game. She could end up like some of 'em you visit. Good at it 'cos they've been doin' it since childhood.'

McNulty thought about Natasha and Melissa and Kim, if that's what their names were. Their expert fingers gliding over his oiled body, arousing, teasing, sexual. Then he thought about Mrs Lemonsucker, the dried prune of a receptionist who had obviously grown too old to perform any more. Or too unattractive for anyone to want her to. Sucked in and spat out by a business that was ruthless and always looking for young blood. Like Michelle. He felt ashamed.

'None of that anal fisting or water sports.'

His voice was small. He was trying to convince himself and failing miserably. He thumped Donk playfully on the shoulder.

'Aw, shut the fuck up and make the tea.'

Donk did just that. Mashed a fresh pot and set clean cups on the tray. He refilled the biscuits. He sat opposite McNulty at the table and didn't seem so stupid any more. The change was subtle and had probably been there all the time. McNulty just hadn't recognized what was in front of his face. Donkey Flowers was no mug. The news came on in the background. Follow-up story to the Mississippi bridge collapse. Donk stirred sugar into his cup.

'You can't protect everyone.'

He stopped stirring, the spoon small in his fingers.

'But you could protect her.'

McNulty paused in mid dunk, not because of what Donk had just said but because the news was showing fire engines outside his flat. The wet biscuit in his hand broke off and plopped into his tea unnoticed.

'Turn the sound up.'

Donk picked up the remote and increased the volume. The fire scene at Weetwood Court changed into the body in the oil drum crime scene at City Road as the newsreader's voice explained that police believed the two incidents were linked. Sparks of electricity shot up McNulty's spine. The short hairs on the back of his neck stood on end. His warrant card photo filled the screen.

'Police urgently want to locate this man, Vincent McNulty, in connection with the disappearance of several girls and the murder of one. McNulty is an ex-policeman and believed to be driving a blue Vauxhall Astra similar to this one.'

Library footage of a CID car flashed on the screen, followed by McNulty's registration number.

'Police say that McNulty is believed to be dangerous. If seen do not approach him. Contact the police immediately.'

Donk dropped the remote on the table.

'Oh shitty death.'

McNulty looked at the soggy biscuit floating in his tea.

'Deep shitty death.'

He wasn't referring to the biscuit.

SIXTEEN

The mistakes people make. A man's life is littered with them. Mistakes, errors of judgement and stupid decisions. Some are small and easily negotiated. Some are huge and come back to bite you on the arse. It felt to McNulty, as he swung the Astra into the twenty-four-hour Tesco car park, like he'd fucked up big time more often than he'd fucked up small time. And every single one of them had come back to haunt him. If the bite-you-on-the-arse was literal, he'd have no backside left.

Weak autumn sunshine broke through thin cloud and highlighted the changing colour of the trees dotted around the grass verges. The leaves were dying, shifting rapidly through the spectrum from golden yellow to dried-up brown. They were dropping like confetti around the foot of the trees, forming drifts that children would enjoy wading through while their mothers bought the shopping.

There were no children at this time of day. Mid morning. They were either at school or too young to be left without their mothers. The supermarket was enormous. It supplied everything from food to clothing, electronic goods to DVDs. The car park was the size of a football field, marked into individual bays with white paint and broken into manageable sections by grass verges and trees. Every section had at least one collection point where shopping trolleys could be left. During peak times the car park would be completely full. At a slow time, like now, only the section near Tesco's front doors was occupied.

McNulty didn't think he'd ever been here when that part of the car park wasn't constantly on the move. In and out. Quick visits to buy a sandwich. Longer visits to get the weekly shop. Some in-between visits for browsers of the DVD releases. The perfect place to leave a car you didn't want people to notice. Dump it in the corner out of the way and sooner or later someone was going to report it. Trolley collectors or mobile security. But hide it in plain sight among the constant bustle of activity and no one was going to notice a blue Vauxhall Astra among all the other Vauxhalls and Fords and Nissans.

He parked next to a red Ford Mondeo that he knew wouldn't be there in half an hour. It would be replaced by another car and then another in an ever-changing tableau of vehicular traffic. He turned the engine off and took a deep breath. The mistakes we make.

Some big.

His mind replayed the slap like a gunshot and the sniffling girl on the bench seat, but that memory was all played out today. It had been a formative experience with far-reaching consequences, but not as immediate as . . .

Some bigger.

. . . the mistake he kept trying to forget. Once a cop always a cop. It was almost like the old joke, when is a door not a door? When it's ajar. Well, when is a cop not a cop? When he's been sacked.

'Now listen here, you pencil-dicked little fuckface.'

DC McNulty held Daniel Roach up by the throat against the custody corridor wall. The pasty-faced teenager flapped his feet in the air but couldn't speak. McNulty's fingers bit into his neck. The heavy door from the cell area slammed shut and they were alone.

'I'm gonna be checking on your sister every week until my dying day, and if I find out you've stuck your curly-wurly anywhere near her tuppence I'll come round in the dead of night and break your fucking neck.'

He was close to breaking the diminutive prisoner's neck now and had to rein himself in. The explosion of anger eased slightly, more through necessity than a reduction of his rage. McNulty's eyes bulged from his face. Spittle dripped from his lips with the ferocity of his warning.

'You slimy little cockroach.'

That was an apt description for the thirteen-year-old child molester, since he only had a little cock and his hands were as slimy as a just-shit turd. Being called Roach simply reinforced the nickname.

McNulty took several deep breaths until he regained control. Once he'd calmed down a touch he glanced either way along the corridor. Inside the heavy door, all angles of the custody suite were covered by CCTV that was recorded on a central hard drive. Outside, in the corridor, a prisoner's rights were thought to be in less danger, so there was just one camera near the foyer entrance. Twenty feet away, covering the area where members of the public accessed the police station proper. In case of complaints and such. Standing in the alcove to the cell area door, they were safe from prying eyes. And recordings.

Daniel Roach was thirteen. His baby sister Chantelle was seven. Since Daniel was only five feet nothing, with a tiny penis that curled like a piglet's, he'd been putting it to his sister since she was four. No self-respecting female was going to be girlfriend to the council estate joke, so his sexual leanings took the route of least resistance. His sister. All three holes.

McNulty tightened his grip at the thought of what this bastard was walking free from, but lowered his feet to the ground.

It was only during a routine doctor's appointment that the anal bleeding was spotted. From there a full examination revealed the extent of the abuse. At first it was thought the mother's boyfriend must have done it, but after exhaustive interviews with Chantelle by child protection officers the truth came out. McNulty just happened to be the detective on duty when the arrest was made.

That was the start of his problems.

The trouble with the Roach family was that nobody cared. Not the mother, nor the boyfriend, nor little Daniel Cockroach. The mother had more boyfriends than a golf course had holes, and deciding which one was flavour of the month was her main concern. What her son had been doing to her daughter wasn't high on her priority list. That meant that witness evidence was restricted to a vulnerable seven-year-old girl. There was no forensics to tie Daniel to the abuse. The last time had been too long ago for any fluids to still be present in her mouth, or vagina, or anus . . .

McNulty squeezed again.

. . . and the mother backed him all the way. She didn't want him sending to prison because sooner or later he was going be a viable source of income. Either by working or collecting benefits.

The interview under caution went badly. Roach's solicitor, knowing the lack of evidence, instructed a no-reply interview where Daniel didn't answer a single question. Since his mother was excluded as being part of the investigation, an appropriate adult was provided by social services. The elderly woman, who was more concerned with feeding her cats, was shocked by the questions McNulty put to Daniel for a response. He read out every allegation in gruesome detail and noted there was no reply. That was so Cockroach couldn't argue later in court that he hadn't been asked. But this wasn't going to court.

A file was put together and placed before a Crown Prosecuting Service solicitor the same night. Despite wanting to prosecute, she had to admit there was insufficient evidence and ordered that the charges be dropped and Daniel released. His solicitor gave him the good news and left to see another client. The appropriate adult left to feed her cats. Leaving McNulty to return Daniel's property and take him to his mother waiting in the foyer.

It was Daniel Roach's sneer that got him walled up in the corridor. There was no sign of remorse. No sorrow for his baby sister. Just a smug, self-important look-down-his-nose expression as he was signed out by the custody sergeant. McNulty held himself in check until they were alone in the corridor and then . . .

'Now listen here, you pencil-dicked little fuckface.'

. . . his career went into freefall. He didn't hit the boy. Didn't break his nose or kick him in the knapsack. He simply slapped him, held him against the wall and delivered his warning. Trouble was his mother was waiting twenty feet away. The vivid red finger marks around his throat stood out like a tattoo and it was all the woman needed to back up her complaint. The lack of physical evidence against the boy converted to strong physical evidence against DC McNulty. The black and white photographs showed it up even more.

Six weeks later Detective Constable Vincent McNulty was asked to resign.

A Tesco lorry rumbled past the cash machines towards the delivery bays round back. Asked to resign? That was the force solicitors' way of easing bad eggs out of the force without having to sack them, a process that would require a tribunal and lots of public mud slinging. The carrot was that you could keep your pension, as far as it was paid up. The stick was that if you were sacked you weren't entitled to anything.

The lorry obscured the CCTV cameras above the main doors for a second and then they were back again. Two cameras angled down to cover any trouble in front of the store. There were more cameras inside and the car park itself was covered by skycams mounted atop the tall, slim lighting stanchions. One at either end of the tarmac and one in the middle. Apart from a couple of blind spots they recorded pretty much all the parking bays, but from so far away that people looked like insects on an anthill. That didn't worry McNulty. He was parked in one of the blind spots directly beneath the centre camera. He might have a temper but he knew how to avoid being picked up on camera.

What did worry him was the sinking feeling in the pit of his stomach. Mistakes that we make. He was confident that leaving the car here would cover his tracks for now, but it was the tracks he'd left already that he felt would bite him in the arse. The naïve assumption that the girl would be safe at Donk's house. On Mean Wood estate of all places. If Obi Wan Kenobi had stood overlooking the rundown council estate he would no doubt have echoed his sentiments about Mos Eisley space-port. *'Mos Eisley spaceport. You will never find a more wretched hive of scum and villainy. We must be cautious.'*

Cautious indeed. And McNulty had taken the girl there.

He got out of the car and locked the door. Trying to put the bad feeling aside, he cut through the pedestrian exit furthest away from the store and began to walk the mile and a half back to Donk's place.

SEVENTEEN

Donk was in the kitchen when the girl got up. He had grabbed a couple of hours' shuteye on the living room settee and found that the power nap refreshed him, as much as he was ever fresh. The cushions had smelled of her perfume mingled with smoke. Standing at the kitchen sink he was torn between keeping her smell on him and removing the smoky memento of the fire at McNulty's flat.

He heard movement upstairs and the toilet flushed.

Using a handful of Fairy Liquid he soaped his face and rinsed it under the hot tap. He ran his fingers through his hair and rubbed his eyes. Then he ran the cold tap until it was ice cold and dunked his face in the washing-up bowl. Wide awake now, his hand reached for the towel but couldn't find it. The hall door opened behind him and he smelled her scent again.

'Is this what you're looking for?'

She gave him the towel and he dried his face. When he looked up he saw a vision of loveliness in the sun-brightened yellow of the kitchen. He hadn't heard the sink running upstairs but she'd obviously had a wash too.

She watched his mouth flopping like a fish out of water.

'Close your mouth or your tongue will fall out.'

She was so self-assured that Donk almost forgot how young she was. A side effect of the hard life she'd chosen. Or that had been chosen for her. Michelle. He had to reach for the name and not think of her as simply the girl. After so many trips to the Hyde Park Picture House she became Lauren Bacall in her first film with Humphrey Bogart. *To Have and Have Not*, he thought. Or maybe *The Big Sleep*. Either way he didn't see himself in the Bogart role. That was McNulty.

Michelle sat at the table and crossed her legs. If she'd been Bacall she would have put a cigarette between her lips and waited for it to be lit. Instead she looked around the kitchen and noticed Bogart wasn't there.

'Where's the other one?'

Donk didn't blush and dither but it felt like he did.

'He's moving the car. Felt it'd be safer not parked out back in daylight.'

He didn't mention the news report or the fact that the registration number had been plastered all over national television.

'Why'd he need to move it? Not stolen is it?'

Donk laughed and sounded even more like he was dithering.

'Stolen? No. He used to be a copper, you know?'

'No. I didn't know. What does that have to do with anything? Don't you think coppers steal things?'

This time he didn't dither and didn't laugh.

'Not Vince. He's a good 'un.'

Michelle seemed to notice the change in Donk's demeanour. She tapped her fingernails on the table as she appraised him. He took that as a request for a cup of coffee and filled the kettle. She leaned her elbows on the table.

'He helped you out, didn't he? Back when your mum was here.'

'You had sugar, didn't you?'

'Your mum liked him.'

Donk turned to face her. So young and yet so intuitive. So hard. Her face hadn't taken on the chiselled features of the old brass yet but time would take its toll. Time and the work she did. For a moment he found himself hating Vince for the choices he'd made. Helping keep a profession going that churned out girls like this one. Then the moment passed as he remembered his mother thanking Vince for arresting her son and threatening him with prison.

'Yes. She did.'

He sat opposite Michelle and spoke non-stop for twenty minutes. By the end of his speech she knew everything that Detective Constable Vincent McNulty had done for Donkey Flowers and his mother. All the good stuff and none of the bad. He didn't mention being sacked, although she knew he was an ex-cop not a current one. He omitted to mention the massage visits too but she knew about that already. She'd met him at a massage parlour.

'He saved me from the road to ruin. And, yes, my mum liked him very much.'

'Because of that.'

'And because he's just a nice bloke.'

Michelle looked down at the table cover. She didn't speak but Donk could see she'd already come to that conclusion herself. He supposed she didn't meet that many nice blokes in her line of work. He stood up to make the coffee as he tried to phrase what he wanted to say. Stirring sugar into her cup, he turned to face her.

'He just likes helping people.'

'Saving people you mean.'

He put the cup on the table in front of her.

'Saving people.'

She put both hands around the cup as if warming them.

'He should have joined the fire brigade then.'

Donk sat and leaned forward.

'He could help you.'

'Save me?'

'Yes.'

She looked him in the eye and her stare burned right through him.

'He saved me once before. Remember? And look how that ended up! Almost chargrilled chicken in his flat. If that's what you call being saved then tell him to leave me alone.'

He had no answer because she was right, but he wasn't going to give up on McNulty yet.

'He'll sort things out. Honest.'

Her stare softened.

'I know you're honest. But you don't know what you've got yourself into.'

'Vince. Not me.'

'What *he's* got himself into.'

Donk reached across the table and cupped one delicate hand.

'Then why don't you tell me?'

'Tell *him*?'

'Yes. Him.'

She swallowed hard and turned away. Sunlight reflected off the white and yellow tablecloth like a buttercup under her chin. Then someone hammered on the front door.

Donk was up like a startled rabbit, and startled was exactly what he was.

'Oh shit. It's the police.'

It was a natural first reaction to the persistent pounding. The coppers' knock. The come out, come out, wherever you are knock. He went into the hallway that ran from the kitchen to the front door and stood frozen with indecision. What would McNulty do?

Donk didn't know. He tried to think one step at a time. McNulty was the one on TV as a wanted man, not Donk, and McNulty wasn't here. So that was one question he could answer truthfully. 'Sorry, officer. He's not here.' The next question would be, 'When was the last time you saw him?' That one was more difficult. How much did they know? Apart from last night's explosion, which he should definitely avoid mentioning, what difference did it make if he'd seen him or not? There was nothing illegal in meeting McNulty at the cinema and having a few drinks. Easy peasy, lemon squeezy. Provided he could keep the lie off his face. Not so easy. Donk's was a notoriously easy face to read.

The knocking grew louder.

The explosion. Donk quickly looked at himself in the hall mirror. No sign of the black smudges apart from a slight singeing of his eyebrows and fringe. He sniffed his shirtsleeves. A slight smell of smoke but not strong. He wished he'd changed clothes after getting in but if he kept his distance he might be OK with that.

Fresh coffee smells drifted from the kitchen and he looked over his shoulder. Michelle stood nervously in the doorway. The white masseuse smock told its own story and he waved her to one side. She stepped to her right so the smock was out of sight but her face still showed, like she was peeking round the corner.

'No. Stay in the kitchen.'

She moved behind the door and disappeared. When Donk turned back to the front door she came out of hiding to watch. She felt safer keeping him in sight. Donk felt safer now that he'd got his mind straight.

The knocking sounded like it would come right through the door.

'All right. I'm coming. Keep your hair on.'

Donk didn't recognize the irony of using McNulty's words from when Donk had been knocking at Flat 7. He went to the door and reached for the key in the lock. It was a solid door. No windows. No windows either side of it. No security chain or fisheye peephole so you could check who was at the door before opening it. His mother had been a trusting soul and Donk had never felt the need to beef up security. His hand hovered over the key.

The knocking stopped. Nobody spoke. Not even a shout for him to open the door. Something felt wrong. Whenever the police knocked on your door the first thing they did was announce themselves as police and order you to open up or else. Nobody had shouted from outside. Just an angry knock.

He bent over and lifted the internal letterbox cover. Nothing. That puzzled him for a moment before he realized he needed to lift the outer flap too. He pushed it open to see who was knocking just in time to see the heavy boot kicking at the door.

The frame splintered. The door slammed into Donk's face. The world went dark. Sparks flashed behind his eyes. Somebody shoved past him. There were violent noises in the kitchen and the girl screamed.

EIGHTEEN

Moving back to Mean Wood was a mistake. McNulty sensed it as soon as he entered Donk's street. Curtains twitched. Faces peered out of upstairs windows. Even birds in the leafless trees seemed to stop and stare. Low wooden picket fences exposed front gardens strewn with discarded toys and footballs but devoid of children. A door slammed shut. He felt more under surveillance here than by the CCTV at Tesco's car park. These neighbours missed nothing and told everyone.

Not a perfect hiding place for a wanted man.

Somebody had mown their lawn. McNulty could smell the freshly cut grass but couldn't hear the lawn mower. He scanned the gardens, noting the overgrown, weed-infested lawns and broken fences, and spotted the only house with a tidy frontage. An extension cord slid out of an open living-room window and snaked round the side of the house. A hover mower was plugged into it next to the well-appointed garden shed, but nobody stood with it. The shed door was open. He half

expected to hear the engine ticking over, but of course an electric mower only worked when the trigger was depressed.

The abandoned mower stood silent. Just like the rest of the street. The only thing missing was tumbleweed blowing across the road. McNulty stopped and waited. Donk's house was at the end of the cul-de-sac next to an oak tree that had dropped most of its leaves. The front garden was tidy but overgrown. The flower borders that had been Mrs Donk's pride and joy needed weeding. The lawn needed a trim like next door's had been getting when the mower was abandoned. When whatever happened had scared the neighbour behind closed doors.

McNulty felt a shiver run down his spine. The bad feeling he'd had at the car park settled into his bones. Just beyond Donk's house, round the back, was the dirt track where his car had been parked. Out of sight for most of the neighbours but not all. In summer the foliage might have hidden it better but now, with the leaves dropping faster than the dollar against the pound, he might as well have parked in the middle of the street. Even the cover of darkness was no cover at all in Mos Eisley.

He turned his collar up against the cool breeze that swirled leaves around his ankles and disturbed the branches of the giant oak beside Donk's house. He stuck his hands in his pockets and walked straight to the front gate. Ignoring it he stepped over the low fence and marched up the path. Not wanting to attract any more attention than he already had, he went round the back to the kitchen door. It was locked. Good. The TV sounded inside, giving him hope. McNulty tapped on the door.

No reply.

He knocked louder.

Still no reply.

He pushed his face to the window but couldn't see through the partly open curtains. Yellow blasted back at his face and he thought of buttercups under the chin proving that you liked butter. The memory made him feel sad.

Then he saw movement inside.

Somewhere in the hallway beyond the kitchen. He couldn't make out what it was but it was so slight he almost missed it. Low down. On the floor. Behind him the breeze grew stronger. It rustled the bushes and made the giant branches of the oak groan. A sudden gust caught him by surprise and he put a hand against the window. Along the corridor a wedge of light blinked on and off, then he heard the front door slam as the wind subsided.

Now he knew something was wrong. The groan sounded again, not the tree but from inside where it had always been. McNulty raced round the side of the house and reached the front door as it creaked open again. It looked intact until you examined the frame, which was splintered and destroyed around the lock. He pushed it open and stepped into the gloom, almost tripping over the bundled heap on the floor.

'I'm sorry Vince. I fucked up.'
  'Didn't you just?'
  'Ouch.'
  McNulty lifted the wet sponge off Donk's ruined face and surveyed the damage now most of the blood had been washed away. Sunlight reflecting off the chequered tablecloth provided fill-in light and McNulty winced at the gaping wounds. He'd seen plenty of injuries during his eighteen years' service but it had always been to strangers with no connection to him. It looked worse on someone you knew.

The front door was wedged shut by the vacuum cleaner and the hallway door was closed. It made the kitchen feel like a cocoon of safety, a feeling that was completely false. It hadn't been safe before and it wasn't safe now. One of the chairs was broken on the floor and the cups were smashed.

The girl was gone.

McNulty rinsed the sponge out in the sink until the water ran clear and returned to Donk sitting at the table. One eye was closed and swollen like a tennis ball. His nose was broken and spread across his face. A deep gash across the bridge of the nose and another split his cheek to the bone. Blood seeped out of both. Donk held his right arm across his stomach and couldn't sit up straight. McNulty pulled a chair out and sat opposite.

'Can you wiggle your fingers?'
  'I can't feel my fingers. Whole arm's just tingly.'
  'Ribs?'
  'Never could wiggle them.'
  'How are your ribs? Fuckwit.'
  'Bad. Heard something crack.'
  'Bastards.'
  Donk didn't respond. He simply leaned to his left to ease the pain in his chest. Blood dripped from his chin onto the tablecloth and that seemed to upset him more than the pain. It was his mother's favourite tablecloth. Tears formed in his one good eye but were indistinguishable from the blood and sweat.

'They didn't even ask any questions. Just kept kicking.'
  McNulty felt guilt choking his throat and he struggled to speak.

'How many of them?'

Donk shook his head and then wished he hadn't.

'At least two, 'cos I heard one in the kitchen while I was getting a kickin'. Grabbing Michelle.'

McNulty had almost forgotten the girl had a name. He felt guilty about that too. What he felt most though was anger. Boiling rage.

'Fuckin' bastards.'

Donk didn't nod this time but he agreed. McNulty fell silent for a moment, turning the sponge in his hands as water dripped onto the tablecloth. He turned and threw the sponge into the sink with a splat. Facing Donk again, he made a decision. This changed everything. The last twenty-four hours had changed everything, but his friend getting mashed to a pulp was the last straw. He had to come clean and call the police. Ambulance first though.

'Come on. Let's get you to hospital.'

Donk held up a hand for McNulty to stay put.

'Just a minute. You'd best go first.'

'I don't need the hospital.'

He knew what Donk meant but was stalling. This was the sort of selfless act Donk's mother would have been proud of. Maybe even the sort of selfless act he wouldn't have considered before McNulty straightened him out all those years ago. Donk leaned forward, ignoring the blood dripping from his chin.

'I had a chat with her this morning. Told her you'd help her out.'

McNulty grumphed an acknowledgement. Helping the girl hadn't helped anyone.

'No, Vince. Don't take the piss. You did help her. Saved her from the fire. It wasn't you put her there. And it wasn't you brought them here either.'

McNulty stared at his hands and said nothing.

'She said we didn't know what we'd got ourselves into.'

'You didn't get into anything. I got you into it.'

'Oh fuck off. This isn't about you. It's about her.'

'Fuck off yourself. Of course it's about me. They used her to set me up.'

Donk shrugged and regretted it.

'OK. That was about you. But today. This. They weren't here for you. They took her back because she was still alive. You're a wanted man. They've fucked you anyway. But she could tell you things.'

'Like what I've got myself into?'

'Like what you've got yourself into.'

McNulty pondered that for a moment. The word had obviously got out on the estate where he'd brought the girl. It had got back to whoever was the cause of this mess. And then they had snatched the girl back. Not him. They could have sorted him at the same time but they'd waited until he was out dumping the car before they came. He heaved a sigh and then smiled at Donk.

'You know, if this was a film, it would be that bit in *Get Carter* where the ugly bloke with the big nose gets beat up for helping Michael Caine.'

'Him off *The Royle Family*? Ricky Tomlinson?'

'No. Alun Armstrong. And Michael Caine drops him a few quid and says he's sorry for getting him into this.'

'You gonna drop me a few quid?'

'No. But I am sorry. I really am.'

Donk went all moist-eyed again.

'Oh fuck off. You're not Jack Carter. Remember the lad says, "You're a heartless bastard, Jack." Well, you're not a heartless bastard.'

That shut McNulty up. He simply stared at Donk and nodded. Whatever kind of person he was, it didn't change what needed doing first.

'You still need an ambulance.'

'I'll count to ten after you've gone and ring for one.'

'Fuck counting to ten. I'll ring before I go.'

'And leave your voice on the tape?'

All emergency calls were recorded and were often used in court later. Evidence of disturbance, sometimes background noises for location, and definitely voiceprint of the caller if he was a suspect. McNulty was a suspect. No point giving the police more evidence than they already had. Circumstantial though it was.

'All right. You make the call. But I'm waiting to make sure you manage it before I leave. What you going to say?'

'The truth. Someone burst in and did me. Don't know who it was.'

No mention of McNulty. He nodded again.

'Thanks. What about the girl?'

'Michelle. Better not mention her or I'll have to explain the explosion. Your flat. And where she worked. Her only chance is you. And that means you staying free to find her.'

McNulty went into the hallway and brought the cordless phone from the bottom of the stairs. He pressed the green button for a dialling tone and handed it to Donk. Donk paused before making the call.

'You know I said you can't save everybody? Well, that's true. But maybe you can save Michelle.'

McNulty barked a laugh that said he didn't believe it. Donk pressed on.

'This isn't your fault. It's not like your sister.'

McNulty flinched as if slapped and Donk realized that was a bad choice of words. He tried to back-pedal but it was too late.

'That wasn't your fault either.'

NINETEEN

The slap sounded like a gunshot in the quiet office. A gunshot followed by a heartbreaking whimper. A wounded animal kind of whimper. The man in charge of Crag View Orphanage stood back and leaned against his desk, sunlight from the window glinting off his glasses.

The gunshot echoed in Vincent's ears. Anger filled him like hot oil.

Mr Cruckshank pushed off from the desk and his bulk hid the bench seat in the alcove. It didn't matter. It was too late. Vincent had already seen the girl who was too young to defend herself holding the torn dress across her chest. The girl he would find out much later was the sister he didn't know he had.

He saw the bright red handprint on her cheek. Picked the biggest book he could find from the bookshelf and hefted it in both hands like a baseball player preparing to swing. The anger boiled over.

The Bible crashed into the headmaster's face and broke his nose.

The heavy gate cracked like a broken nose as McNulty forced it open. The bottom hinge was frozen solid and the top one rusted away, causing Crag View's main gate to lean like a drunken sailor. McNulty held it straight and lifted. It came off the ground slightly and he opened it five or six feet.

There was a dangerous moment when the gate looked like it would fall onto the car as he drove through, but the bottom hinge held. He quickly got out and closed it the way he'd found it, before parking the Astra round the side of the orphanage out of sight. He slid the old number plates and Donk's screwdriver under the passenger seat, then checked that the plates he'd stolen in Tesco's car park were securely fastened. Once he was satisfied he leaned against the car and let out a sigh of relief.

Retrieving his car hadn't been a problem. As an ex-policeman he knew the stolen plates wouldn't be reported for hours yet, and when they were it wouldn't lead to him. He had selected two cars in the far corner and switched plates from one to the other before taking the second pair. People carrying bags of shopping don't check their registration number; they just know where their car is. Only time it stands out is if the plates are missing altogether. By the time the missing plates were on the system both cars would be miles apart and it would be the second car that got pulled by the police. It would only be then that the plates now on McNulty's car were circulated. At least a day, maybe two.

He needed breathing space. Time to think.

After leaving Tesco's McNulty had swung past Ecclesfield Police Station. The familiar fortress gave him a sense of belonging and he parked beside the derelict factory opposite for half an hour while he got his mind straight.

Cell doors slammed in his head.

'Now listen here, you pencil-dicked little fuckface.'

McNulty replayed holding Daniel Roach by the throat, his fingers biting into the teenage child molester's neck.

'I'm gonna be checking on your sister every week until my dying day and if I find out you've stuck your curly-wurly anywhere near her tuppence I'll come round in the dead of night and break your fucking neck.'

Sister. It seemed ironic that this turd had performed such disgusting sex acts with his little sister while McNulty had only tried to protect his, and yet both had been punished. Daniel Roach by Vince McNulty, and Vince McNulty by the custodian of Crag View Orphanage. The girl who McNulty didn't know was his sister was shipped out the next day and lost in the system, papers destroyed by a vengeful headmaster. The slammer came years later when a social worker let slip her existence too late for McNulty to find her.

He had more immediate problems now though. The sense of well-being he felt staring at his old police station was overshadowed by the dilemma about what was the right thing to do. Sensible thing would be to surrender to custody and explain that he had nothing to do with the missing girls or the murder. He hadn't. Therefore, if he wasn't guilty, what did he have to fear?

As an ex-policeman he knew better.

Circumstantial evidence and innuendo could sway a jury twelve months down the line when the case finally came to court, and there was plenty of circumstantial evidence. No. He needed time to sift through all the evidence before he made his next move. Somewhere to hide while he did that, since his face was all over the news.

So Vince McNulty came full circle, cracking the gate hinge like a broken nose as he came home.

The best room to stay in was the last room he wanted to visit. The headmaster's office under the stairs. He reluctantly came to that conclusion after spending half an hour exploring the building that had been his prison for so many years. Nostalgia stabbed him with a poisoned pen. A guitar intro played in his head. The Animals joined in.

> *There is a house in New Orleans*
> *They call the Rising Sun*
> *And it's been the ruin of many a poor boy*
> *And God I know I'm one*

All the carpets had gone. His footsteps echoed through the dusty shell of the corridors as he retraced his past to Dormitory 5 on the second floor rear. Wallpaper peeled off in great sagging strips in the hallway. Damp patches showed through the plaster and there was a hole in the ceiling. The entire place smelled of mould and rat shit. Several of the doors were missing.

His old room was stripped bare. Daylight bled in through a gap in the boards that covered the windows. McNulty had been surprised on his previous visit that the boards hadn't been ripped off and the windows smashed, but now he could see that the vandals had decided on an inside job. Kids had found a way in and smashed every pane of glass and light fitting on the second floor. Broken glass crunched beneath his feet. He tried to remember what it had been like sleeping here but no memories would come. That tape had been wiped.

Every room on the second floor was the same. Broken glass and plaster covered the floorboards. The only thing missing was wind howling through gaps in the boards, but the wind had dropped. There was only silence like a held breath and the smell of decay.

The staircase creaked as he came down. Someone had carved their initials on the balustrade but none of the uprights were missing. He felt an urge to climb aboard and slide down the banister but good sense prevailed. Someone had carved initials on that too and he didn't want to add splinters up the arse to his problems. He ran one hand over a smooth section and took a deep breath. Immediately regretted it. The smell wasn't as bad down here but it wasn't exactly fresh air. Touching the heavy wooden banister rail felt like touching the past. He could almost smell the Sunday roast from the dining room.

The ground floor wasn't as bad as the dormitories. The rooms at the back, storage and kitchens mainly, had sustained some damage but not like upstairs. Several windows had been smashed. Most had not. All the doors were intact. Whatever damp had crept in through the roof hadn't reached the downstairs rooms. Even the rat-shit smell was countered by the scent from the overgrown flower border outside. The boards over the windows held firm but daylight leaked around the edges, giving enough light to see by. At night it would be black as the ghetto. A rolled-up carpet had been abandoned in the dining room next to a pile of curtain hooks.

Back out in the hallway McNulty looked at the staircase and found that his memory tape of down here hadn't been wiped. He could hear the sound of cutlery behind him in the dining room and laughter coming down the stairs. The thunder of racing feet. A barked order to stop running in the corridors. He concentrated on the stairs because he already knew about the office underneath them. Sod's Law always kicked in when you least expected it and Sod's Law stated that if there was one thing you didn't want, it was the thing you got. Today that meant that the one place McNulty didn't want to spend the night would be the place he'd end up spending the night.

The headmaster's office.

Accepting his fate, he opened the door and found he was right. The desk and chairs had gone but it was the only room in Crag View that was still carpeted. There were no curtains. Wallpaper was dry and solid. The bookcase was built into the wall, so that was still there. No books though. No Bible.

And the upholstered bench seat still filled the alcove near the window.

McNulty stared at the seat for a long time but the memory of that day had been overplayed. It was burned into his mind so deeply that he didn't need to see it again now. The girl was gone. His sister was gone. He would never see her again. That was a fact and he dealt in facts. The past is the past. Time to press on with the future. An icy finger ran down his spine. It was cold in here. Better deal with the present first.

McNulty leaned forward and warmed his hands on the fire. There was plenty of splintered wood and he'd found some old newspapers in the kitchen. The ornate fireplace hadn't been used because of the central heating. It had been painted white in days gone by and decorated with dried flowers in a vase. Using household matches he'd brought from Donk's, starting the fire was easy. Two candles flickered on the wide cupboard at the bottom of the bookcase, moulded in place by dripping wax. Donk's old sleeping bag formed a comfortable backrest on the bench seat.

McNulty gave silent thanks to his friend and hoped he was all right.

That sharpened his focus on the problem at hand. As a wanted man with his picture all over the news there was no hiding place in the city where he'd worked the streets for eighteen years. It wasn't a matter of *if* he'd be caught but *when*, and that was the only thing he could control. How many times had he sought a criminal from the estates and simply bided his time? Where were they going to go? Couldn't leave the country on the proceeds of petty crime, and changing your identity only happened in Hollywood movies. Plastic surgery and passports? Forget it. In the real world criminal masterminds didn't exist, just ordinary people and the mistakes they made. If life on the beat proved one thing, it was that ninety-five per cent of crime was committed by five per cent of the population and that the obvious suspect was nearly always the right one. There were no surprise endings. Just time and patience. And gathering the evidence.

What did the police have on him? McNulty closed his eyes, rubbed his temples and concentrated. What linked him to the crime? Or crimes? Right. First there were the missing girls and then there was the dead girl. Almost certainly connected. All worked at massage parlours. That was the place to start. McNulty had visited several of the parlours where the missing girls worked. The dead girl also worked at one of those parlours. That wouldn't be difficult to prove, so there was connection number one.

His flat had been blown up in a gas explosion that should have left another massage girl, and him too, dead, therefore cementing the link between him and the missing girls. QED. Except there were no bodies, so the police only had the explosion. Not provably connected but pointing in that direction.

And he had been sacked from the police because of a violent streak following an unstable childhood. Broke his headmaster's nose even though no charges were brought, and the orphanage had been closed down following the scandal of child abuse. Even more evidence of a dark side that could be used against him. All this was circumstantial, but McNulty knew that a good prosecutor could paint such a compelling picture he might be found guilty. McNulty knew he was innocent, so how had the finger of blame been pointed at him? And why?

A knot of wood popped in the fire. Sparks drifted up the chimney like fireflies. The candles flickered then settled. Daylight bled through gaps in the boards, but it was late afternoon daylight. It would soon be evening and the only light would be the fire and the candles. He would then be able to venture from his cave in relative safety.

He had no idea about the why so he concentrated on the how. How had he become prime suspect in crimes he knew nothing about? When had this all started? That was the key. He opened his eyes and stared into the flames. The first real evidence the police might have was his sweatshirt at Golden Touch when he'd been thrown out after restraining the bully. Everything else – the breaking news about the missing girls, the explosion at his flat, him being named as a suspect – had happened after that. After he returned from his year-long travels.

McNulty put his elbows on his knees, interlaced his fingers and rested his chin on his hands. Heat from the flames burned his face but he didn't flinch. All this had started when he came back to the town where he'd pounded the beat. Back to where he'd arrested hundreds of thieves and perverts. Pissed off all the sex attackers and most of the thieves. Made plenty of enemies.

It came to him like a bolt from the blue. Somebody had seen him. Sometime over the last few weeks he had been spotted coming out of a parlour by someone with a grudge and they had fingered him for the missing girls. Probably followed him around so they could tip the police which parlours he'd visited. After that, good police work would link him to the rest.

There was no point trying to work out who it might be. He had arrested too many people, and if there was a child abuse element, upset too many of them. The seeds of his heavy-handed methods had been sown in this very room on a day that ended with a broken nose and shattered spectacles. It wasn't a stretch of the imagination to believe that one of them had found a way to get back at him.

Then the argument fell like a house of cards.

News hadn't leaked about the missing girls until after he'd come home. After his visit to Golden Touch. His mind grappled with the time-line but it was growing foggy after too much thinking. Could the news have broken in time for someone to set him up? He didn't think so but wasn't sure any more. Whoever set him up must have seen the news first though, otherwise how could they have fitted the frame so quickly?

Another knot exploded in the fire and it sparked a revelation that almost burned his eyes. He sat bolt upright and gasped at the shock of it. The hairs on his arms stood on end. One half of his brain was already working out a plan to turn the tables even before the other half finished accepting the truth. Whoever set him up knew about the missing girls beforehand. Because whoever was setting him up was the one that was taking them.

TWENTY

It was the third massage of the evening when McNulty's plan paid off. He didn't think it was possible to get bored with naked breasts and scented oil, but the third masseuse wasn't even twitching a pulse in the engine room. Her fingers slid under the towel and squeezed his buttocks.

'Mmmm. Hard ass. Rock hard, baby.'

Part of the problem might be the girl's insistence on pretending he was the best thing since sliced bread. Murmuring sweet nothings in his ear and complimenting his musculature with porn-star dialogue had exactly the opposite effect it was supposed to. He'd always preferred the mature, silent type. Lying on his stomach he turned his head and glanced behind him. The girl was barely out of her teens, twenty at most, much younger than he normally selected. Her tight smooth body was exquisite, with no sag or sway in her breasts. Even her nipples looked young, as if they hadn't experienced life enough to crinkle up yet. He thought about the girl from his flat, Michelle, and felt guilty all over again.

The main reason he wasn't aroused, however, was the plan in his head.

The plan in his head was based on line of sight. If someone at point A could see someone at point B, then the person at point B could see the one at point A. Line of sight. Someone had fingered him for visiting massage parlours. That someone must have seen him going into or coming out of said massage parlours. If that person could see McNulty, then McNulty should be able to see that person. He just hadn't been looking until now.

He didn't think he was being followed all the time. That would be too Hollywood, hardly realistic around Mean Wood. The local grapevine was incredible – and no doubt responsible for Donk's house being given up to the bad guys – but shadow tails only happened in the movies. Lowlife bottom feeders in Yorkshire generally couldn't follow their noses to the turd pile.

If they weren't on him all the time that meant they must be on the massage parlours. Being spotted at one might be happenstance, but two or more was no coincidence. Question was, which ones were being watched? Not the ones he'd already visited, especially now his face was on the news, so he picked a handful spread across town and started at number one. A quick massage and a shower but no drink afterwards. Slide out of the side door and watch the front. See if there was anyone hanging around. Watch for suitable observation points and lines of sight. Give it half an hour and then move on to the next.

Turning onto his back at Executive Sauna, he had a feeling about number three that had nothing to do with the velvet fingers sliding down his stomach. Tiny electric shocks ran up his neck and the muscles across his chest tightened. There was a twitch beneath the towel.

'Mmmm. Now it's working, baby.'

McNulty ignored the false encouragement but couldn't ignore the fingers that blatantly encircled him. The girl dribbled oil into her palm and it slid gently up and down. McNulty's nostrils flared at the prospect of action. This was the one. He felt it in his bones. It wasn't the action that excited him, but like any crime he'd ever worked, it was finally nailing the suspect. Gathering the evidence and having enough to bring him to court. An airtight charge. The fingers moved faster. He clenched his jaw. His stomach muscles tensed.

'Ooh baby. That's right. Come on.'

He could practically see the man hanging around outside, collar up against the cold night air. The girl squealed in false delight. And McNulty was getting showered before she'd even finished cleaning him off.

Ten minutes later he was standing in the alleyway down the side of Executive Sauna. The fire exit door closed quietly behind him. His breath bloomed like steam. Muffled traffic noise came from the main road out front. Darkness surrounded him. Dustbins and broken glass reflected light from the street but nothing penetrated the shadows where McNulty stood. The dustbins smelled of rotting fruit. A cat hissed and scampered off. An argument between a man and a woman sounded from an open window above the shops, but it was impossible to tell the direction. Everything echoed. Cars could be coming from the left but the noise bounced off the walls and sounded like they were on the right.

McNulty had scouted the front of the building before he went in and came up with two possible vantage points for anyone watching for him. Beside the bus shelter across the road, where overgrown trees provided the observer some cover, and the alley where McNulty stood now.

He waited for his eyes to adjust and then squinted into the gloom.

The cobbled alley formed a gap between two parades of shops and was just wide enough to get a car down if the dustbins hadn't been in the way. It gave access to a wider passage behind the buildings. The Executive Sauna was the first building next to the alley, hence the fire exit down the side as well as the back door into the walled yard. Main vehicle access to the passage at the rear was at either end of the parade. The only street lamp was broken. The shops to his right weren't as deep as those on the left, starting thin and widening into a strange triangle, and a narrow snicket shot off into the dark six feet from the main road.

A puff of smoke, backlit by the lights from the street.

McNulty relaxed. The junction of the snicket and the alley. Just where he would have hidden if he were doing covert obs. The tension eased. He was right. He took a deep breath that brought his pulse down even further. This was the time to be calm. Measured steps were the ones that paid off, not a headlong rush into action. Whenever the going got tough and the gloves came off, in a volatile situation or a brawl, the man who came out on top was the one who thought before he fought.

He didn't move. Simply observed.

There was no movement in the snicket. The glow of a cigarette flared briefly and then another puff of smoke drifted into the alley. Night seemed to deaden the sounds around him and the only thing he listened for was footsteps up ahead. The man had been there at least since McNulty entered the Executive Sauna and probably long before. His senses would be attuned to the dark and the quiet. McNulty didn't want to do anything that would trigger a feeling in the watcher that he was being watched. It wouldn't take much.

So he didn't move.

A boot scraped on the cobbles as the cigarette was stubbed out.

A blue glow shone out, about head height.

A mobile phone being flicked open. The light picked out an angular chin and a crooked nose. Muffled words were lost in the rumble of traffic. McNulty quickly moved along the alley while the man focused on talking. He got halfway before the phone clicked shut and the light went out. Still in the shadows near an overturned dustbin. Up ahead, a silhouetted hand checked the time.

McNulty breathed easily, not allowing himself to get excited. Nice and easy does it. On a normal massage visit he would be having a drink in the lounge about now. Maybe another half an hour before he'd come out and head for his car. The man hiding in the snicket must know that but appeared to be growing impatient. Now that McNulty was closer, he could make out the man's shape shuffling from one foot to the other. He took out a pack of cigarettes but put them away again without lighting up. Checked his watch again.

McNulty stood completely still. His mind raced through the mug shots of his past. The narrow chin and crooked nose were familiar but he'd arrested hundreds of men with broken noses. Some of them not broken until he arrested them.

The man came out of the snicket and walked to the mouth of the alley. He peered round the corner towards the Executive Sauna's front door and then both ways along the road. He checked his watch again. What was he waiting for? Something more than McNulty coming out of the sauna. He flattened himself against the wall but he was still in deep shadow. Movement would give him away, not light. The man came back and disappeared into the snicket.

McNulty moved fast before the man's senses readjusted to the stillness. He was standing beside the snicket entrance when the figure came out again. A siren sounded in the distance and the man's head turned towards the main road. He was muttering to himself when McNulty grabbed his arm and twisted it up his back.

In a split second the alleyway's quiet serenity turned to boiling anger. McNulty used the leverage on the twisted arm to push the man against the wall but he kicked backwards, catching McNulty's shin.

'Gerroff me, yer bastard.'

He kicked out again but only connected with a dustbin on the corner. It crashed to the floor, sending the lid rattling across the alley. A dog in one of the gardens barked. McNulty tightened his grip and slammed the man's face into the bricks.

'Now listen here, you pencil-dicked little fuckface.'

The voice in his head didn't come out of his mouth. This was a completely different situation. This wasn't the head rush of anger that the teenage child molester had inspired. This was about getting answers, not revenge. Control and contain. First rules of making an arrest. Control the subject so they can't get away or cause injury, to you or themselves. Contain the situation so it doesn't escalate, with angry relatives or passers-by. The head slam into the wall achieved the first objective. There weren't any passers-by to bother about the second.

'Gerroff me, yer fuckin' bastard.'

Another kick backwards but with less conviction. The sirens were louder, but because of the echo McNulty couldn't tell where they were coming from. He tried to see the man's face. In the darkness of the snicket there was only a blur of pale skin and snot.

A squeal of tyres sounded from the main road. The sirens stopped abruptly and car doors slammed. A single flash of blue light as the police car skidded past the alley in front of the Executive Sauna. A plain car pulled up behind it and a voice of reason shouted after the uniformed officers.

'Silent approach, you knob.'

Blue light? The mobile phone. McNulty gave the arm an extra twist.

'You scheming shit.'

With McNulty's attention on the road, the fourth kick came right up between his legs and the wind was driven out of him in an agonized gasp.

'You know the best way to disable a crocodile?'

The back kick to the balls pulled McNulty's teeth and disabled him. The man broke free and set off at a sprint along the snicket. McNulty squeezed tears of pain out of his eyes and gritted his teeth. Ignoring the ache between his legs he pushed off from the wall and raced after him.

The snicket was pitch black. McNulty followed the sound of fleeing footsteps and put his faith in the council. The paving was uneven and he almost tripped. So much for the council. Light from several back windows picked out sections of snicket and he plunged through them into stretches of darkness. His breath came in ragged gasps until he got his second wind. The ache in his knackers eased as he concentrated on keeping his feet.

Up ahead he heard a scuffle and clatter and then the running feet turned right. Seconds later McNulty reached the intersection with another alley bordered by splintered wooden fencing. The allotments. They were moving away from the houses and into a black hole of rented cabbage patches and greenhouses. No lights from windows, just darkness.

Follow the noise. That was easy in the silence of the allotments. There were no car engines. No sirens. No chatting pedestrians laughing on the way to the pub. Just silky quiet and his own breath. His eyes adjusted to the dark. As he kept to the path his feet found a rhythm and his balance shifted with each kink and turn. He focused on the patch of earth rolling out in front of him and ignored anything beyond that. In a foot chase you were in more danger from the ground you covered than the suspect you were chasing. Until you caught him. For now he needed to keep his feet and not go, officer down.

The suspect cut left over the fence. McNulty heard the fence crack and then the rustle of grass and leaves. He was taking a short cut off the path. McNulty crashed through the collapsed fence. The ground was softer, cultivated earth and overgrown lawns. He was catching up. A glass and wood greenhouse flashed by on his right. A garden shed to his left. He vaulted a low wall.

They were almost at the far end of the allotments. Ragged breath sounded close ahead. The man was slowing. McNulty put on an extra spurt and crashed into the opposite alley six feet behind his quarry. The man bounced off the retaining wall and turned left towards the exit. McNulty followed without breaking his stride.

Orange sodium light from the road bled into the mouth of the alley. He chased the silhouette towards it. The ground levelled out. Smooth tarmac instead of uneven gardens. A stitch knifed into his side but he ignored it. The man was almost at the end of the alley.

McNulty leaned into the run and almost toppled forward. His legs were tired. They weren't keeping up with his pace. His upper body wanted to go faster than his legs would carry him. He concentrated on the coat of the man in front of him. It flapped like a cape and he felt he could almost reach out and grab it. He tried and missed.

The mouth of the alley.

Twenty feet away.

Pursuer six feet behind the pursued. They were both flagging, the chase becoming more of an afternoon jog than an Olympic sprint. McNulty's breath burned in his throat. His eyes watered.

Ten feet from the mouth of the alley.

The man was almost there. McNulty reached out for another grab but missed again. Sparkles flared in front of his eyes. The street light glinting off gravel on the path.

Five feet.

The man cut sharp left and disappeared round the corner. McNulty was right behind him. He reached the end of the alley and . . .

A huge shadow as solid as a brick wall bulked in front of him. It reached a tree-trunk arm across the alley at head height and planted it on the sidewall. Blocked path. McNulty back-pedalled but the gravel path gave him no grip. His feet skidded as he ducked the outstretched arm and he went down like a sack of potatoes. Knocking the wind out of him.

A shorter man stepped beneath the tree trunk. Flicked open an ID wallet just in case McNulty didn't recognize the detective leaning over him.

'Vincent McNulty. You're under arrest.'

TWENTY-ONE

I thought you were in better shape than that.'

Tynan sat opposite McNulty in the CID office at Ecclesfield Police Station. McNulty kept quiet. He wasn't going to let anything slip until he knew what was going on. Eighteen years on the other side of the fence had taught him that. Eighteen years of trying to get your suspect to trip himself up before he spoke to his solicitor. Any comments made after caution but before booking into custody, provided they weren't in answer to questions, could be used in court. 'It's a fair cop, officer.' Not in so many words, but admissions of guilt would be difficult to deny once the solicitor came up with a plausible lie.

Except McNulty hadn't been cautioned. He hadn't been read his rights. And he hadn't been booked into custody either. Procedures had not been followed. McNulty wasn't saying anything until he knew why. He sat in a swivel chair in front of a notice board plastered with photographs of missing girls, timelines and linked locations.

Another breach of good practice.

The rest of the office was in darkness, just the last bank of lights switched on. It gave a false sense of security, like sitting in a cosy room in front of a log fire. McNulty rubbed his wrists even though he hadn't been handcuffed. Sort of a habit after seeing all his arrests do the same. Tynan stood up and went to the fridge in the corner. Filled the kettle from the sink and plugged it in.

'Coffee?'

McNulty shook his head. He didn't want a coffee or a hot chocolate or even a cup of tea. He didn't want any of the things he'd offered his own prisoners in order to lower their defences. No cigarettes or chewing gum or a shoulder to cry on. He just wanted to keep his head clear until he knew where this was going. He thought back to his plain-clothes days. Jimmy Tynan. He'd seen him around but never worked with him. From what he could remember he seemed like an OK guy, but that was from a work colleague perspective. He might be a right bastard to his suspects. It didn't look that way at the moment though.

'You sure?'

Tynan indicated the fridge.

'Could've offered you a doughnut if Baildon hadn't eaten 'em all. Gift from down under. Speedhoff's still trying to butt-kiss his way up the ladder. You remember Speedo, don't you? Was your shift inspector for a while, wasn't he?'

McNulty remembered Inspector Speedhoff, the ginger-headed management tool who always annoyed BF Cranston and amused Mick Habergham during briefings that lasted for ever. When McNulty had done a spell in uniform. The memory made him feel sad. He was no longer a part of that great body of men. In fact he was now a prisoner in the very police station he used to work from. His stomach fluttered but he kept the tension off his face. He knew what DC Tynan was doing. Trying to open a dialogue. McNulty shrugged and said nothing.

Tynan stirred his coffee and looked at McNulty. If he was getting annoyed at the silent treatment he wasn't showing it. He appeared to make a decision, sat down opposite and took a sip of coffee. It was too hot, so he put it on the desk and drummed his fingers.

'The other fella's in worse shape than you.'

The detective watched McNulty's reaction. Barely a flicker.

'We got him round the corner. Keith Tellez. Had no running left in him.'

Still no reaction but McNulty's mind raced. Keith Tellez. He thought the face was familiar. Something to do with drugs. Must have been more than one arrest for him to remember the guy. The rest of it was lost among the sheer numbers of arrests he'd made over the years. Tynan tried his coffee again.

'You made quite a mess of his face. He'll live though.'

McNulty wasn't taking the bait. He stretched his arms upwards and arched his back, then flexed his neck. A bone cracked and he rubbed his right shoulder. He glanced at the photographs on the notice board and then down at the steam rising from the detective's coffee. Looked Tynan in the eye. There didn't seem to be any animosity there. No hooded deception. He thought his first assessment had been correct. He was a decent bloke. McNulty decided to let him carry on and see where he was going with this.

'Keith Tellez. Thirty-five. You arrested him three times in his twenties. Minor possession. Put him in the system. He didn't straighten out like I guess you hoped. Got in deeper for maybe ten years. On the methadone programme now. Finally got free of the monkey. Still blames you I think.'

McNulty ran it through his memory and came up with exactly the same. Young man. Good job. Reasonable family. The short sharp shock hadn't worked on him like it had with Donk. Win some, lose some. It explained why he had it in for McNulty though. And why he might want to get his own back with a few phone calls and a bit of creative evidence. Tynan read McNulty's mind.

'Must be why he phoned the police and gave you up.'

The detective gave up on waiting for a reaction and drank his coffee.

'Only he says he didn't. Says he doesn't know who you are and you didn't slam his face into the wall. Fell taking a short cut through the allotments. That's bollocks of course. We've got his mobile. Redial went straight to the control room. Bet his phone bill will show a couple more too. If I can be arsed checking.'

The coffee was almost gone. Tynan swilled it around the bottom of his mug. He glanced at the notice board and then back at McNulty.

'I remember you. When you worked out of Vice. Next stop Major Crime Unit if you'd wanted it. What they did . . .' He nodded upstairs to the top floor. 'Hanging you out to dry. Fuckin' disgrace. Could've happened to any of us.'

McNulty looked Tynan in the eye again, looking for any sign of insincerity. Either the detective was good at faking it or he was telling the truth. Did that mean he could trust him? It was too early to tell.

'Look, Vince. I know you're not talking. Doesn't bother me. I wouldn't. Not in your shoes. But I'm not trying to screw you over. You say what you want to say. Or not. Up to you. There's something closer to home though.'

McNulty tensed. This was usually where the bombshell dropped. The damning piece of evidence that fucked you up and forced a response.

'Donkey Flowers.'

He was right. He waited for the hammer to fall.

Tynan drank the last of his coffee and pushed his cup to one side. Glancing across the desk at the prisoner who wasn't a prisoner, he thought he was finally getting through to him. He knew Vince McNulty had been a good policeman given the short end of the stick. Shat on from a great height by a management team more concerned with performance figures and targets than doing real police work. McNulty had done real police work and got crucified for it. He didn't want to push him. He needed to tread carefully and gain his trust before laying it all out for him.

'Someone booted Donkey Flowers' front door in and gave him a seeing to.'

There was a flicker behind McNulty's eyes.

'That's somebody else you put in the system early, isn't it? Worked that time. Joined the navy. Became a good citizen. Mostly. Lives on his own since his mother died. Your informant, wasn't he? Before they became Covert Human Intelligence Sources.'

He was right to try this. McNulty obviously had compassion for the people he dealt with and it showed. Was probably his downfall. The reason he'd kicked that little pervert's arse and got canned for it.

'Doctors thought he was going to lose his eye but he's going to be all right. Couple of cracked ribs and a broken arm, but otherwise OK. I thought you'd want to know.'

'Thanks.'

Just the one word, but it was like the walls of Jericho tumbling down. The bond was formed. Now to strengthen it. Tynan nodded towards the kettle.

'Now you've talked yourself dry. You want a coffee?'

McNulty smiled. Not a grin but a start.

'Tea. No doughnuts.'

Tynan filled the kettle and plugged it in. Using two fresh mugs he brewed a tea and a coffee. The tension had gone out of the room. The pool of light surrounding the corner desks became the cosy place it had always been. The CID office at night. In fact the entire police station at night. It became a proper cop shop instead of the office block it was during the day. Full of analysts and typists and politically correct senior managers. The only people working here after dark were coppers, the lifeblood of the police force.

Setting McNulty's tea down on the desk, Tynan sat opposite with a steaming mug of coffee. He felt more relaxed, even though there was much work to be done before he'd feel safe letting McNulty into his full confidence. He looked out of the window at the enclosed yard. Most of the marked cars were patrolling their beats, just the sergeants' car parked at the end and Alpha Three in the custody loading dock. Whichever prisoner they'd brought would be booked in and fingerprinted before they moved the car for the next delivery. On a busy night the last thing you needed was to struggle with a violent prisoner twenty feet from the custody door.

When he looked back across the desk he noticed that McNulty was staring at the yard too. He could only guess at what memories were playing in the ex-policeman's head. There was a sad little smile frozen on his lips. Tynan ignored the coffee and began building bridges.

'What's it like? Being out after all those years?'

McNulty blinked and came back to the present. He appeared to consider whether to answer or not and took a swig of tea to cover the pause. When he put the mug down he looked at Tynan.

'It's shit. Like being cut off from your family.'

Tynan empathized. He'd hit forty last month and would reach twenty years' service in the New Year. That was almost half his life as a police officer. He couldn't imagine not being a copper. The boys in blue had become his family. Even though McNulty was trying to hide it, the look in his eyes said a whole lot more. Tynan remembered checking McNulty's personnel file. He was an orphan. Had never known his parents. Father unknown. Mother died. No relatives. For McNulty the boys in blue *were* his only family.

'Yeah. Sorry I brought it up.'

'You don't have to bring it up. It's there all the time.'

'Ever thought of trying to get back in?'

McNulty snorted a laugh. The sickest joke in the world.

'Why? Aren't they bothered about a squeaky clean image any more? They don't want people who get their hands dirty. They want pencil pushers who can make the accounts add up and meet the monthly targets.'

'I know. Aren't any two jobs the same. Tell them arseholes upstairs.'

They both fell silent and drank until their throats burned. Tynan was getting a handle on McNulty. He thought his first impression had been the right one. A good copper with a heart. It was time to push on.

'Where can you stay now? With the flat gone and Donk in hospital?'

McNulty put his mug down.

'You know about the flat?'

'All town knows about the flat. Made the headlines on all channels. Front page news as well.'

A shadow flickered across McNulty's face. The explosion wasn't the only thing to make headlines. He glanced up at the notice board and for the first time really looked at the faces. Tynan pushed his empty mug away. They were almost at the meat of it now. Time to put up or shut up. Shit or get off the pot. This was a judgement call and Tynan made his decision.

'We've got nine reported missing. All below legal age. You can probably double that number with unreported. One dead in a barrel couple of days ago.'

He watched McNulty for a reaction.

'I didn't have anything to do with it. Any of it.'

Tynan nodded. It was time.

'I know. That's why you're here.'

TWENTY-TWO

McNulty sat in silence. He didn't think this was a trick to get him to talk, because even if he admitted killing all the girls it wasn't under caution and would be inadmissible in court. Christ, it wouldn't even be on tape. No. Whatever was going on here, Detective Tynan was playing an off-the-books game. What McNulty saw when he looked across the desk was the kind of copper who was willing to get his hands dirty. A go-fuck-your-target-figures kind of copper.

'And it's not your fault that Donkey Flowers is in hospital either.'

That should have made McNulty feel better, but guilt clung to him like a shroud. If he hadn't visited the parlours he wouldn't have been fingered as a suspect and if he hadn't been fingered as a suspect he wouldn't have taken Donk to his flat that night. Follow on from that, he wouldn't have taken the girl to Donk's house and therefore Donk wouldn't be in hospital.

'Yes it is.'

For the first time since he'd been sacked he opened up to someone in the job. It felt like unburdening himself of his sins without having to light a candle and say three Hail Marys. He explained how it felt whenever he saw the police on the news. Told Tynan about visiting the massage parlours because it was like still being under cover. Related everything about the girl being dumped at his flat when it exploded. About her being snatched from Donk's.

'She told Donk we didn't know what we'd got ourselves into. I guess she got that right.'

'She certainly did. Her picture on the board?'

McNulty didn't need to look. He'd already scoured the photos with their pink ribbon connections but she wasn't there. Not under the Sauna Kabin or any of the other parlours.

'No.'

'Another unreported. I'm not surprised.'

Tynan leaned forward and opened his notebook. He consulted the pages for a moment and then put the tips of his fingers together as if in prayer.

'Let me explain just what you have got yourself into.'

Halfway through the telling, a meeting of minds put them both on the same page. If McNulty had still been in the force he would be making notes and jotting down timelines, but he didn't have a notebook and none of this was going to be evidence later. Not from him. Tynan had all the evidence recorded. All McNulty needed to do was listen.

'I don't work out of Ecclesfield nick. I'm Major Crime Unit. This would normally be a Vice job but it's got too big.'

Too big indeed. Word from the street had filtered up to Vice Squad that there was a new place in town. Snippets of information at first: an offhand remark from a streetwalker here, a dark rumour from an informant there. Nothing specific, but over time enough bits and pieces to confirm that something was going on. The street prostitutes sneered at the prospects of working there. They were too old. Even the youngest were aged beyond their years and rumour had it you needed to be still in training bras to qualify. Real young.

'An old tart down the Lane got Vice thinking there was more to it. Tried to bargain away a soliciting charge. Said she knew girls taken for this new place. Never seen again. Young lass she turned onto the game. Lived in the same bedsit. Vanished off the face of the earth.'

McNulty thought of the girl upended in the oil drum. Anger bubbled under the surface as he listened to the story unfold. Vice Squad had started actively seeking information. They'd checked all their sources and collected enough anecdotal evidence to set up an operation. Trouble was they didn't have a location for surveillance. And no faces to target. It was all just rumour and scare tactics. Someone was setting up very young girls, but where? Obvious first line of enquiry was the massage parlours. They had the premises but were sufficiently open to the public that hiding an underage sex ring would be difficult. Vice Squad used undercover officers to check them out but everything was fairly above board. Above consensual age anyway.

McNulty shuffled in his seat. Tynan noticed and shook his head.

'Hey Vince. I'm not judging here. You want your pudding pulled, go for it. This other shit though. That's seriously fucked up. Only thing the undercovers came up with was if they wanted younger, there was a place out of town. Our man. New boy. Pushed a bit too hard and the woman sussed him out.'

Lack of resources had forced Vice Squad to ask for help. Division were just as short of staff trying to meet stop-and-search targets and keep recorded crime down in the hotspot areas. That, and the first reports that some of these girls were being taken against their will, pushed the entire file up to Major Crime Unit. It took them three weeks of beating the brush before somebody spilled the beans.

'Someone's been recruiting through the Northern X chain. Signing up the young and really young. Then snatching them away to stock this new place. A body farm for sex slaves. Secure unit. Exclusive. Do anything you want. Very high price.'

'Jesus Christ.'

'Yeah. Age being the prime mover here. Makes you wonder what happens when they get too old, doesn't it?'

'Body in a barrel?'

'That'd be my guess. And she was still pretty young. What the fuck they call too old?'

McNulty looked at the faces on the notice board. Young fresh-faced girls who looked like they should still be at school. Vulnerable. In need of protection. What backgrounds had they come from to lead them into this sordid game? Where were their parents? McNulty's neck flushed. Not everyone had parents and not everyone charged with looking after you looked after you. He clenched his fists beneath the desk.

Blue lights flashed in the yard and a siren blared. He looked through the window. Two patrol cars sped across the yard and paused while the electronic gate slid open. As soon as the gap was wide enough they shot through onto the street for another emergency. In the silence that followed, the pool of light in the CID office seemed to close in around them. Tynan broke the spell.

'We got a name. Fella doing most of the recruiting. Muscle. Don't know if he's the money and you wouldn't think he's got the brains.'

McNulty's ears pricked up.

'Telfon Speed. Ruthless bastard. Ran his own stickup crew down in South Yorkshire. Armed robbery. Nicknamed Teflon because nothing sticks. Managed to slip out of any charges. Apart from his youthful thuggery. Likes to think he's Mister Big. Not the forgive and forget type.'

'Don't know him.'

'Non-stick knows you. Wasn't Keith Tellez set you up. He only called the last couple of times 'cos he'd seen you on the news. No. It's Teflon who's taken a dislike to you.'

'Since when?'

Tynan leaned forward.

'Since you almost broke his arm at the Sauna Kabin.'

Heat burned up McNulty's neck. He remembered the girl from his flat, Michelle, being manhandled in the first floor lounge, but it was the man doing the manhandling who sprang to mind. The square-jawed, no-necked bulk of the man called Telfon Speed.

The man was quick but McNulty was quicker. He grabbed the man's lead hand below the wrist and yanked it towards him and up. He bent the joint down into a gooseneck and the man had no choice but to follow or get a broken wrist. He lost his balance and toppled forward. McNulty slammed the heel of his free hand into the exposed throat.

The girl had disappeared down the fire escape and McNulty had saved the day. It was obvious now what had been happening. Another recruitment snatch by the man running Northern X. He couldn't believe that he'd shown the bastard his usual level of compassion.

'You know. If this was a film. I'd be asking what movies you'd been in? Like in Get Shorty. *Remember? After Travolta gut-punched*

Gandolfini – before he did the Sopranos *– and asked what movies he did? 'Cos Gandolfini's character had been a stunt man.'*

The man was breathing better now. McNulty looked into his eyes.

'You aren't a stunt man are you?'

Tynan sat back in his chair.

'I see you remember him.'

'How could I forget?'

'Seems like he hasn't forgotten you.'

McNulty nodded. Tynan closed his notebook and toyed with the mug. His eyes gleamed. This was the moment of truth, when all Detective Tynan's groundwork would either pay off or fall flat on its face.

'And I have an idea we might turn that to our advantage.'

TWENTY-THREE
NEWS REPORT

Montage of shots from previous reports showing the crime scene tent at City Road. Police tape flutters in the breeze. An officer in a fluorescent jacket holds a clipboard.

'The suspect in the death of a young girl last week, and abduction of several others, has been released pending further enquiries. Vincent McNulty, an ex-police officer, was arrested last night outside the Executive Sauna, and questioned overnight at Ecclesfield Police Station. He must answer police bail in four weeks' time.'

Closing shot using archive footage of Ecclesfield Police Station.

PART THREE
House of the Rising Sun

'I stopped by here to tell you two things. Number one is that you're gonna die tonight. Number two, I'm gonna find your wife. And I'm gonna kill her too.'

TWENTY-FOUR

T he mistakes people make. A man's life is littered with them. Stupid decisions. Errors of judgement. Bad choices. But maybe some of them aren't really mistakes at all. Just choices made that will affect choices in the future. God's plan to ensure that all is right with the world. As McNulty sat in his car outside Golden Touch he wondered just how many decisions had led him to this point in his life. The point where only his past made him eligible to change the future.

Another day had passed and another night was settling in. It was cold and clear and windless. Along the street the leaves had dropped and only the naked branches of lonely trees remained. McNulty touched the tattoo on his neck. Naked, dead branches reaching across the gothic house of his childhood. Across the road the discreet sign above the front door could have been advertising a hairdresser's or a beauty parlour. Maybe a Chinese takeaway. Golden Touch.

What goes around comes around. It felt strange that the place he'd been thrown out of was the place chosen for his triumphant return. The car windows steamed up and he turned the fan on to demist. The Astra pumped exhaust fumes into the night, the only sign that the engine was still running. This was like a hundred stakeouts at a hundred locations; the only things missing were a flask of coffee and a bag of sandwiches. Stakeout. Another Americanism, right up there with once a cop always a cop. More appropriate than doing covert obs, or undercover surveillance, but for a different reason. This wasn't a stakeout. McNulty was being staked out. Bait to tempt the predator.

He glanced along the road to the junction, where sky-high street lamps flooded the crossroads with light. Traffic network cameras covered each approach but one of them was being manoeuvred to a new target. McNulty stared up at the distant lens and smiled.

'What are you smiling about?'

The CID office two hours ago. DC Jimmy Tynan handed ex-DC Vince McNulty a police radio, adjusted to channel nine. Secure talk-through from unit to unit within two miles. McNulty was smiling a contented little smile as he took the radio.

'You remember that film, *Midnight Run*? Robert De Niro?'

'I don't go to the pictures.'

'No? You should. Great way to unwind.'

'I thought you unwound by firing one off.'

'That's great too. But, *Midnight Run*. De Niro plays this ex-cop turned bounty hunter who never really wanted to be an ex-cop. The Feds are taping a wire to him to catch Dennis Farina, this real nasty bastard gangster, and one of them asks why he's smiling. And he says, "I feel like a cop again."'

He hefted the radio in his hand.

'Well. I feel like a policeman again.'

Tynan nodded as he shrugged into his shoulder harness, handcuffs and CS spray on the left balancing his baton on the right.

'Yeah? Well don't forget there's nowhere to hide a wire where you're going. The radio stays in the car. We've got a man at the magistrates' with the warrant. Soon as you get a location he'll swear it out, and we'll be right behind you.'

The bustle in the CID office was reassuring. All around him plain-clothes detectives strapped on their stab vests and shoulder harnesses. Two traffic officers in fluorescent jackets waited by the door. Pursuit car if needed. In the yard outside, the PSU team zipped up their black overalls and loaded shields and the door ram into a police van. Twilight sucked the last vestiges of daylight out of the clear autumn sky. A stray dog in the station kennels barked.

It had been a long day as Tynan explained his dilemma and why McNulty could help him out. Sitting in a corner of the police canteen on the third floor with McNulty's first free lunch since being asked to resign. Ecclesfield canteen was one of the few left, after force-wide cutbacks, which still had catering staff and a hotplate. Mainly because any major operations in the city were run from Ecclesfield Division, so catering was needed for whatever extra staff that entailed. McNulty had the all-day breakfast of bacon, eggs, sausage and beans. Tynan had scrambled eggs on toast. Both had steaming mugs of tea.

'Problem is, we can't get an undercover female in there.'

McNulty sliced a chunk of sausage and loaded it with beans.

'Too young?'

'The girls are, yes. Even our youngest policewomen don't look as young as they're recruiting.'

McNulty stopped eating for a moment. He stared at his plate and thought about the girl from his flat. Michelle. Telfon Speed had been recruiting her when McNulty got in the way. How young did she look? He remembered thinking pretty young at the time. Even younger when he'd pulled her out of his flat, smoke-begrimed and unconscious.

'I should have asked her what was going on.'

'Asked who?'

'The girl from my flat. If I'd talked to her first instead of moving the car she might have told me where the new place is.'

'If she knew. She got away from Speed once.'

'But he must have got her back, otherwise how'd he dump her in my flat?'

Tynan swallowed a mouthful of eggs.

'Don't get hung up on that. We won't know what happened until we ask him on tape. We never do. It's all about gathering pieces of evidence. You know that as well as I do. An eyewitness here. Bit of forensics there. My guess is only a guess until we prove it.'

McNulty put the sausage and beans in his mouth so he didn't have to comment. All police work was best-guess work unless you witnessed the crime yourself, and that hardly ever happened. He could count on the fingers of one hand the number of crimes in progress he'd stumbled across. Maybe an occasional robbery he'd been called to and got there quick enough to catch them at it. A few vehicle stops that turned out to be stolen cars or hidden drugs – but that didn't count. Most crimes he'd investigated, it was a case of putting the pieces together until you could prove guilt beyond a reasonable doubt. The evidence of a civilian witness was the most unreliable and always second best to physical evidence or CCTV. Bottom line, unless you saw it yourself, it was still an educated guess what had really happened.

'And what is your best guess?'

'About the girl? Haven't the foggiest. How he got her back, we may never know. What he was using her for. My best guess is Speed heard we were looking into the missing girls and wanted to close us down. Easiest way is to give us a suspect and then make sure we can't interview him. That'd be you. Give us enough evidence to link you to the parlours the girls were missing from so we'd look at you hard. Blow you up in the flat. Have one of the girls found in the ashes. Neither one of you could deny anything. Case closed.'

McNulty folded a piece of bacon into a slice of bread and dipped it in his egg. He waited for the excess yolk to drip off then took a bite. It amazed him how stupid the average criminal was. Did Telfon Speed really think the police would stop looking just because they'd found one girl dead in a flat? They might lean toward blaming Vince McNulty, but it wouldn't take long to disprove that theory once they hadn't found the other girls. It was as stupid as expecting McNulty to turn the light on after smelling gas in his flat. Ridiculous. Like he'd

thought before, there are no criminal masterminds on the estates of
Yorkshire.

'And you wouldn't have fallen for that of course.'

Tynan took a swig of tea.

'Not me. The top floor you've got to worry about though. It'd keep
the detected crime figures up if they could write them all off to you.
But even the bosses aren't so blind they can't see the problems with
that. Doubt if they're worried about false accounting, but any of
the other girls turn up and they've got egg on their face on national
television.'

'So why'd Speed pick me?'

'Like everything else he does. Instinct and availability. Not a lot of
thought goes into it.'

McNulty was eating so Tynan carried on.

'You pissed him off back at the Sauna Kabin. Since he runs Northern
X it wouldn't be hard to track you around the chain. Brought you up
on his radar and just like that he made a snap decision.'

McNulty swallowed and took a drink. When he looked across the
table, Tynan had stopped eating. The detective pushed his half-finished
meal away and ignored the steam rising from the mug in front of him.
McNulty put his knife and fork down and waited. He sensed a change
of direction coming. After a few moments Tynan began drumming his
fingers on the table. He didn't speak again until the drums stopped.

'That's why we want you to go undercover again.'

'You got to be fuckin' kiddin'.'

McNulty didn't need a pregnant pause to think about his response.
He'd been shafted out of the police force, circulated as wanted for
murder, and almost blown up in his flat. Add to that his only friend
had been beaten up and the girl they'd rescued kidnapped. And now
the police force that had shafted him wanted to put him back undercover against the very person who'd set most of that in motion.

'How the fuck can I go undercover? My face has been all over the
telly.'

Tynan waited him out.

'Fuck that for a game of soldiers. Shitty fuckin' death. Fuck no.'

The storm blew itself out and McNulty fell silent. He sat back from
the table and set his jaw against any further questions. Tynan just
smiled at some internal private joke.

'You finished?'

McNulty nodded. All the things he'd said were true and none of
them mattered. Given the chance to do some police work again, there

was no way he was going to turn it down. Tynan knew that but explained his reasoning anyway.

'I've checked around. You were the best undercover that Vice Squad had. Nobody ever made you as police.'

McNulty thought about what Donkey Flowers' mother had once said. *'You're not like a policeman at all.'* It was the best compliment he'd ever been paid. Her experience of the police had always been heavy-handed swaggers knocking heads at the Mean Wood terminus. Showing a little compassion had gone a long way.

'They won't have to make me as police. The news has already told them.'

'That you're ex-police.'

'Like that'll cut some ice.'

Tynan wasn't put off.

'Think about it. If Speed's learned anything it's that you're a disgraced ex-copper who hangs around massage parlours. You've just been arrested and bailed by the people you used to work for, so there's no love lost there. And when you fronted him up at the Sauna Kabin you were asking when a very young girl would be free.'

That was true. Looked at from a different perspective, McNulty might not be seen as the knight in shining armour saving a damsel in distress but the dirty little scum bucket wanting the young girl for his next massage.

'You've got a point.'

'I know I've got a point. That's why I want you to go for another massage and ask for someone younger than they've got.'

McNulty shivered at the thought of even asking for that.

'Not nice, but . . .'

Tynan shrugged. Sometimes you had to do unpleasant things in order to get the conviction. Nobody ever said this was an easy job.

'Tell them you've heard about a new place for that kind of thing. My guess is they aren't going to tell you without checking with Speed first. If they do, that's a bonus.'

McNulty could see where Tynan was coming from and began to admire the detective for the way he'd handled this. By drip-feeding McNulty the possible scenarios he'd allowed him to work this out for himself. Now that he had, he came to the same conclusion as Tynan.

'And Speed doesn't like me anyway. So either they'll let me visit the new place because I'm a perv or Speed'll let me visit because then he'll get me alone in a dark place.'

'A very dark place. That's why it's your decision.'

*   *   *

As darkness fell over the city the CID office was abuzz. Radios were being booked out. Stab vests and harnesses being put on. The RIPA forms required before authorization for any kind of covert surveillance were almost complete and ready for signing by the Divisional Superintendent. McNulty sat quietly amid the bustle. Tynan came over and leaned against the desk.

'Don't forget. We'll be set up on the roads in each direction to pick up your trail. Radio when you get to Golden Touch then turn it off. He might jump in with you or even take you in another car. Whatever. We'll be watching. Once you get to the new place, confirm it's got the sex ring and call the nines.'

Tynan slid a mobile phone across the desk.

'I doubt they'll feel threatened by a mobile if they search you. If you can't speak just hit three nines and send. The control room are monitoring this phone so they'll know it's yours.'

McNulty checked that the phone was turned on and put it in his pocket. Tynan sat on the edge of the desk. They both fell silent. Tension was building in the air. Out in the yard a police van reversed up to the PSU shield store. Tynan didn't have to say be careful. They both knew what life in the trenches could be like. Tynan handed McNulty a police radio, adjusted to channel nine. Secure talk-through from unit to unit within two miles.

'What are you smiling about?'

I feel like a policeman again, McNulty thought as he smiled at the traffic camera high up on the distant lamp post. Across the road the discreet sign above the front door could have been advertising a hairdresser's or a beauty parlour. Maybe a Chinese takeaway. Golden Touch. McNulty lifted the radio to his mouth and pressed the transmit button.

'Alpha Six-Nine in position.'

It felt strange having a call sign again after all this time. He didn't have an official one since he wasn't on the job any more, so sixty-nine had been allocated as a sort of in-joke. There was a crackle of static and then Tynan's voice, barely recognizable as he acknowledged.

'One-Twenty. Be good.'

Once again, not 'Be careful.' Police officers weren't as superstitious as actors so there was none of that 'Break a leg' shit, but they were practical enough to know that the most redundant saying when entering a dangerous situation was to tell someone to be careful. McNulty's heart thumped in his chest. His breathing became shallow and rapid. He took several deep breaths to calm his nerves. Switched the radio off and slid it under the driver's seat. A few minutes later he turned the engine off and got out of the car. Careful not to get run over on his first assignment in twelve months, he crossed the road.

TWENTY-FIVE

The décor hadn't changed, same dark red wallpaper and leather settees, but the atmosphere was thick with anticipation. Thicker than the damp-carpet smell from the Jacuzzi in the basement or the scented oils from the massage rooms beyond the first floor lounge. Behind the stripped pine doors, muffled sounds indicated that both rooms were engaged. The fire exit door was open a couple of inches for fresh air but the tension wouldn't shift.

A different woman than on his last visit showed McNulty up the narrow stairs, then quickly retreated to the safety of the cubbyhole behind the reception desk. A middle-aged bottle blonde sat on the nearest settee. A brunette moved behind the corner bar. Bottles of Robinson's fruit squash lined the back wall beside a stack of clean glasses. A dark stain spoiled the cream carpet. The spilled blackcurrant had obviously proved more stubborn than the cleaning lady.

The blonde stood up to greet him but didn't seem too enthusiastic. McNulty wondered if Kim, the strawberry blonde who'd oiled his muscle last time, was working and found himself hoping that she wasn't. This might be better with a cast of unknowns. He didn't bother reading the name badges on the clean white smocks. It used to be a good excuse for sizing up the women's breasts but that wasn't necessary this time. Neither of them would be working on him tonight. The blonde pointed to the corner bar.

'Would you like a drink?'

The brunette clinked a glass against the bottles, a rehearsed move that would generally raise a smile, but neither woman looked in the mood for smiling. McNulty nodded and tried to lighten the atmosphere.

'Orange. No ice. Shaken not stirred.'

The brunette must have been the only person in Leeds who hadn't seen a James Bond film.

'Shaken?'

McNulty gave a little it-doesn't-matter wave.

'As it comes.'

He glanced around the room and then nodded towards the stripped pine doors.

'How many girls working tonight?'

The blonde took her cue and went into her sales routine.

'We have four girls on duty tonight. Stella.'

She indicated the brunette who was making McNulty's drink.

'Me. Also there's Cindy. Thirty-six twenty-four thirty-six. Dark hair. Oriental. Very friendly. And Emma. Thirty-eight double D. Very experienced. They are with clients at the moment but will be available in half an hour or so.'

McNulty took the offered glass of orange squash and looked undecided. He made a show of eyeing the two women up and down and gave an embarrassed smile. He glanced at the mirror behind the bar and then back at the blonde.

'I don't want to offend you two fine ladies.'

The brunette came around from behind the bar and sat on the furthest settee. The blonde didn't look as if she could be offended no matter how hard you tried.

'But do you mind if I wait until you're all available before making a choice?'

'Of course not. Make yourself comfy. They won't be long.'

McNulty sat opposite Stella. Damp-carpet odour from the Jacuzzi battled the smell of scented oils and both clawed at his throat. Cool night air from the partly open fire exit door tried hard but couldn't fight it off. He took a sip of his drink; mixed so thin it was almost water with an orange tinge. For the first time he felt awkward in the waiting room. He wondered if this was what married men felt like while they waited to cheat on their wives.

'What time are you working 'til tonight?'

His small talk felt stilted and forced. It was directed at nobody in particular. The blonde moved towards the office door beside the bar. The brunette looked pale and tense but managed to answer.

'Should be midnight but it depends how many customers we have.'

'Sort of flexi time shift then?'

The blonde went into the office. McNulty continued chatting to Stella but the conversation quickly dried up. He checked the cheap electric clock on the wall. Time was crawling. He hadn't been here half an hour yet. The blonde returned and sat next to Stella. She seemed a little happier. McNulty drank slowly, not wanting to be offered a refill.

Forty minutes.

The nearest massage room door opened and an oriental girl came out straightening her white smock. Cindy. She stepped aside to let a middle-aged man with hunched shoulders come past her. She asked

if he wanted a drink and he looked like he was going to say yes until
he saw McNulty.

A cheating-on-his-wife type of customer. A shy type of punter. There
was no way this man was going to feel comfortable having a drink
with the next customer. His bonhomie evaporated like spilled milk on
a hot day. He quickly made his excuses and, avoiding eye contact,
went downstairs. The front door closed quietly as if nobody would
notice him leaving.

Cindy smiled at McNulty and made herself a drink. When the blonde
thought he wasn't watching she threw a warning look and the oriental
stopped smiling. It would have been comical if it weren't so serious.
Whatever had been said about him, it certainly got their attention.

Fifty minutes.

The second massage room door opened. As with all good advertising, Emma bore no resemblance to the description sold by the blonde
earlier. She looked careworn and haggard and wore enough make-up
to Polyfill a rendered wall. The only thing you could say was that she
was certainly experienced and definitely had thirty-eight double Ds.
Her chest came out of the room five minutes before the rest of her.
The man who followed her looked even more pussy-whipped than the
first and disappeared even quicker. When the front door closed this
time, McNulty heard the distinctive double click of the latch being
dropped and a bolt slammed home. Emma didn't bother with a drink.
She sat on the middle settee without a hint of a smile.

McNulty glanced at the mirror behind the bar. He imagined the office
on the other side with its viewing window into the lounge. The main
threat. It was time to play this little scenario out and see where it led.
Standing up he set his empty glass on the bar and faced the room. He
could just make out the office door from the corner of one eye.

'I'm sorry, ladies. Is there any . . .'

He paused as if embarrassed to ask.

'Are there any younger girls available?'

The blonde indicated the oriental.

'Cindy is only nineteen.'

Another lie, said without much conviction. Cindy was difficult to
age because of the smooth Chinese skin and slanted eyes but she hadn't
been a teenager for a good few years. McNulty felt that the blonde
was only going through the motions too. Everyone knew where this
was leading.

'I mean a lot younger.'

He felt dirty even saying it. Something stung behind his eyes.
The slap like a gunshot in the quiet office. A gunshot followed by a

heartbreaking whimper. He tried not to blink but was afraid that would only make his eyes water. His palms began to sweat. The office door. He concentrated on that even though he was addressing the lounge.

'I heard you had a new place. For, like, young girls.'

The four women looked at him. The blonde was obviously the spokesperson but even she kept quiet. The old brass, Emma, actually looked sad. The blonde nodded once but McNulty was focusing on the office door.

Any moment now.

He braced himself for the rush because he felt this was going badly wrong. The women were too aware of him. Expecting him. The front door had been locked. Despite being back in the fold he felt more exposed now than when he'd had no backup. The heavy gang were parked in a back street. Tynan was waiting for a signal. But McNulty was alone in here. No radio. No stab vest. No partner to help him out.

The office door handle.

He felt the first pulse of a headache as his eyes strained to watch two things at once. The handle didn't move. The blonde stood up. She went to the bar and made a fresh drink, clinking ice around the glass before diluting the orange squash. She looked into the mirror, adjusted her hair and turned to face the others. If there was a hint of disgust in her face she hid it well. McNulty's tongue swelled in his throat like the first day giving evidence in court. It was hard to talk.

'Somewhere private.'

He didn't know what he'd expected but the entire operation felt stupid now. Did they really think that Northern X would simply give him an address and send him on his way? What the fuck? The office door didn't move. The voice behind him was deep and close.

'So that's why you stuck your nose in? Like a bit of fresh meat, eh?'

McNulty didn't need to turn round to know it was Telfon Speed. The fire exit door clicked shut.

TWENTY-SIX

S peed sounded different to how McNulty remembered him. There was no anger in his voice, just a quiet intensity. Despite the body-builder physique and faded rugby shirt, he sounded almost educated. He smelled of soap and aftershave. His fingernails were neatly trimmed and scraped clean.

'That explains a lot. I hope you're not going to lose your temper again.'

McNulty shrugged and gave an apologetic half smile.

'And, no. I'm not a stunt man.'

Speed clicked his fingers and the blonde darted behind the bar and mixed an orange and blackcurrant drink. She dropped two ice cubes in and added water from the tap. Speed accepted the drink with a nod and stood in front of the settee where Stella was sitting. She stood up quickly and he sat down.

'Ladies. Haven't you got some cleaning to do?'

All four disappeared downstairs without a word. Speed waved towards the opposite settee.

'Being compared to James Gandolfini was a compliment though.'

McNulty sat down and faced Speed. He tried to gauge the mood behind the words and decide on his best response. He didn't want to seem too eager but he didn't want to come over too aggressive either. This was the crucial point. When he would either convince Speed to let him use the new facility or be blown out. Keeping a neutral tone he settled back against the hard leather.

'It wasn't meant to be.'

'I'm sure it wasn't. Or were you just making small talk to defuse the situation? That says something about your character. Same as what-ever you say now says a lot about why you're here.'

'You know why I'm here.'

'Do I?'

'Supply and demand. You've got what I want.'

'Yes I have, haven't I?'

He took a deep swig of orange and blackcurrant.

'The question is, why would I give it to you?'

'Sell it to me.'

'Why would I do that? To someone who has been a copper for eighteen years?'

'Emphasis on has been.'

Speed put the drink on the arm of the settee and leaned forward. The muscles beneath the rugby shirt tightened as he rested his fore-arms across his knees. Cords stood out on his neck and his eyes gleamed.

'Right. The kind of has been who was kicked off the force in disgrace. Why the fuck should I sell you anything?'

McNulty's neck flushed with suppressed anger. This was as stupid as expecting someone to switch on the light in a gas-filled room. What on earth made him think this was going to work? He stood up in one movement but Speed didn't back off.

'That's up to you. I didn't know you'd be here or I'd have gone somewhere else. But if we're throwing insults. What kind of pimp only pimps to people he likes?'

'Trusts. People he trusts. I don't like any of my customers.'

'Whatever. Fuck this.'

He started towards the stairs, his neck burning at the stupidity of this simple plan. The light switch in a gas-filled room. But someone had flicked that switch. So that simple plan had worked. Speed stood up and folded his arms.

'If I reminded you of Gandolfini in *Get Shorty*, then you remind me of Clint Eastwood in *Tightrope*.'

McNulty stopped and turned to face Speed.

'Detective Wes Block.'

'Used to go with prostitutes. Liked to get whipped. Handcuff them. Carried a lot of hidden baggage. Not exactly Dirty Harry.'

'Dirtier.'

Speed put his hands in his pockets and considered McNulty.

'You've got a lot of hidden baggage too, haven't you?'

'Mind your own business.'

'I do mind my own business. That's how I know who to trust.'

The light switch in the gas-filled room. A stupid plan but this was going to work. McNulty's anger subsided but was replaced with shame. He'd been using this man's services for almost a year and now this man recognized something in McNulty he didn't want to acknowledge about himself. This was a dirty little business, and like Detective Wes Block he was a dirty little man.

They stood facing each other in silence. The tap dripped in the sink. Distant traffic noise rumbled past outside. Speed gave an almost imperceptible nod.

'You liked that girl, didn't you? Wanted her?'

McNulty swallowed his shame.

'Yes.'

'Well, this is your lucky day. She's one of my bestsellers.'

TWENTY-SEVEN

They used McNulty's car. Telfon Speed sat in the passenger seat giving directions, while McNulty turned left and right and tried to keep track of where they were going. He couldn't decide whether using his own car was safer than Speed taking him in his. The feeling he got was that this way it left Speed's hands free while McNulty had to concentrate on driving. That wasn't a good thing if the bodybuilder was after revenge.

On the other hand, at least using the Astra gave Big Fish the chance to follow his route using the traffic network cameras. Tynan had programmed the registration number into the system and the control room were monitoring his progress. Two unmarked CID cars were keeping their distance. The traffic car even further. Nobody wanted Telfon spotting the tail.

The police radio was turned off under McNulty's seat. He felt its presence but it didn't reassure him. In eighteen months the GPS tracking system would go live and the control room would know exactly where each of its units was at any given time. Like in *Beverly Hills Cop* but without the big screen. Most uniformed officers weren't happy about that because they'd have to clear from every job before sloping off to do enquiries, the only way to avoid being sent to another job straight away. On a busy night you could meet yourself coming back and the only way to get essential follow-up enquiries done was to use creative accounting. Lie about when you'd finished at the scene. GPS would ruin that. On the plus side, if you ever got injured on duty and couldn't radio for help, control would know your exact location. None of that helped McNulty tonight, so the radio was turned off.

'Next right. After the takeaway.'

McNulty flicked on the indicator and slowed down. None of the trail cars would be able to see but at least indicating gave them a fighting chance. Speed had directed him through the town centre and this was the first time they'd turned off the main road. Compton Street. Just like his early days on foot patrol, McNulty memorized the street name. Any other turnoff and he would memorize that one instead, always keeping a mental tag on which street he was in. It was an old habit. The last thing you wanted if you were suddenly chasing on foot was to not be able to yell your location into the radio. He'd learned that the hard way, after a lengthy pursuit that ended on waste ground behind a factory. He'd caught the lad but he was kicking off and McNulty had no idea where he was. It took backup half an hour and McNulty several bruised ribs before they found him.

'Left at the end.'

Rows of terraced houses drifted past. The street lights were modern and bright, but when he turned left into Compton Avenue and then right into Tavistock Road the houses became more run down and the lights changed from white to orange. The older lamp posts were cracked concrete. Several didn't work at all and the ones that did barely threw out any light.

'At the end. Sharp left and cross the canal.'

Several of the terraced houses looked empty. Only every third or fourth had lights on and curtains drawn. Towards the end of the street there was a gap and a pile of rubble where one of the houses had been demolished. Beyond that was a sharp left-hand turn with no street lamps at all. The Astra's headlights swept across a high stone wall with broken glass cemented into the top and settled on the cobbled road. The side of a derelict factory butted up against the canal. A narrow bridge spanned the waterway. McNulty drove slowly.

Two more lefts and a right and McNulty's sense of direction was completely shot. The last two didn't even have street signs, just blank spaces where they'd been removed, probably decorating some teenager's bedroom. Worse than that, they had been off the main roads for so long that the Big Fish cameras were useless. They only covered the main roads into and out of the town centre and arterial roads surrounding it. Nobody organizing the operation had thought the new premises were going to be far enough out of town that this would be a problem.

'Head for the chimney over towards the right.'

Speed's voice had the same flat and even tone but McNulty tensed. They were so far off the beaten track now that he had a sinking feeling. He spotted the tall chimney pointing skyward like an accusing finger in the distance. There were no houses any more. Just small factories and industrial units. Lighting was almost nonexistent. If Telfon Speed wanted to get McNulty somewhere private he couldn't have picked a better place.

There was no sign of life at all. No passing motorists. No pedestrians. A burnt-out Ford Transit van with no wheels stood on bricks at the side of the road. A bicycle tyre hung from a telegraph pole. A single shoe lay in the gutter.

The chimney grew closer. It belonged to an old brickworks at the end of the street. The factory windows were boarded up and cemented. A high brick wall surrounded what looked like a delivery yard. Curls of barbed wire on top glinted in the headlights. Not rusty. Not broken glass cemented into the top. It was the first new thing McNulty had seen in twenty minutes.

'Flash your headlights.'

McNulty flashed twice as he approached and in the full beam he noticed a large wooden gate in the wall. Faded green paint peeled like dead skin and the bottom right-hand corner had rotted away. A rusty oil drum filled with splintered wood and old newspapers stood in front of the rotting planks. The gate looked as if it hadn't been opened for ten years. After the headlamps dipped, the green paint became black in the shadows. So dark that McNulty didn't notice it moving for a few seconds until the gate slid halfway open.

'Drive in and park.'

The gate slid to the right on rollers, supported from the top by a track beneath the brick archway. It screeched and complained, not like the secret doors in a James Bond film, and shuddered to a halt at the far end. McNulty's headlights swept across the enclosed yard as he drove in and pulled over to the right. They picked out the usual detritus of a long-dead industrial past. More oil drums, some with the tops cut off. A six-foot skip with metal shavings and brick offcuts. A pair of aluminium ladders. To the right a delivery door was padlocked shut. In the left-hand corner of the yard the office windows were bricked up and cemented over. There was a single door up a short flight of stairs.

The main gate screeched again. McNulty turned the engine off and watched a man in dark clothing push the gate closed. The bottom corner, where rotten wood left a gap outside, was plated with black-painted metal sheeting.

The engine ticked as it cooled. With the headlights off the yard was plunged into darkness. Now. It would happen now. McNulty toyed with the idea of reaching under the seat and turning the radio on. He might have just enough time to press the panic button and hope that Tynan had been able to tail him. The passenger door opened and Telfon Speed got out. The interior light showed his hands to be relaxed and unthreatening. Not the hands of someone about to attack him. McNulty got out too.

The yard was big enough to have accommodated a large truck at the delivery door in its heyday, and maybe a couple of cars in front of the office. The manager's car, no doubt, when the factory had been running. It could probably park half a dozen cars now but there was only one other in the far corner. A black BMW four-wheel drive with alloy wheels. In the glare from the Astra's interior light McNulty noticed moisture dripping from the exhaust. It had only just arrived. Probably Telfon Speed's car, brought over from the Golden Touch parlour.

McNulty closed his door. Moonlight compensated for the extinguishing of the interior light. It painted half of the yard silver blue while the rest hid in the shadows. The gateman had disappeared. Telfon Speed walked towards the office door and waited for McNulty. When the expected attack didn't come McNulty walked over and joined him. Speed nodded his approval.

'Are you ready to step through the looking glass?'

He didn't wait for an answer. He opened the door and stepped into dim red light. A single red bulb above the door like a darkroom during film processing. McNulty didn't hesitate this time. He followed Speed inside, and the gateman crowded in behind him and closed the door.

The red bulb went out and bright strip lights came on. McNulty kept his face straight, but inside he gasped. The contrast with the outside was extraordinary. The bright lights and soft furnishings of a five-star hotel replaced the desolation and gloom of the yard. Deep-pile oatmeal carpet, beige vinyl wallpaper and a purpose-built pine reception desk made McNulty feel like he'd stepped into a high-end dentist's surgery. Matching curtains, closed over false windows, added to the picture. A wooden bowl of fragrant pot-pourri stood on the desk. Neutral grey wall safes were set in the partition behind it. Each safe had a key in the lock. Burt Bacharach music melted from hidden speakers.

A middle-aged woman wearing a white blouse and grey business skirt stood up behind the desk to greet them, her dental receptionist smile cementing the impression that McNulty had stepped into a parallel universe. He felt like Sean Connery in *Dr No*, only the woman didn't know his inside leg measurement.

'Good evening, Mr McNulty. Your room is ready.'

She knew his name though. Although that wouldn't be difficult if Telfon Speed had organized this. She took a beige plastic tray from one of the safes and slid it across the desk.

'Could you put all your valuables into the tray, please? For security.'

McNulty paused. He generally kept his wallet and badge with him at the parlours, but this wasn't like any massage parlour he'd ever visited. Individual safes for each customer was a new one on him. He put his wallet, cash and car keys into the tray. He felt the mobile phone in his pocket while he rummaged for anything else. The keypad was active. Careful to hit the right buttons, he pressed the nine three times, allowed a few seconds and then hit cancel.

'Is that everything?'

The smile never left her face. McNulty brought the phone out of his pocket, turned it off and dropped it in the tray. Once she was satisfied there was nothing else she put the tray back in the safe and locked it. She handed McNulty the key attached to a safety pin.

'Would you like some refreshment before meeting the girls?'

McNulty said he would, but in the back of his mind he was noting the locked door behind him and hoping the control room staff weren't taking a leak when he dialled three nines. This felt very much like a mink-lined prison. And he had no idea how long backup would take to reach him.

TWENTY-EIGHT

'He's in.'

Baildon hung up the car phone and looked across at Tynan, who was slumped forward, his forehead resting on the steering wheel. He sat up and rubbed his eyes. The strain of the last half hour showed as dark rings of tension.

'In where? That's what I want to know.'

'Can't say. Control room says they got three nines but no speech. Then the phone was switched off.'

'Damn.'

Considering how tight Tynan was feeling, that was pretty mild.

'Damn, fuck, shit, bastard.'

That was more like it. The traffic camera had picked up McNulty and another man, presumably Telfon Speed, crossing to McNulty's Vauxhall Astra and Big Fish had tracked the registration number through the city centre heading south. It was then that the bad news started to bite. The Astra had taken to the back streets somewhere near Compton Street and the follow cars were too far away to see where it went from there. They didn't want to risk stumbling into McNulty and blowing his cover so they pulled back on the outskirts, waiting for Big Fish to pick him up again. It didn't. It had been Tynan's decision and now he was beginning to regret it. Baildon tried to be diplomatic.

'Maybe we should have tailed him closer.'

'Maybe you should have eaten fewer doughnuts.'

Baildon held up his hands in surrender. Tynan sighed but didn't apologize. They both knew how serious this was. How badly it could go wrong. But it was the only play they had at locating the girl farm, so the risk assessment had been made and the most dispensable unit despatched. The unit that wasn't even in the police any more. Tynan felt bad about that too. He liked McNulty.

'If I'd eaten less doughnuts I could have gone up in the chopper.'

'Your chopper's got you in more trouble than your doughnuts.'

Tynan smiled. The tension was broken and he silently thanked Baildon for using the policeman's coping mechanism. Humour. He leaned forward and looked up through the windscreen at the clear night sky. An icy moon glinted off the rooftops on his right, terraced houses that would become unoccupied houses further down Compton Street.

'Even if the force 'copter was available they'd have heard it a mile off. It's not like LA around here. News choppers all over the place. Only helicopter up after dark is ours.'

He was talking to himself. Trying to argue that his decision had been right. It was a hollow argument. An officer had been placed in danger on his instructions and that sat heavy on his heart. He realized he'd just ignored the fact that McNulty was an ex-copper. That made him feel better. He knew how much McNulty missed being in the job. Small consolation at the moment.

'Where did they lose Non-Stick's BMW?'

Baildon tapped his forehead as if that would help remember. Covert obs at Golden Touch had spotted Telfon Speed's 4 x 4 in the back alley. The reg number was known. It was probably how Speed had been dropped at the parlour. Baildon had the control room programme it into Big Fish. After McNulty had set off in his Astra the BMW had set off too. Taking a more direct route, and not trying to throw off any tails, it had driven through town and out on the main road.

'Across the canal. Southside Industrial Park.'

'Not a million miles from where McNulty turned off.'

His fingers began to drum on the steering wheel, his private aid to concentration. This was his operation. The next move was his to choose. The drumming stopped.

'Call the magistrates'. Tell him we've nearly got the address.'

Southside Industrial Park covered a large area of derelict factories and phoenix-from-the-ashes business units, but apart from two narrow bridges it was penned in by the canal on three sides and the main road on the fourth. If he kept the traffic pursuit car on the main road and a unit watching each bridge they'd at least be able to see if McNulty left the area.

'Let's tighten the net.'

He lifted the radio and began to give instructions.

TWENTY-NINE

The mink-lined prison's lounge was every bit as plush as the reception area, except with more subdued lighting. The oatmeal carpet was so thick it felt like walking on soft grass. The colour scheme was the same, all creams and beiges, but the curved reception desk was replaced by a pine bar that ran the length of the far wall. Floor to ceiling curtains hung from the right-hand wall, not to hide false windows but to cover the six-foot cinema screen. Neutral coloured floor-standing speakers on either side of the curtains gave it away. The centre speaker was behind the screen for perfect dialogue placement. Judging by the DVDs on the bookcase behind the bar, dialogue would be at a minimum.

'Some clients need help getting in the mood.'

Speed waved the bartender over, another middle-aged woman with the same dental receptionist smile. She looked like a Stepford Wife for the sex trade. Her white blouse was complemented by a black skirt, the only difference in the corporate uniform.

'What would you like, Mr McNulty?'

This bar was stocked with everything, not just soft drinks. It might be the hotel bar at any city centre accommodation. The optics were fully loaded. A small glass-fronted refrigerator held mixers and carbonated drinks. Several varieties of squash stood against the mirrored backboard. Heavy-duty serviettes on the counter beside fancy plates of peanuts. Gold leaf patterning on the plates.

'Orange squash, please. No ice.'

The room was large enough that the little groups of soft leather chairs and coffee tables didn't appear cluttered, but small enough to feel intimate. Each glass-topped table had a bowl of pot-pourri. The scent filled the room. There was no damp-carpet Jacuzzi smell. No damp at all. Central heating kept the lounge at a pleasant temperature without being too warm. Speed pressed a button on the bar, but no bell sounded. Almost immediately a discreet door in the corner opened.

'No point wasting time. Let's see what you've come for.'

McNulty tensed. Did Speed suspect what he was really here for? McNulty waited for the hired muscle to come through the door, but felt even worse when he was greeted with the parade that followed.

Seven girls wearing silk dressing gowns came into the room and formed a line in front of the cinema curtains. The gowns were tied at the waist and clung to their figures. Some had large breasts that swayed gently as they moved. Some had pert little breasts that looked so firm there was no movement. All were slim and tight, with no suggestion of a saggy arse or fat thighs. And not one of them was over the age of fifteen.

'We can get younger on special order.'

McNulty kept his face blank. *The slap like a gunshot in the quiet office. A gunshot followed by a heartbreaking whimper.* But it wasn't easy. He wanted to turn on Telfon Speed and rip his throat out.

'Our clients have specific needs. Unfortunately that means we have a very fast turnover. Like boy bands. Once they're not boys any more they need replacing.'

In contrast to the receptionist, none of the girls smiled. They looked like catwalk models, keeping a deadpan expression while striking the right pose. Seven pairs of eyes stared at McNulty with no emotion at all. McNulty caught movement out of the corner of his eye. Speed twirled one hand in a let's-get-on-with-it motion and the girls undid their belts in unison. The silk gowns hung open a few inches and each girl, one at a time, hooked her right hand on her hip in a synchronized move from left to right, exposing a tantalizing glimpse of naked flesh. The sweeping curve of one hip. A single breast.

The twirling hand again, and this time the girls dropped their gowns one at a time in reverse order. Standing naked before him it was easy to see just how young they were. Children. Some of them so immature they hadn't even begun sprouting body hair. McNulty tried to look away but knew that Telfon Speed was watching. He seemed to sense McNulty's unease.

'You said you wanted them young.'

There was an element of sarcasm in his voice. Speed was gloating at McNulty's discomfort. The smooth richness of his tone became harder. He moved in front of the ex-policeman and stood eyeball to eyeball.

'Or maybe you wanted something more specific.'

He waved his hand in dismissal and the girls gathered their gowns and left the same way they'd come in. The woman behind the bar went through to reception. As McNulty tracked her towards the door he noticed the two men standing behind him. Speed's voice became a harsh whisper.

'I think I know who you want.'

McNulty relaxed his arms, ready to move quickly.

'And here she is.'

Speed stepped aside to reveal the discreet door in the corner. Michelle stood alone, wearing a silk gown like the other girls. The door closed behind her. She walked into the room and stopped in front of the cinema curtain. Speed walked around her, appraising the merchandise. McNulty watched Speed, not the girl. Anger was boiling inside him, almost to overflowing. A defenceless girl. The man in charge. A secluded room. These thoughts filled his head so much he didn't recognize the distraction technique. Not a glass of orange juice this time. The girl. McNulty was paying so much attention to Telfon Speed that when the men behind him moved it caught him by surprise.

Strong hands grabbed his arms. Before he could react, handcuffs shackled his wrists behind his back and he pulled away from the men. Speed locked one arm around Michelle's throat.

'Take it easy. You don't want her getting hurt.'

McNulty stopped resisting. The hands released him. He stood in the centre of the mink-lined prison, handcuffed behind his back, and waited. Speed let go of the girl and moved back in front of him.

'You like your film quotes, don't you? Well, here's one for you.'

He leaned into McNulty's face and lowered his voice.

'I stopped by here to tell you two things. Number one is that you're gonna die tonight. Number two. I'm gonna find your wife. And I'm gonna kill her too.'

McNulty grunted a wordless reply and nodded. *Midnight Run*. Dennis Farina, that nasty bastard gangster, threatening Charles Grodin's captured accountant in the back of a limousine. The threat was implicit here. The simple plan had been stupid in the extreme, just like the light switch in the gas-filled room. Only this time there was nobody foolish enough to flick the switch.

'I don't have a wife.'

Defiant talk. Macho posturing that had never been part of his make-up during eighteen years in the police force. He'd always preferred the softly, softly approach. Defuse the situation. Talk your way out of trouble. He didn't think there was any talking his way out of this. Speed smiled but there was no warmth in it.

'No you don't, do you? You don't have any family at all.'

McNulty felt his neck burning. The smell of pot-pourri clawed at his throat. He stared ahead so intently that his eyes began to water. Rage. It boiled up inside him like oil in a cauldron. If he could only get his hands free he would do murder here tonight.

'Except you do. A sister.'

McNulty's hands snapped forward but were held tight in the cuffs. One of the heavies grabbed the rigid central bar to stop him lungeing at Speed. *The slap like a gunshot in the quiet office. A gunshot followed by a heartbreaking whimper.* His sister. Too young to protect herself back then. Gone from his life now. Pain flooded his heart.

'Well, guess who I've got in chains next door?'

THIRTY

Tynan pored over the map book spread out in front of him. The Bradford *A to Z* was open at the page covering Southside Industrial Park. It was large scale, but still only showed the streets and passageways and a rough outline of some of the larger buildings. Trouble was the street atlas was three years old and most of the factories that had made up the industrial heartland of the city were either standing empty or just so much rubble. Several of them were now tarmac parking bays for smaller businesses and industrial units.

He racked his brain trying to concentrate on the layout. Working out which premises he could disregard because they were paint shops or car spares warehouses. The inner-city regeneration had only spread so far. Moving a finger along the back streets he traced the redevelopment programme. Most of the newer complexes started on the main road and worked back towards the canal. Work was well under way preparing the ground for the next phase, halfway into the derelict hinterland. That meant he needn't worry about half of the area.

The radio crackled and the control room's disembodied voice filled the car.

'Helicopter's grounded. Frost on the wings or something.'

Tynan had tried for the aerial unit now that contact had been lost, but hadn't held out much hope. The force only had one helicopter and the chances of it being available at this time of night were pretty slim. Divisions all across the force area used it for vehicle pursuits, disturbed intruder scenarios, whatever else the on-duty inspector might think of. Frost on the wings was the last reason he expected. He fingered the transmit button.

'OK. Thanks for trying.'

Baildon waited for the finger drumming to start up again. He knew better than to interrupt. The fingers drummed on the page, dancing a tattoo on the area of Southside nearest the canal. Some of the smaller factories and an abandoned brickworks lived there. Next to them was mainly waste ground and rubble. The drumming stopped.

'Bill? Who's in the van?'

'Pat and Col.'

The surveillance van was a battered red ex-Post Office Ford Transit with video equipment and spy holes. They were using it tonight because it was less conspicuous than the CID Astras. It wouldn't be able to chase anyone but it was ideal for covert obs. It had been the vehicle nearest Golden Touch at the start of the operation and now it was parked in a back street near the second canal bridge. Tynan spoke into the radio.

'Pat. It's Jimmy.'

'Go ahead.'

'Take a slow drive through the west side. Beyond the new projects and the waste ground. Check out the buildings for lights. Any vehicles. They won't be on the street, so anything with a hidden yard.'

'Right you are.'

'Thanks.'

Tynan took one more look at the map and then closed the book. He knew where he was going. He slid the car into first and pulled away from the kerb. The west side was a mile and a half to their left and he wanted to be closer if Pat and Col identified a target premises.

'Fuck the warrant. We've got an officer in danger. That gives us power of entry to preserve life. I'll worry about admissible evidence later.'

All they needed now was the target premises.

THIRTY-ONE

McNulty's mind was reeling. The extent of this man's information stretched beyond even Donkey Flowers' local knowledge, but the more he thought about it the less surprised he became. Telfon Speed was a grass-roots criminal. He survived by having his finger on the pulse and his ear to the ground. Spending most of his life in or around Mean Wood estate meant he could pick up more than enough dirt on anyone that grew up there. Even at Crag View Orphanage.

That might explain how Speed knew about McNulty's sister, but there was no way he'd managed to find her and snatch her up in the short time since McNulty came up on his radar at the Sauna Kabin. This was bullshit. A bluff designed to wind him up. He tried to think of it in those terms but his anger wouldn't subside. Using his sister as leverage, even if it was just talk, was unforgivable. He relaxed his arms. The urge to lunge forward eased but the hand gripping the cuffs' centre bar did not.

The room fell silent. Nobody moved. Michelle stood in front of the curtains, frozen to the spot. Speed's hired muscle kept station behind McNulty. Telfon Speed looked McNulty in the eye for several seconds. Just observed his face.

'I see you don't believe me.'

He didn't sound disappointed. The deep-pile carpet and heavy curtains soaked up the noise of him crossing the room. He grabbed the girl's arm and brought her over to McNulty. The rustle of her silk gown was barely a whisper. Speed wedged her arm in the crook of his and forced her hand out. He gripped the middle finger in his fist.

'Let me show you I mean what I say.'

The girl whimpered but said nothing. A heartbreaking whimper. The fist began to twist upwards, taking the finger with it. Straight out. Against the joint. McNulty jerked his arms but the handcuffs were yanked back.

'Leave her alone.'

Speed stopped. He appeared to think for a moment and then smiled. He released Michelle's finger and she sagged into the nearest chair, rubbing her hand. Three paces and he was in front of McNulty.

'You're right. You need to know personally.'

McNulty tensed. The grip behind him held firm.

'Here's another quote for you. "*Which finger do you use least, Mister Bond?*" Remember that? And then, "*On reflection, I expect you will say the little finger of the left hand.*"'

McNulty squeezed his fingers closed into a fist. Both hands. That had been Mr Big to James Bond in *Live and Let Die*, and he knew what came next. Sweat beaded on his forehead. Speed didn't move but the men behind McNulty crowded in.

'Of course the film cheated and only had Tee Hee clamp the finger in his claw. A bit lame after what happened in the book.'

McNulty didn't speak. He squeezed the fists tighter. All thoughts of waiting for backup vanished. He concentrated on surviving the next few minutes.

'While we're acknowledging creative alterations, we'd better change something else. You're left-handed, aren't you?'

No reply.

'Of course you are. So that would make it the little finger on your right hand.'

Speed nodded to the man on McNulty's right.

'Tee Hee, break the little finger on Mr McNulty's right hand.'

Strong hands began to pry McNulty's right hand open. Unhinged the little finger and straightened it. McNulty tried to imagine the pain so that he could control it. Sweat began to run down his forehead. The man held the tip between finger and thumb and slowly started to bend it back. McNulty braced his legs. To struggle was pointless. It would simply prolong the agony while they restrained him. Might even make the fracture worse.

He stared into Speed's eyes and tried to keep his face straight. Pain built in his right hand. The finger stood upright. He gritted his teeth but couldn't keep the pain off his face. Tears of concentration welled in his eyes as he tried to outstare Speed and ignore the pain. The finger began to bend backwards towards the wrist. And suddenly there was a loud snap.

McNulty's legs gave way and he sagged in the arms of his captors. The girl winced at the sound. Speed nodded to one side and the men dumped McNulty in the soft leather chair next to Michelle's. Speed went to the bar and picked up the ice bucket. It sloshed as he came back. McNulty's head was pulled back and Speed poured the contents of the bucket over his face. Ice and water spilled down his sweatshirt and he snapped awake.

His right hand throbbed like no pain he'd ever experienced. The finger stood out at right angles like a broken twig. He had underestimated this man. He wasn't just a council estate thug who made decisions on the spot and thought little beyond the moment; this was a criminal mind with a bit more vision. To be able to keep a place like this hidden from the police was no mean feat. What McNulty had truly underestimated though was how cruel this man could be. He'd always known there were some nasty bastards out there on the streets, people so lacking in moral fibre that they were capable of anything if the restraints of society were relaxed. The sort of people who would become concentration camp guards or torturers or snuff movie makers.

'We can't leave you like that now, can we?'

Speed put the empty bucket on the table and waved a hand upwards. The men dragged McNulty upright by the armpits. His legs wouldn't lock and he sagged into their arms. They yanked him up again and this time he forced himself to stand. Speed came round McNulty's right side and looked at the broken finger.

'Just to show I have a little compassion.'

He grabbed the finger and forced it back down. There was another crack, duller this time, and McNulty screamed in pain and surprise. The hand looked normal again. It was only the pain that told him otherwise. Speed stepped back.

'Now that I have your full attention . . .'

The smile was so cruel he looked like a snake.
'. . . let's go meet the family.'

McNulty was frogmarched through the door in the corner, leaving the girl alone in the lounge. There was nowhere for her to go. Speed led the way. The bright lights and comfy furnishings were left behind, replaced by a hardwood floor and dark red vinyl wallpaper. It was more like the Northern X that McNulty had come to know.

Discreet ceiling lights painted the walls at intervals along the corridor, giving it an uneven look of shadows and light. The central heating obviously extended through here because it was still pleasantly warm. A swing door to the left led into a fully equipped commercial kitchen. McNulty could see steam rising from a boiler through the porthole window in the door. There were several other doors along the right-hand side of the corridor. These didn't have windows and reminded McNulty of cell doors in the custody suite. He assumed they were massage rooms. The first door was marked Staff Only, the rest were numbered one to four.

McNulty was walking better now. The handcuffs were released, allowing his arms to relax. The pain in his hand subsided to a constant throbbing ache. He followed Speed past the first couple of cells and half expected to hear the heavy slam and echo of doors closing. His mind was in turmoil. Fractured images whirled in his head. Little Daniel Roach held up against the custody suite wall by his throat. The slap and whimper in the headmaster's office. The look in Telfon Speed's eyes when he said, 'Except you do. A sister.' That last one stabbed pain into his temples like the mother of all migraines.

He didn't know what to believe any more. What to expect. Speed's intelligence had found out things about McNulty he thought were buried deep in his past. It wasn't inconceivable that he could succeed where McNulty had failed in tracing his long-lost sister. That being the case, he wasn't sure how to feel about that. Meeting her again after all these years. Would he recognize her? Would she recognize him? Or even know who he was? McNulty had only known about her through a social worker's slip of the tongue.

The familiar smell of scented oil drifted out of the cell door to his right. They were halfway along the corridor now, and were passing a second portholed door on the left. The far end of the kitchen. A trace smell of gas.

There was a utility door at the end of the corridor. The last cell door was partly open and red light spilled out. McNulty tried to breathe evenly as they approached the door. His heart thumped as if it were trying to burst out of his chest. Was he really going to meet his sister for the first time since the headmaster's office? And if so, having protected her from the predatory paedophile back then, was he about to be the cause of her downfall now? His mind was moving into a very dark place.

Telfon Speed pushed the door open and stepped into the cell. Darkness engulfed him, tinged with red from the bulb above the door. McNulty stood in the doorway and looked inside. The floor was bare stone flags, no deep-pile carpet or hardwood flooring, but everything else was shrouded in darkness. He could just make out Speed standing in the middle of the room. There was an unsettling smell that McNulty couldn't quite put his finger on.

A shove in the back pushed him into the cell. He stood beside Speed on the hard stone. It wasn't cold but the comfortable warmth of the lounge and corridor was sucked down a notch. A red bulb in a wire cage was fastened to the wall above the door. There was no inside door handle. In all his time undercover he had never been in such a dangerous place. With no way of contacting backup or the outside world, he was completely alone. Whatever happened now, it was all down to him.

His eyes adjusted to the gloom and he noticed a solid wooden massage table on the left. Next to it was a smaller, chrome trolley on wheels. Red light glinted off several items on the trolley and he didn't need to see them to know what they were. His nostrils flared with fear. Speed turned to face him.

'I told you we had a quick turnover of staff.'

McNulty prepared himself for the shock he knew was coming.

'But it isn't age that determines the end of their usefulness.'

He indicated the wall on the right. Dull metal shackles hung from chains at shoulder height. Ankle bracelets below them. Something hung from one of the shackles. McNulty tried to focus on what it was. A dead cat? A small dog? About two feet long and thin, whatever it was. A message to frighten the disgraced ex-copper even further.

'It's the fact that you can't use a girl with no arms more than once.'

Shock blasted McNulty's eyes wide open. A severed arm hung from the shackle. He doubled over and vomited on the floor. Coughing the last strings of phlegm he forced himself upright. Tears of anger spilled down his cheeks but he was too weak to do anything about them.

'She was too old for my clients' taste, but what the hell? Why don't you shake your sister's hand?'

This time McNulty found enough energy to lunge forward, roaring his defiance. He bared his teeth as the only weapon he had left, but before he could clamp them on Telfon Speed's throat the handcuffs were grabbed from behind and a black bag snapped over his head. With the smell of his own vomit in his nose, the world went dark.

THIRTY-TWO

T he surveillance van pulled up beside Tynan's Astra, facing in the opposite direction. Driver's window to driver's window. Pat wound his window down and Tynan did the same.

'Well?'

There was a hint of pleading in Tynan's voice. They were parked on a levelled section of waste ground that would soon be a building site for more industrial units. Street lamps were practically nonexistent and the detectives sat in the dark with engines running and lights off. In the distance a police siren signalled another emergency somewhere else in the city, but Tynan was concentrating on the emergency he had right here. Not quite an officer down situation, but the next worst thing. Officer missing. Baildon kept quiet in the passenger seat.

Pat shook his head.

'There're three or four streets it could be on. Too many buildings to isolate any premises for sure. Some in better shape than others.'

Tynan rubbed his chin.

'Any vehicles?'

'No. A couple of factories with enclosed yards but none of the gates look like they've been opened in years.'

'Shit.'

'My sentiments exactly.'

Tynan didn't drum his fingers this time. He simply stared out across the ruins of the industrial north and nodded to himself.

'Thanks, Pat. You park here. We'll take the bridge.'

His mind played with various scenarios, but none of them produced an ID on the target premises and all of them gave the suspects plenty of warning they were coming. You can only kick in so many factory doors before anyone listening knows you're kicking in factory doors.

His fingers drummed a short tattoo on the steering wheel, then stopped. Listening. The last thing mobile patrols did any more and the best thing about foot patrol on night shift. He remembered his early days in uniform. Pounding the beat in the town centre and hearing the city's heart beat across the silent night.

'Get on the radio and guide the PSU van in. Keep them here with you.'

He turned the headlights on and put the car into reverse.

'I think I'll take a walk.'

THIRTY-THREE

The cold metal bit into McNulty's wrists as he sagged in the shackles. He was a big man built with solid muscle and everyone knew that muscle weighed more than fat. His weight had made it difficult for them to manhandle him into the restraints and now that he was shackled it was his weight that brought him around. Dragging his wrists down into the metal jaws until the pain forced him to stand upright. His legs were weak. His head spun in the blackness beneath the hood.

He heard movement in front of him and tried to kick out, but his legs were manacled as well, forcing his feet a yard apart and giving him a wide base. The chains rattled.

'Don't get excited. I haven't told you what's in store yet.'

Speed was just in front and slightly to McNulty's right. At least that meant he wasn't at the trolley selecting a scalpel or a saw, or whatever else was over there.

'There'll be plenty of time for kicking and screaming later.'

McNulty breathed evenly, trying to bring his heart rate down. The stench of vomit had diminished, replaced by the more comforting smell of leather. His eyes had adjusted to the dark but couldn't see anything apart from a glimpse of red light through the nose and mouth holes. This wasn't a black bag. It was a leather bondage mask tied tight at the throat.

An exchange of movie dialogue flashed through his mind. *'Bring in the gimp.' 'The gimp's sleeping.' 'Wake him.'* The scene from *Pulp Fiction* that followed the dialogue made McNulty clench his butt cheeks. The sight of Ving Rhames gagged and bound and bent over a table was right up there with *Deliverance*'s 'I'm gonna make you squeal like a pig' scene. McNulty suddenly knew what was in store and he didn't like it one little bit.

Warm fingers stroked his throat and he jerked his head back, banging against the wall. Speed's voice whispered close to his ear.

'That's an interesting tattoo you've got there.'

His breath smelled of mints.

'When we've finished skinning you maybe we'll tan it. Make a leather book cover or something.'

McNulty tried to reply but his mouth was gagged. He remembered Ving Rhames again, the rubber ball strapped tight into his mouth. Whoever labelled this sort of thing auto-eroticism needed a good spanking. There was nothing even remotely exciting about being strapped down and butt-fucked. A pang of guilt made him blush beneath the mask. Anger at himself for feeling self-pity when the underage girls he'd seen earlier would no doubt suffer a similar fate if he didn't get out of this. Underage girls who needed saving.

'You can't save everyone.'

Donk's words had never felt more accurate.

McNulty tried to focus on the things he could control. It was an old technique for combating the frustrations of the job. Whenever the senior management team moved the goalposts, or the Crown Prosecution Service refused to take a case to court, he'd concentrate on what he could do to work around the obstacles. There are more ways than one to skin a cat. The analogy sent a shiver down his spine.

Minty breath and whispered conversation again.

'Like I said. My clients have all sorts of different tastes. Mostly for young flesh of the opposite persuasion. Teenage girls. Pre-teens sometimes. And whatever they want to do is all right with me. They pay for the meal, they can do what they want with the food.'

McNulty couldn't clench his teeth because of the ball in his mouth but his nostrils flared. There was no controlling what Speed was saying so it was best to ignore it. Focus only on what he *could* control. These taunts were aimed at angering him further. When the time came, he would remind Speed of that. For now he had to bide his time. Sooner or later, whatever they were going to do to him would entail getting him down off the chains. Can't get butt-fucked with your back to the wall.

'Mostly young females. But some like a bit of man flesh.'

If McNulty could have smiled he'd be trying to hide it. The threat was supposed to scare him but it was playing right into his hands. Sooner or later they'd try and bend him over the massage table. Speed lowered his voice.

'And guess what? You're on next.'

Sooner rather than later then. McNulty listened but couldn't tell if there was anyone else in the room. He sensed rather than heard Telfon Speed walk to the cell door. His voice echoed faintly from the corridor.

'He won't be long. Just having a drink in the lounge while we clear his payment. In advance.'

The door closed and McNulty was left alone. He assumed he was alone. To make sure, he slowed his breathing until it barely registered in his ears. The only sound was his beating heart. In the silence of the room it sounded loud. Everything else, dead quiet. Like a blind man's senses compensating for his loss of sight, McNulty's hearing fine-tuned until he could have heard a mouse fart if there was one in the cell. There was no mouse and nobody else either.

Once he'd confirmed he was alone he relaxed. The chains rattled as he settled into them, letting his arms rest in the shackles. His wrists were sore but the pain was good. It spurred him on. He twisted his head to gauge how much movement there was in the mask. The leather creaked under the strain like a fat man sitting in a Chesterfield. The dry leather smell reminded him of the barber's shop at Mean Wood Bottom where he'd had his first grown-up haircut after leaving Crag View. The trace memory was almost as positive as the experiment. His head managed a full turn to either side and a good twelve inches forward.

He shuffled his feet. There was only a few inches leeway. No kicking out while he was still chained up, but he could head-butt if necessary. He didn't think it would be. Whoever wanted to abuse him would have to unfasten him first. Even with Speed's henchmen helping, that was going to be his chance.

The dark became a part of him. His lack of vision soaked into him like fog and took away all sense of time and place. It eroded his confidence too. He tried not to think of the worst-case scenario but the longer he waited, the more his mind played tricks on him. This place could ruin him. The room was quiet and yet the strains of a hard guitar came from a long way off. A long way inside him.

'There is a house in New Orleans
They call the Rising Sun
And it's been the ruin of many a poor boy
And God I know I'm one'

McNulty had always associated 'The House of the Rising Sun' with the place that had decided his future and ruined his past, but now he put a different slant on it. In the folklore that defined the original ballad, the phrase 'House of the Rising Sun' was a euphemism for a brothel. Well, what else could you call the premises of Northern X, if not brothels in all but name?

He tuned the song out of his head. In the darkness behind the mask he lost track of how long he'd been here. Unless you were counting, seconds could be minutes and minutes could be God-knows-how-long. He stood very still. No more creaking leather. No more clanking chains. Just the dull red silence of a cell that had been the last resting place of his sister and was intended to be the last taste of freedom for the poor boy from Crag View.

He closed his eyes and took a deep breath. Both were futile exercises since he could only see blackness and smell dry leather. He listened to the steady rhythm of his heartbeat. Despite everything he'd told himself, fear began to creep up on him. Fear of the unknown. Fear of the dark. Time crawled forward. He didn't know how long. Then suddenly a noise sparked shockwaves down the back of his neck. And the door began to open.

THIRTY-FOUR

Tynan leaned against the lamp post at the corner of the street and let out a sigh that plumed smoke around his head. The futility of his search was beginning to get to him. The street corner was in the shadow of an old mill complex and a deserted brickworks. Across the road moonlight painted the pavement an unearthly blue-white. Frost stood out like silver whiskers on an old man's chin.

At first he'd felt optimistic. Walking the streets at night gave you a totally new perspective on your surroundings. There was no engine noise to distract you. No cosy heater to warm you in the safe cocoon of the driving compartment. Detached from the night around you. On foot everything became more immediate. It had been that way in his uniform days, before mobile patrol became the norm and foot beats a thing of the past.

He'd started at the edge of the cleared waste ground and worked methodically along the deserted streets towards the canal. It was only maybe half a square mile, but when you were walking it was surprising just how many streets that entailed. He walked slowly. Every footstep sounded loud in his ears.

The siren he'd heard earlier started up again. Or a different one. It was true that the city never slept and if you stood outside in the middle of the night the noises that you'd hear would amaze you. A late-night bus on the main road. Across the canal, a freight train rattling along the tracks. Somewhere over towards Compton Street a boom box in a cruising car reduced the music it was playing to pulses of bass and silence. There wasn't much silence. The music faded into the distance. Nobody was going to cruise the streets around the derelict factories of Southside Industrial Park.

Derelict factories were all that Tynan found. He checked for lights in the boarded-over windows. He listened for the faintest sound of conversation or laughter or argument. He watched for the slightest movement in places where there should be none. And he drew a blank. A big fat zero. There were no cars parked round the back. There were no doors left partly open. The secure yards behind high brick walls were just that. Secure. No breaches that someone might have crawled through. No gates that looked as if they had been opened recently. Nothing.

But there must be something. Telfon Speed hadn't simply disappeared with the ex-policeman and there were only three ways out. The two canal bridges and the main road. Leaning against the lamp post, Tynan began to wonder if he'd made a mistake. He'd triangulated this position because of where they'd lost sight of McNulty's Astra and where Big Fish had lost track of Speed's BMW. His thinking had been that the Astra was trying to shake off any tails but that the BMW had no reason to. Therefore, since the BMW had turned into the industrial estate, that must be where the Astra was heading too.

Maybe that had been a false assumption.

Maybe they had both just been passing through and had left the area before Tynan's team arrived to secure the exits.

'Fuck.'

The muttered curse under his breath plumed more steam around his head. It hung around him in the still night air until it dissolved to nothing. Even the night sounds had drifted away. He stood in silence and looked at the rubble-strewn road. Even the half bricks and broken bottles were coated in frost. Moonlight glinted off the jagged edges of glass on the floor. He looked up at the high wall opposite. Broken glass cemented into the top. To his left, the brickworks wall was a couple of feet lower but security had been just as tough in its heyday. Curls of razor wire festooned the top of the yard wall. Silver barbs glinted in the—

Tynan pushed off from the lamp post. The razor wire gleamed in the moonlight. Not rusty old barbed wire or broken glass cemented onto the top of the wall. Shiny new razor wire. Emphasis on the new. He moved to his right so he could see round the corner. The heavy wooden gate looked rotten and the faded green paint flaked like dead skin. A rubbish-filled oil drum stood in front of it like a sentinel. Giving the impression that the gate hadn't been opened in years. So why fix the wall with new razor wire? Steam plumed around his head as he let out an appreciative breath. It matched the steam pluming above an outbuilding along the derelict brickworks sidewall. The first movement Tynan had seen in half an hour.

Careful not to kick any of the broken glass, he walked across the road to the oil drum. There were scuff marks on the paving stones where it had been dragged to one side and then replaced. His heart began to race and he had to force himself not to give a little yell of delight.

He placed one hand on the flaking paintwork and pushed gently. The gate rocked slightly but remained solid. He half expected to see a padlock and chain, the usual security employed at an abandoned factory, but was unsurprised to see there wasn't one. Just a rusty handle with no lock. Grabbing the handle in both hands he took up the pressure and then pulled slowly. The gate slid half an inch along its runners and then stopped. Whatever was keeping it locked was on the inside.

He moved to the edge of the gate and peered through the narrow gap that had opened at the end. Half of the yard was in shadow. The other half was lit by pale moonlight. It picked out more oil drums, some with the tops cut off. A six-foot skip with metal shavings and brick offcuts. A pair of aluminium ladders. And the tail end of Vince McNulty's Vauxhall Astra.

Tynan stepped away from the gate and lifted the radio to his mouth.

THIRTY-FIVE

McNulty held his breath and waited. The door closed and there was silence for a moment. He listened for signs of movement but there were none. He began to think whoever had looked inside the room had gone back out, but then he heard the rustle of clothing and measured footsteps. Not coming towards him but going to the massage table. A clink of metal on the trolley.

Something being selected from the surgical tools.

He tensed. Maybe he had been wrong and butt-fucking over the table wasn't on the agenda. Maybe the client only wanted to toy with his captive; peel a slice of man flesh here and there. He tried to detect a change in the shadowy light that oozed through the gap in the mask but the customer was keeping his distance for now. McNulty relaxed his muscles and prepared to move fast. The only plan at the moment was to play dead and hope for the best. Be ready when the time came for action. Not a very substantial plan.

Another clink of metal on the trolley. Something being rejected and another instrument selected. Footsteps came towards him. He waited for the pain.

Shock sparked through his system as cold fingers touched his neck. His head jerked back involuntarily and banged the wall. He wanted to lunge forward. To try head-butting the dirty bastard who was going to use him like a piece of meat. A pang of guilt flushed his cheeks. What had he been treating the masseuses as over the years if not pieces of meat? He felt a sea change in his attitudes and hoped he would last long enough for it to take effect.

Fingers took hold of the leather strap around his throat. He almost gagged on the rubber ball as he took a sharp intake of breath. He felt a presence close to the side of his head. Perfume filled his nostrils.

'Shush. It's me.'

It was the girl from his flat, Michelle.

'Keep still. This is sharp.'

He felt a tug of the strap and then it was cut free. The rubber ball came out of his mouth and he heard it drop to the floor.

'Lean your head forward.'

He did. The fingers pulled the back of the mask away from his neck and again there was the gentle tug, once, twice, three times. The laces holding the mask in place gave way and it was yanked off his head. He could see for the first time since he'd been ambushed in the cell. He took a deep breath and flexed his neck. The girl looked up at him with a deadpan expression.

'If there's nobody to look after you, you should learn to look after yourself.'

McNulty responded with something *she'd* said in Donk's kitchen.

'This sort of thing happens all the time. Goes with the territory.'

False bravado didn't fool either of them. The sudden relief of being set free dumped adrenaline into his system and he began to shake. His teeth chattered. Tears welled up in his eyes but didn't spill. He shook his head to clear it.

'Get me down.'

Michelle dropped the scalpel on the floor and unfastened the shackles on McNulty's wrists before bending to do the same with his ankles. He flexed his fingers and rubbed the circulation back into his hands. After he'd spent so long in the dark the dim red bulb felt like a blazing street light. He could see everything as clear as day. The massage table

in the corner. The trolley load of surgical instruments. And the cell
door closed against the far wall.

His heart thumped. There was no inside handle. Michelle saw the
look on his face and followed his gaze. She walked over and pulled
the folded serviette that prevented the lock from engaging. It created
a gap wide enough for her fingers and she opened the door. In the
white light from the corridor McNulty saw the bruise for the first time.

The girl's right eye was almost swollen shut and the socket and
cheek bruised purple. A trickle of dried blood showed out of one nostril.
McNulty didn't say anything, just touched her cheek gently. *The slap
like a gunshot in the quiet office. A gunshot followed by a heartbreaking
whimper.* It felt like he'd spent his entire adult life getting over that
gunshot. He wanted to find Telfon Speed and smash the Bible into his
face. But this wasn't the headmaster's office at Crag View, this was a
torture cell at the House of the Rising Sun. And this wasn't the time
for slaying his demons; it was time to get the fuck out of here. Or,
more importantly, get the police in to round up this gang of child-
molesting bastards.

'I need a phone.'

Michelle glanced along the corridor towards the lounge door.

'There's one in the bar, but it's only internal.'

'No. An outside line.'

She nodded beyond the lounge and winced. The bruise looked sore.
Her swollen eye wept pus. McNulty could only imagine the headache
that must be banging around her head.

'Reception. And there is an office upstairs.'

'Where are the stairs?'

'In reception.'

McNulty huffed his disappointment. Reception meant going through
the lounge, and the lounge was where Telfon Speed and two henchmen
were entertaining at least one more man, the client. That made three
heavily muscled men and one unknown quantity. McNulty would back
himself against any two out of the four but he was no Jack Reacher.
He was tall and strong but no giant. Getting through to reception with
enough time to make the call was low percentage. He glanced at the
utility door at the near end of the corridor.

'What about this way?'

Michelle didn't nod this time, simply blinked her one good eye in
a yes.

'Service area. Washing machines and waste disposal . . .'

A smile spread across her face.

'. . . and the back staircase.'

McNulty smiled back. All he needed to make was one quick phone call giving his location and Tynan could bring the cavalry. Then McNulty could have a private word with Telfon Speed and make sure the case stuck this time.

'You'd better stay with me.'

Michelle looked like she wasn't going to leave his side no matter what. Her days were numbered if she didn't get out of here. If McNulty didn't get her out. *'I once told you Von Ryan. If only one gets out it's a victory.'* Donk had told him he couldn't save everybody. This was going to be McNulty's little victory.

'Come on.'

Two steps and he reached the utility door. He glanced back along the corridor and listened for a second. No sound. No movement. He remembered the thick padding on the lounge door. Speed didn't want anyone having a drink in the bar to be disturbed by screams coming out of the massage rooms. Satisfied that nobody was going to hear him, he turned the handle. The door didn't move. He turned the handle again. The door was locked.

He didn't curse and he didn't yank the door. The lounge might be soundproof but he didn't know just how soundproof. He took the disappointment on the chin and tried not to show it. The girl had been through enough. He tapped the door with his fingertips. Hoping for the dull echo that would signify a basic egg-box door. Thin plywood skins filled with hollow cardboard spirals. A door like that would be easy to burst through without too much noise. There was no encouraging echo. This was a solid hardwood fire door. He could break his shoulder on it trying and still not force it open.

He glanced back along the corridor. Four massage room doors and a staff room on the left and two kitchen doors on the right. Lounge door at the far end.

'What's in the staff room?'

'Easy chairs and sofas. TV. No telephone. We're locked in there whenever there are customers in the lounge. Otherwise we're allowed full use of the facilities. All the outside doors are locked anyway.'

McNulty thought about the underage girls locked in the staff lounge, waiting for the call to arms when they must display their wares like cattle at the market. The pang of guilt flushed his cheeks again. They were nothing more than children and this bastard had turned their world into a living nightmare. He wondered, did they know just what awaited them in the torture cells that were euphemistically called massage rooms? Did Michelle know?

He decided to be tactful. 'How long do they work here?'

'Some are here a few weeks. The clients can get pretty rough. Some only stay for one or two sessions and then leave.'

He couldn't tell if she knew more about the horrors enacted just down the corridor or if she was pretending for her own sake. Hoping for the best while ignoring the worst. McNulty nodded.

'What about you?'

Again, he didn't come right out and ask how many sessions she'd been engaged in. How rough those sessions had been.

'I'm new here. I started at the Sauna Kabin. When you saw me.'

He remembered Telfon Speed manhandling the girl towards the fire exit and the struggle she put up not to go. If he'd only known then what he knew now she might not be stuck in this place today.

'You didn't volunteer then.'

Michelle set her jaw tight.

'No. I did not volunteer. Nobody did.'

Another thought struck him.

'And the dead girl in the oil drum?'

'I don't know about her. She never came here. I think she must have struggled too hard when he took her. I heard she'd been dumped in plain sight as a warning to the rest.'

Her face went pale. The implication was clear. If she had struggled any harder she might have ended up dead in a ditch somewhere. Or an oil drum. If a tattooed client hadn't stepped in and floored the bully without knowing what was at stake. That made him feel good and bad. Good that he had saved her and bad that he'd used Northern X's services in the first place. As a Northern ex himself, formerly of the North's premier police force, he felt ashamed. He needed to redeem himself and . . .

'I once told you Von Ryan. If only one gets out it's a victory.'

. . . the best way to do that was to get all the girls out. Donk may have been right about not being able to save everyone but he could at least save everyone here. He was halfway along the corridor before he realized that letting them out now would only put them in more danger unless he got a message to Tynan first. And the only route to the telephone was through Telfon Speed and his heavies.

He stopped in his tracks. The girl almost bumped into the back of him. The trace element of gas from the kitchen drifted into the corridor. He glanced through the porthole window at the geyser bubbling steam up the chrome exhaust pipe. For a moment he saw Donk reaching for the light switch. Without speaking he pushed the swing door open and went into the kitchen. It swung shut behind him, flip-flapping until it was closed.

Michelle followed and stood beside him.

The kitchen was long and narrow. All the food preparation surfaces and cupboards were along the corridor wall. The outer wall had a fridge, water geyser, twin range gas cooker and microwave oven. The sink and draining board was at the far end. The window above the sink had been bricked up and painted white to match everything else. The kitchen was spotlessly clean. White-tiled walls and shimmering chrome blasted light from the fluorescent strips back into the room. The only colour was green lino floor and matching worktops.

McNulty opened a cupboard and shut it again. A second cupboard. Not what he was looking for. He found the plates in the third cupboard and took one out. Glazed white with gold leaf patterning around the edge. He hefted one in his hand and smiled.

'Go wait by the end door.'

Michelle looked at him as if he were stupid. Did he really think he could get past Telfon Speed using a dinner plate? She didn't move until he went to the cooker and turned on all the gas rings. Then she moved pretty fast.

The trace smell became a flood of gas. It hissed from the four rings on top of the cooker. McNulty turned on the overhead grill. Opened the oven door and turned that on too. The smell was so strong it made him gag and he buried his nose in his sleeve. He waited for the gas to fill the room, mind skipping from memories of his flat to scenes from *The Dirty Dozen*.

Lee Marvin puts the can of petrol down and empties a bag of hand grenades with the pins still in them into the last vent.

McNulty reached behind the geyser and yanked the narrow gas pipe out of the wall. More gas flooded the kitchen. Room killer. Gas from floor to ceiling.

Jim Brown pulls the pin on the grenade and pauses beside the first uncovered vent. The cobblestones are shiny and wet. Lee Marvin climbs aboard the German halftrack and signals to go ahead.

The gold leaf pattern on the edge of the plate glinted in the harsh light from the fluorescent. McNulty opened the microwave door and paused. Michelle stood by the far door, her eyes widening with horror as she realized what he was going to do.

Jim Brown throws the grenade into the vent and sets off at a sprint.

The kitchen was full of gas. McNulty threw one last glance at the girl and put the plate in the microwave. In one movement he shut the door and twisted the timer. The internal light came on. The platform began to rotate, giving the gold leaf an even heat.

He set off running at full speed.

Behind him the hum of the microwave sounded loud in his ears. The fridge was a blur as he flashed past it. The cooker too.

Brown throws a grenade into each vent as he passes them. One. Two. Three. Four. When he reaches the last vent he stops. The pin is stuck.

Gas made it hard to breathe. McNulty gagged as he reached the sink and had to double over and cough. The humming behind him became a crackling of static. The gold leaf began to spark.

Finally Brown yanks the pin out, slams the grenade into the hole, and races across the cobblestones towards the waiting halftrack.

Still coughing up phlegm, McNulty put on a final burst of speed. His mind was racing ahead of him, merging the present with the past and the past with his cinematic heroes. The gas-filled kitchen became his room-killer flat. Kitchen worktops became air vents of the chateau as they flashed by. The door handle became the guardrail of the departing train with Trevor Howard holding a hand out to grab him. He ran for his life. From a past that was too painful to accept and a future that was no future at all.

Imperceptibly he began to slow down. Somewhere deep inside he wasn't sure if he wanted to make it to the train. Wouldn't it be better to die a hero's death, striving to make the world a safer place? Like Jim Brown gunned down racing across the cobbles? Or Frank Sinatra stumbling on the aggregate between the railway tracks?

Sparks grew louder.

Popping and banging sounded inside the microwave.

McNulty reached his hand out but didn't really believe he was going to make it. The train was just in front of him. The door handle just out of reach. His legs were growing tired but he stumbled on.

Nine feet.

He saw the girl step to one side.

Six feet.

The kitchen door swung closed. Sparks crackled behind him.

Three feet.

His fingers brushed the door handle. Frank Sinatra almost touched Trevor Howard's outstretched hand. A German officer snatched a Schmeisser from one of his soldiers and opened fire on the American's retreating back.

Contact.

McNulty grabbed the handle. The crackling of machine-gun fire became . . .

The slap like a gunshot in the quiet office.

... sparking gold leaf in the microwave.

Everything merged into one to create the defining moment of his life. The sister he'd tried to protect. The films he'd grown up with. The rage he felt at a system that had abandoned him. Fired him. Spat him out like a piece of half-chewed meat.

He lunged at the door handle.

The microwave sparked.

And the kitchen exploded in a ball of flame.

THIRTY-SIX

One minute Tynan was watching steam rise from the chrome exhaust vent and the next the factory's sidewall blew out like an erupting volcano. A ball of flame blasted into the night air, spewing broken tiles and half bricks across the road. A mushroom cloud plumed like a mini Hiroshima.

'Officer needs assistance. Take the gate down.'

He was shouting into his radio before the explosion died down and the PSU van sped round the corner, bull bars over the headlights and grille protecting the windscreen. It slammed through the factory gate with a splintering of wood. Flakes of green paint and rust powdered the concrete. Blue lights flashed across the yard and in a totally redundant move the police siren wailed into the night.

Baildon's Astra skidded to a halt in the middle of the road. The red surveillance van was half a minute slower. Pat and Col jumped out. Tynan waved them towards the sidewall, which was still venting flames.

'Cover the wall. Nobody gets out.'

Pat looked at the flames and then back at Tynan.

'No fucker's coming out of that, Jimmy.'

'Then you'll have an easy night. Bill. With me.'

Tynan could hear the other CID cars screeching through the back streets to get there before the action was over. He clambered through the wreckage of the main gate just as the PSU were disembarking from the van, black overalls and riot helmets blending with the shadows. They left the shields in the back. A huge officer built like a brick shithouse carried the metal door ram by one handle. Tynan indicated the office door in the corner of the yard.

Transferring the ram into both hands the giant balanced front and rear handles and flexed his knees. He swung it twice to build up momentum and then . . .

Wham.

. . . the door flew open. Tynan shouted above the noise as the other officers charged through the door.

'Everyone gets arrested on suspicion. I'll work out what later.'

Baildon came up beside him, puffing and panting. He'd only run from the car to the office door and was already out of breath. Tynan ignored him. He was looking at the oil drum across the yard and remembering the dead girl behind Kwik Save. As the PSU barked orders inside the office he hoped he wasn't going to find any more dead girls inside.

The lounge was full of smoke. Flames licked through a crack in the wall from the adjoining kitchen. The mirror behind the bar was broken and a large section crashed onto the stacked glasses. A bottle of orange squash rolled into the sink.

The two heavies used what limited brain cells they had, took one look at the smoke and flames and headed in the opposite direction. A short fat man with glasses followed them through the reception door. Whatever sadistic plans he'd had for the night, this wasn't part of them. He whimpered like a cornered puppy that had been caught pissing on the carpet.

The reception area was thankfully clear of smoke but the oatmeal carpet was already trampled dirty brown by the retreating staff. The receptionist threw her hands to her face at the mess. This was her domain. Keeping a tidy ship was her pride and joy. The fluorescent bathed the room in antiseptic light. No smoke alarms went off because the only thing that Northern X had skimped on was fire safety. There was no sprinkler system and no smoke alarm but somewhere outside a siren wailed.

The first bodyguard was almost at the front door when it burst open. A giant of a man wearing black overalls stepped aside and three more came rushing in. It was a nightmare. The barmaid screamed and the second bodyguard diverted up the office stairs.

Tynan followed the first wave of storm troopers through the door. A woman screamed. The expensive surroundings surprised him for a moment, all beige curtains and neutral carpet, but he quickly got his bearings. Smoke poured through an inner door that obviously led to the site of the explosion. A pine reception desk took up most of that wall. Heavy-duty curtains covered nonexistent windows. And deep-pile carpet muffled the cavalry charge.

A heavily muscled man lungeing towards the front door put the brakes on and tried to turn around but the lead PSU officer tackled him by the throat. They both hit the ground. The prisoner kicked out to get free. Two more black-clad policemen dived on him, one disabling his legs while the other grabbed his left arm. The first officer shouted something into his ear and twisted his right arm behind his back. More PSU streamed through the door and two more detectives from the briefing. It was pandemonium.

A short fat man who looked completely out of place tried to go back into the smoke. The giant with the door ram grabbed him with one hand and lifted him over the reception desk. Tynan didn't think he was given his rights but he was definitely under arrest. Baildon took the easy option, cautioning and arresting an attractive woman with her hands to her face.

A second bodyguard changed direction and ran up some stairs in the corner. Tynan went after him. The stairs doglegged immediate left and then straight up to the first floor. A narrow landing at the top turned left again into an office above the reception area. Heavy foot-steps sounded behind him as he followed the bodybuilder through the office door. Good. He didn't want to start fighting with a man twice his size.

The office wasn't as plush as downstairs. The chipped wooden desk and grey metal filing cabinet looked as if they belonged to the old brickworks and the curtains over the office window were dull, grey and moth-eaten. There was no other door. Dead end. Tynan wondered if there really was a window behind the curtains but didn't have time to ponder too long. The bodyguard picked up the swivel chair from behind the desk and threw it at the curtains. Glass smashed into the yard. The curtains ripped off their runners and followed the chair into the night.

'Hold it right there.'

Tynan needn't have bothered.

The man was barely over the windowsill when two black demons grabbed him and yanked him back inside. A PSU helmet head-butted him in the face and he collapsed like a sack of potatoes on the office floor. He was flipped onto his stomach and handcuffed behind his back before anyone spoke. No caution. No reading him his rights. He damn well knew he was under arrest and Tynan would bet a pound to a pinch of shit he already knew his rights. No. One of the PSU officers leaned into his face and stage whispered.

'How d'ya like them apples, fuckface?'

It always amazed him how the adrenaline rush affected some people.

He was about to laugh when he turned to examine the office. There was an address book next to the telephone on the desk. He stepped over to the filing cabinet and opened the top drawer. Manila envelopes and stationery at the front. Beige folders in a hanging frame at the back. He did laugh this time. Surely they weren't this stupid? He flipped open the first folder. They were.

The entire operation took fifteen minutes from bursting through the front gate to lining up the prisoners against the reception desk. Baildon was noting everyone's name on a clipboard when Tynan came downstairs with the final arrest. The man with the cut forehead joined the others. Baildon threw Tynan a funny look and Tynan shrugged an apology. It wasn't my fault. He stood next to Baildon and glanced at the clipboard.

'What we got?'

Baildon ran his fingers down the list.

'Five. Two bodyguards and a customer. Receptionist and a barmaid.'

'Searched all the rooms?'

'All we can. Door on t'other side of the lounge is blocked. Won't open 'cos of the explosion. Rest are clear. We've got 'em all.'

Tynan looked at the ragtag bunch leaning forlornly against the reception desk. He was getting a sinking feeling. Only three males, one a paying customer. None of them were Telfon Speed. And there was no sign of Vince McNulty.

THIRTY-SEVEN

McNulty blinked dust out of his eyes and tried to move. A heavy weight across his back and legs pinned him to the ground. His ears were ringing. He coughed bits of plaster and chipboard. Spat to clear debris from his mouth. His throat was dry. He blinked again and shook his head.

The corridor came into focus. It was strewn with splintered wood and plaster. A section of kitchen wall had collapsed across the floor. Scattered cutlery and broken plates. Gold leaf from a cereal bowl glinted in the light. Smoke drifted around him like fog. McNulty was lying on his stomach. He pushed up with his arms but the weight didn't shift. Twisting his head he saw the kitchen door pinning him down. It had protected him from most of the blast but now wouldn't let him go.

Michelle? He lay still for a moment, gathering his thoughts. The girl. She had been standing beside the door as he raced through the kitchen and then the world had turned upside down. Where was she now?

His head was turned to the right. Part of the kitchen door frame was wedged across the lounge door. She hadn't gone through there. He scanned the narrow view. No sign of the girl. The door had saved him, but what had saved the girl? He daren't look to his left. Achieving the victory of getting just one out had eluded him. He had failed again. He didn't think he could bear the sight of her broken body beneath the debris. What had he been thinking? Blowing the fucking kitchen up? It had seemed like a good idea at the time, like thumbing his nose at Telfon Speed by repaying the debt with another gas explosion. But what about the collateral damage? Had he achieved what Speed had failed to do in his flat and killed the girl?

He shoved upwards as hard as he could, anger and guilt giving him strength. The door shifted and he managed to pull his left leg out. Another heave and a pile of bricks tumbled off the door. The weight eased. Drawing his left leg up to his chest he pushed with that as well. The extra leverage tipped the door to one side and he knelt up, taking a deep breath. Dust made him cough again. A cold breeze cleared the smoke around him and he looked over his shoulder.

He could see into the kitchen and beyond. Half of the back wall had been blown into the night and the wooden cabinets trickled flames. The gas pipe from the geyser shot blue fire into the sky. A section of roof had collapsed. The gaping hole sucked the smoke outwards and let fresh air in. McNulty took another deep breath and this time it was clean night air.

He knelt for a long time, afraid to turn towards the rest of the corridor. Not wanting to see the girl crushed by his folly. Slowly and with great deliberation, he pushed himself to his feet and patted the dust off his clothes. His hands were peppered with tiny cuts. Both knees were torn. The throbbing of his broken finger was joined by an all-encompassing pain throughout his body. Everything ached. Even his teeth.

Movement to his left. Chipped porcelain crunched underfoot. He finally plucked up courage to look. Michelle was there, standing six feet from him, but she wasn't alone. Telfon Speed stood behind her with one arm locked across her throat. The other hand held a fisherman's knife, the serrated blade thumbed open.

Once a cop always a cop. It had a certain rhythm to it. Rolled off the tongue. An Americanism that should be embraced, not derided. McNulty embraced it now. He had known thirty-year retirees who still regarded themselves as cops. Some had taken other jobs and some had stayed retired, but whenever they were asked what they were they never said security guard or pensioner, it was always a retired policeman. An ex-cop. That's what McNulty was. An ex-cop. A Northern ex. The play on words made him smile as he faced the head of Northern X.

'What are you smiling at?'

Speed had lost all of his cultured charm. His voice was hard and dangerous, like Dennis Farina. That made McNulty smile even more, only not as twisted as De Niro's.

'I feel like a cop again.'

'Very fuckin' funny. You look like shit to me.'

Speed had his back to the wall. McNulty slowed everything down, carefully brushing dust from his sleeve. First rule of a potential violent encounter was defuse it as much as you could. Fast movement and aggression caused more injuries on duty than anything else. Standing back and taking stock worked every time.

'One man's shit is another man's *Coronation Street.*'

He took a step forward to get away from the debris he'd been standing in. Looking behind him he ignored Speed and gently kicked a piece of brick off his shoe. Slow movements to build up a rhythm. Non-threatening movements. Like ordering a glass of orange squash and waving it around until the glass became a non-glass. Just something that was there but wasn't a threat. He didn't have a glass this time. Only his hands and his feet. He needed them to seem harmless.

The single step forward put him two feet closer to his target. Speed tensed and raised the knife to Michelle's throat. McNulty stood still. The bully obviously wasn't going to be fooled twice. McNulty noticed the bruise down the side of the girl's face, but what he saw was a vivid handprint . . .

The slap like a gunshot in the quiet office.

. . . on a pale face in the headmaster's office. Another girl from a different time, but both in the clutches of a man who thought he had power over them. A strong man who used his authority to take advantage of those he should be protecting. McNulty tried to hide the anger boiling inside him. The explosion was sure to come. He needed to time it for the best effect.

Slow movements. Calm voice. That was the ticket. He continued to dust himself down. His sleeves. His trouser legs. The chest of his coat. Even his hair. The hands patted gently but Speed's eyes never left them. Distraction technique wasn't working. He glanced over his shoulder at the door to the lounge. At the kitchen door frame wedged across it. Then back to Speed.

'Can you pull rabbits out of a hat as well?'

The hand holding the knife tightened its grip.

'Rabbits?'

'It's just that getting through that door was something of a magic trick.'

Speed glanced at the door and straight back at McNulty.

'Born lucky I guess.' He nodded towards the staff door. 'I was picking a winner for the client.'

The staff rest room with its easy chairs and sofas. Its TV. But no telephone. Where the girls were locked in whenever there were customers in the lounge. Until a dark-hearted bastard came to pick a winner, the unlucky lady who would be chained up and dismembered in one of the torture chambers labelled massage rooms. The door was closed.

Muffled voices and shouting came from the lounge. Thumping foot-steps running upstairs. Speed and McNulty both looked at the door and then back at each other. They knew what those noises meant. Speed's knife hand tensed until cords of muscle stood out on his forearm. The blade stroked Michelle's throat. Anger boiled up McNulty's neck and it was all he could do to keep it off his face. This bastard was going to pay. McNulty's expression said he didn't care.

'Maybe you'd better start practising the rabbit trick.'

He stopped dusting himself down, arms hanging by his sides, hands relaxed. His legs looked straight but they were flexed slightly at the knees. Everything about him indicated complete relaxation. Everything inside him signalled the moment for action. He slowed his breathing to control his heartbeat. After the constant motion of patting himself down he looked like a statue. A rock. Something so solid it could not be moved.

Speed hesitated and then squeezed his arm across Michelle's throat.

'I've still got a couple of tricks up my sleeve.'

'Hat. You're supposed to pull the rabbit out of a hat.'

'Fuck hats. And fuck rabbits too.'

McNulty's breathing was almost zero. There was a faint twinkle in his eyes.

'What about crocodiles?'

'What?'

McNulty stared into Speed's eyes but it was the girl's eyes he noticed. A flicker of recognition that was instantly hidden. McNulty shrugged his shoulders and flexed his neck. A bone popped like a knot of wood in the fire.

'You know the best way to disable a crocodile?'

The moment was drawing near. He kept one eye on Speed's expression and the other on the knife. Any sudden movement would be signalled in the eyes first, a split second before the knife could be dragged across Michelle's throat. He sensed more than saw the girl shift her weight onto one leg. The noises from the lounge faded into the background. The dust settled. Flames crackled in the kitchen but the corridor descended into complete and total silence. McNulty pushed his chin forward and winked.

'You stick your hand in its mouth. And pull its teeth out.'

Speed opened his mouth to reply but the breath was knocked out of him. Michelle's leg kicked backwards from the knee and crashed her heel into the bully's knapsack. His balls were squashed, forcing a yelp of pain. Auto reflex doubled him over and his legs wavered. The arm clamping the girl's throat loosened and the knife hand relaxed.

McNulty moved like lightning. In a single movement he stepped forward, grabbed the knife hand below the wrist and yanked it towards him and up. He bent the joint down into a gooseneck and Speed had no choice but to follow or get a broken wrist. The knife dropped from his hand. He lost his balance and toppled forward. McNulty slammed the heel of his free hand into the exposed throat.

Michelle ducked out of Speed's grip and sidestepped his fall. She leaned against the wall, taking deep breaths of lung-filling night air.

Speed hit the floor in a cloud of dust. A loud bang slammed into the lounge door. McNulty twisted the wrist until the arm was held straight up from the fallen bully and then twisted it some more. He stood over the man known as Teflon and felt anger boil over. He roared his pain and rage like a primal scream and stamped hard between Speed's legs. If his balls weren't squashed already they were now. McNulty stamped on them again, roaring like a lion. In his mind he saw the sister he would never see again. The job he would no longer hold. And the fragile girls who were cannon fodder in a sex trade that turned his stomach. He didn't hear the lounge door burst open.

The door ram splintered the door off its hinges and black-clad hands yanked it to one side. Tynan was first through the gap. Two PSU officers followed. Tynan dragged McNulty off the figure moaning on the floor and slammed him against the wall.

'Sshhh. Hush now.'

He might have been calming a baby crying for its bottle. Slowly McNulty's roar diminished. He let go of Speed's broken arm, the crack of bone lost beneath the sound of McNulty's rage. His nostrils flared.

His breath came in vicious gasps. Eventually he subsided into sullen silence. Eyes dead and emotionless. He was empty. Finished.

Tynan released McNulty and stepped back. He was breathing heavily himself but from exertion, not anger. This was the job for him. Not personal. When he thought McNulty had calmed enough to hear him, he spoke softly.

'You know. You've got two means of expression. Rage and silence.'

A flicker of recognition forced a smile onto McNulty's lips.

'Charles Grodin to Robert De Niro.'

Tynan nodded. McNulty grinned.

'You bastard. You said you hadn't seen *Midnight Run*.'

'I said I didn't go to the pictures.'

The grin brought tears to McNulty's eyes. He was quiet for a moment, wagging a finger in Tynan's face.

'You fucking lying bastard.'

'See? Rage and silence.'

'TV or video?'

'Both. It's one of my favourite films.'

'You fucking bastard.'

One of the PSU officers led Michelle into the lounge. The second handcuffed Speed behind his back despite the screams of pain. He dragged him to a sitting position and then to his feet. Tynan nodded towards him and then smiled at McNulty.

'You got any other favourite lines?'

McNulty knew which one he meant. He smiled a thank you and stepped over to face Speed.

'You like your movie quotes, don't you? Well how about this one? "*I've always wanted to say this. You're under arrest.*"'

Then he leaned in close and lowered his voice.

'You really aren't a stunt man, are you?'

The PSU officer dragged Speed away. Flames still crackled in the kitchen. The geyser still blasted blue fire into the night sky. Everything smelled of smoke and gas and adrenaline. McNulty and Tynan were alone in the corridor. McNulty suddenly felt tired. He sagged against the wall. At a moment like this there should be words of male bonding. Pats on the back and manly hugs. But both kept quiet.

Then a thought forced its way into McNulty's tired brain. A memory that he was annoyed with himself for disregarding. He pushed away from the wall and walked along the corridor. Chipped porcelain and plaster crunched under his feet.

'I once told you Von Ryan. If only one gets out it's a victory.'

He opened the staff room door and waved the girls out. Fear was etched across their faces until they saw Detective Tynan's police badge hanging around his neck. McNulty didn't need to say anything. If getting one out was a victory, then rescuing seven went a long way to saving everybody. Tynan took the girls into the lounge. McNulty looked at the desolation around him for a few more minutes and then stepped through the door to follow them.

THIRTY-EIGHT

The woman massaged unscented oil into McNulty's back, leaning forward so that all her weight pressed down through her hands and drove the air out of his lungs. He lay face down on the hard table, head resting on folded hands, and glanced behind him. It was the first massage he'd had where the woman kept her clothes on, and looking at the hospital physio it was just as well. She made the lemon-sucking receptionist at Golden Touch look like Angelina Jolie, but she certainly knew what she was doing.

She changed position and, using her knuckles, kneaded each individual vertebra from his neck down. The pain was excruciating. The bruising across his shoulders and back had faded from vivid purple to sickly green but they were still tender. He grimaced as she dug her fingers in, loosening the tension in his spine that was only partly due to the kitchen door slamming into it. When he spoke, it was from one side of his mouth as his face buried itself into the table.

'At least if they ever close the hospital you know there's a job for you at Helga's House of Pain.'

The lemon didn't unsuck even a little bit. She obviously hadn't seen Steve Buschemi in *Armageddon*. McNulty glanced up at the wall clock. Half an hour to go. These outpatient appointments seemed to last for ever, whereas his previous massages had felt like they were over in a flash. It was a well-known fact that good times rolled while bad times strolled. He remembered someone back in his uniform days saying, 'All good things come to an end. It's the bad things last for ever. Feels like I've been married a hundred years.' Just before the poor fella's divorce, that was.

A thumb dug in beside his shoulder blade.

'Clock watching won't make this go any quicker.'

McNulty gritted his teeth and shook off the pain.

'Did you do that on purpose?'

'Of course I did. This is no accidental physio. You've still got a lot of tension in there. And whatever hit you twisted your spine out of alignment.'

'Well, I can live with being bent a lot easier than the pain.'

She stopped massaging and gave him a funny look.

'Hey. I'm straight that way. Just twisted.'

'So I've heard.'

The thumb dug in again. He wondered how much information his medical notes contained. Of course, the newspapers had revealed a lot more than he felt comfortable with, turning him into some kind of hero with a troubled past. His photo hit every front page the day after the raid on Northern X and the television news filmed him being stretchered out of the ambulance at Bradford Royal Infirmary. Tynan had his hands full keeping a lid on the story until all the arrests had been made. Key members of Northern X.

With a lack of early information from the police the newspapers had run with the story on their own, surmising that McNulty's circulation as a suspect for the missing girls had been a ruse to give him credibility in the eyes of Northern X. The brief press release named him as an undercover officer injured during a countywide vice operation. The papers lapped it up without thinking that if he was an undercover officer, why were they naming him? McNulty felt good about that part though. About being acknowledged as an officer after being sacked by the people who were acknowledging him.

The thumbs worked their way down his spine, allowing him to flex his neck and shoulders. He had to admit they felt looser. This was his third appointment and the woman definitely had the magic touch. Clothes or no clothes. She continued the massage in silence. Just his back. The National Health Service didn't stretch to a full body massage when it was only his spine that was twisted.

When she'd finished he sat up and swung his legs off the table. Both knees were still bandaged under his tracksuit bottoms, although the numerous cuts to his hands were almost healed. Each knee had half a dozen stitches, plus three to a cut on the back of the head he hadn't even known about until the ambulance arrived. He stood up and flexed his spine.

'You know? That feels a lot better.'

'Good. Two more appointments and you should be good as new.'

The physiotherapist's mouth still looked like it was sucking lemons but McNulty noticed a twinkle in her eyes. Almost a twinkle anyway.

'Now you go straight home and don't be a naughty boy.'

McNulty straightened his tracksuit bottoms where they'd been rolled down at the waist and towelled off the residual oil from his back. There wasn't much. The woman took the towel off him and rubbed the parts he couldn't reach.

'Are those girls going to be all right?'

It was the first time she'd mentioned why he was here. McNulty felt a change in the atmosphere. As if the lemons had become oranges or something sweeter. He didn't look at her as he reached for his sweatshirt.

'Compared to what?'

When he turned round he regretted the short reply. The woman looked embarrassed for asking. She took his towel and dropped it into a laundry basket in the corner of the room. McNulty unfolded the sweatshirt.

'Sorry. I don't know. They've had a bad childhood. Probably take a bit of getting over. With a bit of help they should be OK though.'

He considered that but didn't think it was true. What happened in your youth set some things in stone. He wasn't sure you ever got over them. The loss of innocence was irreversible. You could never get it back. 'We wear the chains we forge in life.' He'd heard that somewhere. Probably in a film. It's where he heard most of the things he'd learned. Something else popped into his head, accompanied by a lone guitar.

> Well, I got one foot on the platform
> The other foot on the train
> I'm goin' back to New Orleans
> To wear that ball and chain

The woman must have seen something in his eyes because she suddenly seemed almost human. Miss Whiplash at Helga's House of Pain disappeared and the maternal woman she no doubt was emerged. There wasn't even a hint of lemon sucking in her expression. She patted his arm.

'I'm sure they will get all the help they need.'

McNulty paused and looked into her eyes. People working in the emergency services always built a shield around themselves, whether it be police, fire or ambulance, but you couldn't hide the good that was inside. He added hospital staff to that list because the eyes were a window behind that shield. He saw that briefly now, before she shut the visor and became all business again.

'And don't forget. Straight home.'

He pulled the sweatshirt over his head.

'Can't do that. Got a hospital visit first.'

McNulty was plotting his route to Ward 13 before he opened the door.

Donkey Flowers was fourth bed along the ward and McNulty could see him through the window in the door. He was about to go in when he heard footsteps racing along the corridor behind him. In the normally measured atmosphere of the main hospital away from Accident and Emergency, the noise sounded urgent and out of place.

'Hang on there. Wait a minute.'

McNulty turned to see who was shouting and saw Jimmy Tynan trotting along the corridor towards him. Early afternoon sunshine shone in through the third floor windows, glinting off the rooftops of the old hospital outside. Ward 13 was part of the modern extension and the corridor overlooked the original section two floors below. Winter sun did nothing to warm the grey slate of the angled roofs and the few trees in the hospital grounds were bare and leafless.

'They said you'd be up here.'

Tynan was out of breath. Dark rings under his eyes made him look like he'd been up all night. His police radio squawked in the shoulder harness under his coat. Something about units leaving the scene at White Cross. Tynan turned it down and sat on the low windowsill opposite Ward 13.

'Glad to see you're up and about.'

'I was always up and about. It just hurt so much it was easier to stay down.'

McNulty glanced out of the window at the A and E entrance, just visible beyond the old building. Three patrol cars were parked opposite the ambulance bays. A gaggle of uniformed officers stood behind the cars, some smoking, some talking, all looking very serious indeed.

'What's going on?'

Tynan followed McNulty's gaze.

'Team two from nights. One of theirs got assaulted last night up at White Cross. He's in a bad way. Steve Decker. You know him?'

McNulty shrugged his shoulders and shook his head.

'Know of him. We never met. He gonna make it?'

It was Tynan's turn to shrug.

'Too early to tell. All hands to the pumps. They've even got me in helping with enquiries. It'll keep you off the front pages at least.'

McNulty grunted and turned away from the window. Last week he had been the officer-down story. Now it looked as if there was a more serious tale to tell of a man injured in the line of duty. The press loved

a bad news story. The only good thing to come out of a story like that
was it reminded the public how dangerous the job was. The sacrifices
made to keep the streets safe.

He smiled and felt sad at the same time. There he was, thinking
like a copper again. Feeling like he was still part of the family that
was dipped in blood and bathed in blue, the blue serge of a uniform
that was no longer blue and hadn't been serge for twenty years.

'That what you came to tell me?'

Tynan avoided McNulty's eyes and looked at the ground. McNulty
had a sinking feeling in the pit of his stomach. The Northern X investigation had lots of loose ends to tie up but only one of them affected
him. It was a difficult subject to broach whichever way it went. The
only way was to come straight out with it, so Tynan stood up and
looked McNulty in the eye.

'The woman in chains.'

The arm in chains, he meant. They both knew what he was talking
about.

'It wasn't your sister.'

McNulty's legs wobbled and he almost sagged against the wall.
He'd been pushing the nightmare of his sister to the back of his mind
even though he'd never really believed the severed arm belonged to
her. That was simply Speed trying to get a rise out of him. It would
have been too much of a coincidence. Even so, being told officially
what he believed in his heart was a weight off his chest. He immediately felt guilty. The fact that it wasn't his sister meant it was someone
else. Someone else's sister or daughter or mother. Tynan looked as if
he understood.

'The girls you released. They identified her as one of the barmaids.
Thought she'd handed her notice in the week before. No pun intended.'

Police humour. Gets you through the day.

'Distinctive nail varnish and a ring. We'll do full DNA tests later
but I thought you should know.'

'Thanks.'

There wasn't anything else to say about that. They both stood in
silence for a few moments before Tynan pulled a folded sheet of paper
from his inside pocket. He nodded towards the door to Ward 13.

'You still visiting Flowers?'

'Visiting but not bringing.'

'I'd worry if you were bringing pink carnations.'

McNulty laughed and the mood lightened. He'd been visiting Donkey
Flowers every day and never brought anything apart from a bottle of
orange squash and the *Racing Times*. Donk had no family, just like

him, and McNulty felt responsible for him being here. He was due to
be discharged in the next few days. Tynan hadn't finished.

'What you going to do now?'

'Visit Donkey Flowers.'

'In the future I mean.'

McNulty shrugged. There would be plenty of time to worry about
the future once he'd sorted out the present. Statements. Identification
parades. Court hearing a long way down the line. He'd consider his next
move after the dust had settled. Tynan nodded at the ward door again.

'Maybe you could go private. You know. Private detective. I can
just see you and Flowers digging up the dirt.'

'McNulty and Flowers.'

'Has a certain ring to it.'

'Getting his nose splattered, Donk might have something to say
about that.'

Tynan waved the sheet of paper and handed it to McNulty.

'Here's another option.'

McNulty unfolded the paper. It was a leaflet headed *RIG Police
Recruitment*. Underneath the familiar chequered banding there was a
two-line heading, bold and underlined.

FORMER POLICE OFFICER?
WE VALUE YOUR EXPERIENCE . . .

The rest of the letter described RIG as a specialist recruitment agency,
supplying ex/retired officers of all ranks, with specialist skills, to police
forces across the UK on a temporary basis. McNulty scanned the posi-
tions available.

'Statement takers? Control room operators? OIC inputters? You've
got to be fucking kidding.'

'Enquiry officers and district investigators as well.'

McNulty saw those jobs on the letter but said nothing.

'You'd be back in the fold.'

'Temporarily.'

'But back. I know you miss it.'

McNulty acknowledged that with a sad smile and a nod. He did
miss being part of that family but it was too painful to talk about in
a hospital corridor. Maybe over a few drinks in a police bar. He had
to admit it was nice of Tynan to think about him. He folded the paper
and slipped it into his back pocket.

'Thanks. I'll give it some thought. Good luck with this White Cross
thing.'

'He's going to need it. See you around.'

Tynan turned to leave but McNulty felt there was something else the detective wanted to say. Tynan took two steps and stopped.

'There is one more thing.'

He looked sheepish, as if he wasn't sure how to say this, and the look on his face seemed out of place on a hardened detective.

'Your sister.'

McNulty tensed.

'You ever try to find her?'

McNulty thought about those awful days when the social worker had let slip that he had a sister. The long and fruitless search of the council records. He'd even tried searching her name on all police databases periodically during his eighteen years' service. He couldn't answer so he simply blinked his eyelids.

'No joy, eh?'

A shake of the head.

'It's just that. Well. I've got a few contacts. If you wanted . . .'

Tynan's voice trailed off. McNulty's mind raced. He had given up on finding his sister a long time ago but now he had to consider something else. Did he want to find her after all this time? Would she want to be found? In the end there was only one answer.

'That would be great.'

'OK then. I'll be in touch.'

Tynan headed back towards the stairs and McNulty watched him go. The future. Until recently he didn't think he had one. Now he had to choose which one to take. After a few moments he pushed the door open and went in to visit Donkey Flowers.